SALLY LUNN

Leo Walmsley. (Photograph copyright Peter Woods.)

Sally Lunn

Leo Walmsley

Foreword by Stephanie Walmsley

First published in 1937 by Collins

This edition published in 1992 by
Smith Settle Ltd
Ilkley Road
Otley
West Yorkshire
LS21 3JP

ISBN Paperback 1 85825 003 X
Hardback   1 85825 004 8

British Library Cataloguing-in-Publication Data:
A catalogue record is available for this book
from the British Library.

Printed and bound by
SMITH SETTLE
Ilkley Road, Otley, West Yorkshire LS21 3JP

Foreword

Sally Lunn is a first-rate novel set against a background of high drama at sea. With narrative skill and strong powers of observation, it tells of the hair-raising adventures of a family of fishers, the Lunns, who put to sea in all weathers. The action takes place on the east coast of Yorkshire.

The male members of the family, father (Henry) and sons Marney and John, are real men. They lead strenuous, hazardous lives, governed always by the weather. The risks they take are perilous. The rewards not high. But their courage is. Hauling their catch, facing and fighting overwhelming odds, their zest for life is unquenchable. Unselfconscious, without self pity and constantly risking their lives, they face each challenge with grave optimism. For these are the men who laugh at danger.

One of the most exciting moments takes place at night when a trawler goes aground near the rocks. In a dense fog, with a freshening wind that threatens a gale, the Lunns set off in their coble to the rescue. The sea is dark, angry and heaving. Huge waves are crashing round the shaking coble. It is a tense, thrilling scene.

Sally Lunn is so vividly told, its characters so warmly human, that you feel you know them all and share their dangers. You feel you are really there in the quaint, charming village of Bramblewick (Robin Hood's Bay), walking along the cobbled alleyways that weave in and out between the stone-walled red pantile roofed cottages sloping down to the sea. Or you could be down at the slipway watching the men launch their coble.

Inside the Lunns' cottage, all is warm and bright. It may be quaint now to read about folk who are quite content to be without electricity and gas, who cheerfully take a bucket and go and draw water from a tap at the bottom of an alley. But it is good, too, to read about a way of life now gone forever; where fish come straight from the sea to the table, to be served with home-fried potatoes and hot mugs of tea followed by jam tarts warm from the oven and Yorkshire cheese-cake. These were the days before the deep freeze and fast foods, when a cottage loaf not a sliced one was placed on the tea table, and women were contented to be at home looking after their families and knitting guernseys and stockings for their men, and 'skaning' bait or mending nets.

Owing their good looks to their Scandinavian descent, all the Lunns are fair, with blue eyes and complexions tanned by the sun.

Running like a thread through the story, along-side shipwrecks, sudden storms and threatening seas, is the slowly developing romance between Sally Lunn, the only daughter, and Tom Fosdyck. He is tall, lean and handsome with high cheekbones and a swarthy complexion. But Tom is the son of the rival fisher family. As the saying goes, love doesn't run smoothly; not at first.

Like all good stories this one has conflict and suspense.

Of all the characters, my favourite is Marney Lunn. He has such sturdy, worthwhile qualities. I admire his restless energy, contagious enthusiasm, his toughness at sea and refusal to be beaten, his endearing swagger, ironic sense of humour and his sheer joy in living. I like, too, the warmth he has for his wife and 'bairn'.

In the closing chapters of the book there is mounting excitement when such a catastrophe overtakes the fishermen out at sea that they nearly lose their lives.

Leo Walmsley wanted to pay a tribute to the splendour of the fishermen of Robin Hood's Bay, to put down on record that, in his time, such men existed.

In this book he has certainly done that.

Stephanie Walmsley

For our darling Boodles,
whose home is the sea

WHEN Luke Fosdyck, veteran cox of Bramblewick Lifeboat, neared retiring age, most folk naturally thought that Henry Lunn would be cox in his place. True that Tindal Fosdyck, Luke's brother, was next in seniority among the crew, but Tindal for some time past had suffered from failing eyesight, and, besides, he was only a year younger than Luke himself. The Lunns might be foreigners, but after all, Henry Lunn had lived and fished in the place most of his lifetime, and knew the bay and the coast as well as any living man; and as there were only him and his two sons, and young Tom Fosdyck, nephew of Luke and Tindal, to choose from, there was not likely to be any haggling about it. There were no real fishermen among the rest of the crew, who, it was admitted, were a scratch lot. Only two of them had been sailors and they were both well over sixty years of age. There was the fishmonger, the foreman of the gasworks, a gardener, a joiner, a publican. They were all right for pulling an oar, for doing what they were told; but it needed an experienced chap to launch Bramblewick lifeboat down the slipway on a dark winter's night, to steer her out of the Landing, and thread the narrow channels between the scaur ends, where an inch too much helm one way or another might tear the boat's bottom out.

7

Aye—Henry Lunn was the chap, said local gossip. It would be the first time since Bramblewick had a lifeboat that her cox hadn't been born and bred on the spot—the first time, for that matter, her cox hadn't Fosdyck blood in his veins. But, seeing there were only two boats fishing where once there had been fifty, and no choice to make where once there'd have been at least a dozen men as good as Luke or Henry, least said the better. Main thing was that there'd be some one always fit and ready to get the boat out sharp when she was wanted, whether to save lives or make a bit of brass out of a salvage job. Bramblewick was lucky enough to have a lifeboat these days. How many villages along the coast had had their stations closed because there were not enough men to launch and man the boat? As for Henry, he'd be glad to take it! In spite of his motor coble, he hadn't done so well out of fishing lately he could afford to turn up his nose at a certain ten quid a year (which was the retaining salary of a lifeboat's cox) and a pension when *his* time for retiring came.

By custom, the choice of a lifeboat cox lies first with the crew. The man picked by them is considered by a local honorary committee. He is formally asked then if he will accept the post, and if he agrees, there remains nothing but the formal approval of the Institution. The Fosdycks as a family did not like the Lunns, and the Lunns did not like the Fosdycks. True that the Lunns, father and sons, had served under Luke in the lifeboat, that both families had helped each other in the daily toil of launching and hauling up their fishing boats, that for a long time there had been no open quarrel. Yet with the possible exception of young Tom Fosdyck—there smouldered in the heart of each of them at least the embers of that hostility born when the Lunns, along with several families of foreigners, had emigrated to Bramblewick from a village a few miles down the coast, and started to fish grounds which for generations the local men had regarded as exclusively their own.

In spite of this, it seems there was no opposition among the Bramblewick element of the crew to Henry's appointment. Indeed, it is doubtful whether there was any real discussion; and no one troubled to ask Henry himself about it. His name was brought before the local committee, which, under the chairmanship of the vicar, consisted of 'Up-Bankers,' inhabitants of the modern and genteel part of Bramblewick, elevated, socially as well as physically, from the old village, lying in a hollow close down by the sea. There were Fosdycks on the committee, belonging to that branch of the family which had followed the more lucrative profession of the Mercantile Marine—retired, of course, and well-to-do. Individually, they were not enamoured of their 'Down-Bank' relations, yet had there been any choice to make between a Bramblewick candidate and a foreigner, their vote would undoubtedly have been Bramblewick. There was no such choice. The approval of the committee was unanimous, and the vicar was empowered to acquaint Henry Lunn with this decision and obtain his consent.

The vicar had been in Bramblewick only one year.

In that time he had done his best to make himself
popular; and, so far as his 'Up-Bank' parishioners
were concerned, he had apparently succeeded. Per-
sonally, he was just what the vicar of a quiet rural
parish ought to be. He was in the prime of life,
athletic, handsome, and possessed of a very fine voice,
only faintly Oxford in its accent. He came of a good
family, and had a private income. It was not to his
disadvantage from the point of popularity that he was
a bachelor, for there were several spinsters and widows
in his flock to whom an unattached male (and a parson
at that), however remote he might have seemed, was
at least a glamorous possibility. The fact that his
housekeeper was old and plain, that he had a gardener
who 'slept in,' placed him beyond the breath of
scandal. He was attentive to his spiritual duties. If
his sermons were conventional and dogmatic, if they
suggested that to him all human behaviour was simply
divided into doing wrong or doing right according to
the Law of God (as interpreted through the Church
of England) they were eloquent; and his voice, his
distinguished appearance in the pulpit, compensated
for their occasional dullness. He took an interest in
the social activities of the parish, church and otherwise.
He was president and patron of the cricket and football
and lawn tennis and bowling clubs, and gave them his
personal support. He made a good and witty chairman
whenever there was a concert or bazaar in the church
room, and he subscribed handsomely to any local
charity or special fund like the Institute, the district
nurse, and the Bramblewick Brass Band. He was a

happy man, and wanted every one else to be happy. He would not have been human if he had not been agreeably conscious of the liking and respect he inspired among the greater part of his flock.

'Down-Bank' he had not been so successful. For one thing, there were not so many folk left 'Down-Bank' now that fishing had come almost to a standstill. Nearly half the cottages of the old village were used for summer letting and were empty in the winter. What folk were left were mostly Wesleyans, attending their 'Down-Bank' chapel, and, except for weddings and funerals, never seeing the inside of the modern 'Up-Bank' church. Again, Bramblewick's traditional hostility towards foreigners had always been stronger 'Down-Bank.' Yet, of all his lay activities, none interested the vicar more than his chairmanship of the lifeboat committee. He was a townsman. It was not surprising that he should be susceptible to the glamour of the lifeboat service, that even in his capacity as chairman, presiding at a meeting in the warmth and security of the church room, he felt that he was sharing a little in its glory. Indeed, on the occasion of Lifeboat Day, celebrated in the height of the summer visiting season by a ceremonial launch of the boat, he might have felt a more direct identification, for it had been his duty, when the boat, on its massive steel carriage, was launched to the bottom of the slipway, to stand on her deck, close by Luke Fosdyck, and make an appeal to the crowd of spectators for support for the Institution funds.

The day was hot, the sea dead calm. The crew in

their oilskins and thick kapok life-jackets were hot,
too; their faces were red, so they looked big and
healthy. It could not have been easy for that crowd of
holidaymakers to visualise what even a practice launch
would have been like in winter. Many of the male
spectators had actually helped in the first stage of the
launch, manning the thick hawsers by which the
boat was steadied down the steep and narrow slipway
slanting between the walls of the breakwater and the
old coastguard lookout. They had done this in a
spirit of fun, eagerly obeying Luke's summons to
'take hold,' and none of them could have guessed
what concern there was in that summons, for it was
the steepness, the narrowness of the slipway, that
made Bramblewick the most difficult and dangerous
station on the coast. There was no such extra help
in winter time. The peril might be accentuated by
snow and frost. Let the boat (with her carriage,
weighing several tons) get out of hand for a second,
and no human power could stop her taking charge and
crushing any of the crew or launching party who
stood between her and the sea. Even the vicar was not
aware of this latent peril peculiar to the Bramblewick
station, which had not been so grave in the prosperous
days of fishing. But he had closely studied the official
records of the local lifeboat, and he had found ample
material on which to base his address. That record,
with a total of more than two hundred lives saved,
was indeed a magnificent one, and perhaps the most
stirring incident was the loss of the original boat fifty
years ago when, putting out to the assistance of a

stranded sailing ship, she capsized, and all her crew (including no less than three Fosdycks) were drowned. Over this, and one or two other noteworthy incidents in which Luke himself and several members of the present crew had taken part, the vicar had grown eloquent, and in winding up with an almost unnecessary appeal to his hearers to patronise the collection boxes, he had laid his hands on Luke's shoulders and called for three rousing cheers for the gallant coxswain and his crew.

True that in subsequent meetings with Luke, the vicar had not recaptured that sense of intimacy he had experienced while standing by him in the boat. Luke was never communicative with his own folk. He was practically dumb with strangers. Henry Lunn could and would talk, and could be extremely affable to any one who had the tact and time to break through his reserve; but, as he was a busy man, and was usually either fishing or in the warehouse when the vicar chanced to be 'Down-Bank,' they had never got beyond wishing each other good-day. Marney Lunn definitely avoided all parsons on principle. John was the only one of the Lunns with whom he had made any contact at all, for John was the prime mover behind the brass band, himself playing the cornet. It was John, in fact, who had touched the vicar for a five-guinea subscription; but, as John belonged to the Wesleyan choir, even this contact had been slight.

Yet the vicar could not have had any misgivings as to the outcome of his mission when he set off 'Down-Bank' to pay his official call on Henry Lunn. It was

a night in January. The weather was wild, with a
freezing gale from the north-east, the sea rough, and
roaring on the scaurs. Even the old village, protected
from the north by a ridge of cliff, did not entirely
escape the storm, which during intermittent squalls
was accompanied by blinding showers of hail. The
narrow streets and cobbled alleys, lit by flickering
gas-lamps, echoed to the sound of wind and surf, and
although it was only an hour after dark, were deserted.
The tide was flowing. In the dock, that open space at
the lower end of the village, where the lifeboat house
stands and the slipway slants down to the shore, the
roar of breaking seas was louder, and already the
spume was drifting up between the walls, where at
full tide the seas themselves would be breaking, rushing
up to the very doors of the lifeboat house. A wild,
perilous night, the sort that might make even the
remotest shore-dweller think in sympathy of those
whose livelihood is on the sea. But the two cobles
belonging to the Fosdycks and the Lunns were drawn
up to the village end of the dock, behind the lifeboat
house, well out of range of the biggest high-tide seas,
and Henry Lunn's cottage was unusually bright and
cosy, for Sally was just home for her holidays.

2

SALLY LUNN was Henry's only daughter. He had five sons. John, the eldest, still unmarried, was twenty-seven. Marney, with a thriving family of three (the latest addition another son) was twenty-five. Sally was next. Eddy and George, nineteen and eighteen, were both in the Mercantile Marine, serving 'out foreign,' and Steve, the youngest, had recently gone to join the Navy as a boy.

Sally was twenty-one. She had always been a great favourite with her father. It had been strongly against his feelings that she had ever left home. But Henry had never allowed his personal feelings to stand in the way of his children, and he had realised without mother's persuasion that Bramblewick was no sort of a place for a girl like Sally to stay in for ever. Although he would not openly admit it, he knew in his heart that inshore fishing—at least the sort that he'd been bred to—was played out. He wanted to give all his children a chance to better themselves. Even John and Marney had first of all gone into the Mercantile Marine. It was of their own choice that they had come back to Bramblewick—and fishing.

Four years ago a well-to-do London lawyer had taken a furnished 'Up-Bank' villa for the summer holidays. His wife had just recovered from an illness, and he had a family of three small children, whose nurse, after two days in Bramblewick, had suddenly, without notice, departed. Sally was then helping mother with the house, and also in the special jobs that belong to a family of fishers, knitting guernseys and stockings, 'skaning' bait, baiting. But summer was Henry's slack season, with little baiting to be done, so Sally could be spared to take a temporary post with the distracted lady. The children at once took a strong liking to Sally, a liking that was shared by the lady herself. When the time came for the lawyer to return to London she had asked Sally to come with her and, referred by Sally to her parents, had made a personal appeal to Henry and his wife. There had been much quiet family argument, much thinking it over. Sally had become devoted to the children. She wanted to go, but the ties of her own home were strong. Henry's feelings were against it, but he wanted Sally to have her chance, and there could be no doubt that the lawyer and his wife were very decent folk, that Sally would be going to a home where she would be secure and happy. It would mean more work for mother, of course. But mother had scoffed at this argument. If she'd done for him when all the bairns were small and helpless, she could go on doing for him now they were all grown up.

Perhaps in mother's seemingly wholehearted approval there was the expression of a subtle jealousy of her daughter, a subconscious fear that her own place in the home and in her husband's affection was being usurped—for Sally, apart from the physical attractiveness that had been mother's when Henry courted her,

had inherited most of the other virtues which made
her such a successful wife. Even before she had left
school she could cook the family dinner: she could
knit the complicated patterned guernseys which Henry
and all the male members of the family wore. She
could sew finer than mother herself. She could
'skane' mussels almost as quick, bait, mend nets.
But this jealousy, if it existed, was a more wholesome
instinct than the possessive love that ties a parent to
an adolescent child, that holds when it should let
go, and mother's conscious attitude towards her
children was as unselfish, as unpossessive as Henry's.
If Sally stayed at home she'd only be learning to be a
fisherman's wife, and if mother was content to be
one, she knew too much of its hardships, its anxieties,
above all, its failures, not to wish something better
for her daughter.

So Sally had gone to London, out of sight and sound
of the sea. The children had continued to adore her,
and she them. She had given more than satisfaction
to her mistress. Yet the latter was wise. She had
realised that in Sally she had found a treasure, but
she had not taken advantage of her seemingly
inexhaustible energy, her liking for hard work, her
astonishing dexterity. She had the foresight to realise
that in a few years all the children would be at school,
that Sally's present occupation was somewhat of a
dead end, and she had the decency to act upon this
knowledge. Sally, she saw, had the makings of a
first-class nurse. This had not impressed her so much
as her gift for making clothes, for fine needlework—

which, with a training shorter and less arduous than that of a nurse, might give her a lucrative profession. So she had made it possible for her to attend classes in dressmaking at a polytechnic. She had allowed her gradually to assume charge of her own wardrobe, which was that of a woman who likes to be un-pretentiously well dressed. Thus, to their mutual advantage, the dexterity which once had gone into knitting fishermen's guernseys and household sewing had been directed to the mending, the alteration, the making of elegant garments, and it would have been difficult for Sally not to have acquired some of her mistress's liking for good clothes, and, above all, her taste.

The fact that on her yearly visits home Sally had provided growing evidence of this taste, that her speech was acquiring a certain softness, that in many other ways she was showing the influence of an urban environment, had produced a subtle constraint between her and the family, particularly apparent in the first few days of reunion. Indeed it was in the minds of every one (save Sally herself) that Sally had grown into a lady. Spring cleaning was a mild affair compared with the preparations made for her homecoming. The cottage would be turned inside out, every washable article in it washed, windows cleaned, carpets taken up and beaten, floors scrubbed, and enough cakes and pastry baked to supply a Sunday School treat. And for her actual arrival (like the present occasion, it was always by the five o'clock train), the best tea-service would be on the richly-laden table, the polished kettle would be boiling on a fire in which even the very coals seemed to have been dusted and tidied up. Henry and John would be shaved, and in their best Sunday guernseys, and mother in her best Sunday black.

Secretly, Sally hated this. Although she was happy in London, appreciative of its lights, its shops, its bustle, although she had made plenty of friends, including at least two young men who on any free evening were only too willing to indulge a quiet passion of hers for the movies, although she had no particular liking for Bramblewick as a place and often wished her family out of it, now that fishing had become such an unprofitable drudgery, she suffered at times from an almost unbearable nostalgia. She longed passionately for her parents and her family; and when she pictured them it was always as they would be on an ordinary working day; father and John, and perhaps Marney with them (if Amy was washing), just come up from the boat, unshaven, smelling of fish and the sea, their faces reddened and salt-encrusted, mother bustling between fireplace and table (clothless and with honest mugs and stout dishes on it) attending to their great appetites and keeping up a constant chatter. And mingled with this longing for her family was often a longing for the life itself as she pictured it in her vivid memories of childhood—the drama of bad weather, the boats rushing in to escape a sudden storm, the excitement of shipwrecks and lifeboat launches, of the changing fishing seasons, the feverish making and repairing of nets and lines and lobster pots, the thrill of heavy catches following periods of unprofitable fishing, the rivalry (it was stronger in those days) between her own family and the Fosdycks, which provided an eternal topic for discussion in the kitchen, and the warehouse, where she and mother would be 'skaning' or baiting lines. She didn't actually want to come back to this sort of life. She had made the best of the advantages which had come her way, and she found plenty of satisfaction in her job. But when she thought of her holidays and coming home, it was never with the idea of rest, but as a change of occupation. She wanted to be Sally again, not Miss Lunn; to come straight back into the life of a home, to clean and cook and wash, and look after men's garments as a change from silk. She didn't want to be treated as a lady.

The mother she pictured in these periods of nostalgia was always busy, always chattering. Now, stiff and uncomfortable in her best black clothes, trying desperately to be the genteel hostess, she was like another person. It put a constraint on Sally herself. The conversation was confined almost entirely to questions and statements about the weather past and present, at Bramblewick and London, and the health of various members of the family. Henry and John were practically dumb. In spite of the abundance and variety of food on the table, every one seemed to be afraid of touching anything except bread and butter; and Henry and John handled their teacups (the service had been brought from Japan by John on his first voyage, and normally rested behind the glass doors of the corner cupboard) as though they belonged to a doll's set, and the tea was make-believe.

Yet Sally knew and appreciated how much her family looked forward to her rare visits home, that they were all intensely proud of her having done so well, and if the admiration was mute and so uncomfortably mingled with awe, there was real affection behind it, and she could repress her own mild disappointment and irritation in the thought that the ice would thaw before she had been home long. The ice indeed gave signs of thawing when the present meal ended, and father, with an involuntary sigh of relief, turned his chair round to the fire and picked up a piece of rope he had been splicing, and mother got up and started putting her apron on.

"I'll help you to wash up, mother," said Sally quickly.

"Eh—you'll do nowt of t'sort," mother answered. "Muckying your best clothes! Have another cup of tea, love, and turn your chair round to the fire. I'll soon get everything tidied up. . . . Give the fire a poke, Henry. . . . I expect Marney will be round to see you soon, Sally. Eh, those bairns of his have grown. You'll hardly know them. Little one's the very spit of Marney!"

Mother in her apron, mother chattering, was more like the mother Sally knew. Father was more like father when he had got a piece of rope in his hands instead of a china teacup. John, too (who had met her at the station and had maintained an almost unin-terrupted silence all the way down), looked more natural when he pushed his chair back, yawned, and then lit a Woodbine. And Marney, her favourite brother, who never stood on ceremony or tried to be anything different from what he was, could be trusted to brighten things up the moment he opened the door; and she looked round eagerly when there was a sound of footsteps outside, just audible through the muffled roar of the storm. But the sound was followed immediately by a knock. It couldn't be Marney. John, who was nearest the door, got up and opened the inner door, half closing it behind him so that for a moment the identity of the caller was not known to the family. The very fact of the knock, however, indicated an unexpected visitor, and mother stopped still in the act of tying her apron. Henry looked up from his job, and there was a silence in which shortly they heard John's very respectful "Good-evening, sir," and the vicar's hearty, "Good-evening, John. It looks as though I'd found the right place after all. Is your father at home?" And then: "Aye, he's here, sir. Will you step inside?"

Mother gave a nervous glance at the table, then, realising she had no time to do anything about it, slipped off her apron. Henry stood up. The vicar entered the room, John coming behind him and closing the door; and for a moment there was a silence more embarrassing than any during the now concluded tea-party, for the vicar himself was be-numbed with the cold, and the heat of the room, the glare of the unshaded incandescent gas-lamp temporarily dazed him. But Henry's "Good-evening, sir," if it was slow in coming, put him at his professional ease.

"Good-evening, Mr. Lunn," he said heartily, stepping forward and shaking Henry's hand. Then he turned to mother.

"There's no need to tell me I'm speaking to Mrs. Lunn—eh? I expect you know who *I* am? How do you do!"

"I'm in the best of health, thank you," mother answered, a little overcome. "And I hope you're keeping well. Isn't it bitter weather?"

The vicar shook mother's hand. Then he looked at Sally, and for a moment some of his professional heartiness went, for there was something in Sally's face that most men, except those of her own family, would have found arresting and disturbing. All the Lunns were good-looking. They were fair, with blue eyes, and very fair complexions which in the men were only slightly toned down by the weather. Both Henry and mother looked superbly healthy. Henry, at fifty-five, had not a grey hair, and would have passed for ten years younger. Mother's hair was nearly white, her figure had suffered with child-bearing and years of incessant domestic toil, but she was extraordinarily youthful looking and vital. Henry, perhaps, was more stolid in body and mind. He talked slowly, moved slowly, except in any emergency connected with his job, when he could spring to action like a jungle animal. John, inclined to be pessimistic and gloomy, showed Henry's predominant hereditary influence. But the rest of the family, combining the health and good looks of both parents, had inherited a strong measure of mother's abounding vitality, and it was this quality, more perhaps than her purely physical beauty, that made Sally so disturbing to men. It was not blatantly sexual. If the expression of her clear blue eyes, of her full and very mobile lips, the slight tilt of her nose, the way she moved her head, the subtle movement of her body were sexually provocative, her eyes at any rate conveyed a strength of character, a complete self-mastery that was not moral, but selective, proof (as her London men friends had quickly realised) against promiscuous surrender.

The vicar was startled by the look Sally gave him, which was at once inquiring, provocative and vaguely mocking; he was embarrassed by her clothes (an excellent tweed coat and skirt originally in her mistress's wardrobe, skilfully altered to her own slender figure, with a very neat silk blouse she had made from an American fashion magazine.) She didn't look like a fisherman's daughter, and he was relieved when his hesitant, "And this is——?" was completed by Henry.

"—That's our Sally, sir. She's at work in London. And only landed home for her holidays by the five o'clock train."

There was a genuine warmth in Sally's handshake that helped to restore the vicar's confidence, which was further restored when mother said:

"Won't you sit by the fire, sir? I hope you won't mind the table being so untidy. I was just starting to clear up when your knock came to the door. You needn't mind us if you want to talk to Henry. Unless it's summat private."

The vicar smiled, unbuttoned his coat and sat down. If his manner was a little pompous, he looked extremely handsome.

"No, there's nothing private in my business with your husband. And it won't take me long. It's just a little official duty, and a very pleasant duty, too, as far as I'm concerned."

Indeed, at that moment the vicar's task must have promised to be wholly pleasant. There was a warmth, a friendliness in the air such as he had never encountered in the 'best rooms' of his 'Up-Bank' parishioners. He liked Mrs. Lunn. He was agreeably conscious of Sally. Glancing at Henry, who had sat opposite him, he was impressed, more than he had been impressed by Luke Fosdyck, by the sturdiness of his physique, with the resolute cast of his face, so patently that of a man of deep experience and great strength of character. Certainly the committee had made a wise decision in asking Henry Lunn to be the new cox; and while he could not believe that the object of his visit was still a mystery to Henry and his family, it was pleasant and encouraging to feel that all of them were waiting very intently to hear what he had to say.

"Well," he began with a broad smile, "I suppose you've got a pretty good idea what my business is, Mr. Lunn. As you know, Luke Fosdyck is retiring from the lifeboat at the end of the month. I don't suppose there is any doubt as to who is best fitted

to take his place, but of course the business has got
to be done in a proper manner, so it has been brought
before the committee, and I'd like to tell you at once
that only one name was mentioned at the meeting,
and that the vote on the choice was unanimous."

The vicar paused, and with the professional skill of
a preacher, took stock of the impression he had so far
made. He was pleased. The whole family seemed to
be hanging on his words, and all of them gazing at
Henry, whose cheeks it seemed had grown slightly
red. But the expression on his face remained unchanged. His keen blue eyes were fixed upon the
vicar, and gave no clue, beyond complete interest as
to what was moving in his mind. He said nothing.
The vicar went on to complete his official duty.

"Well, I need hardly say that the name chosen was
yours, Mr. Lunn. Although I am almost a stranger
to the place, I've seen and I've heard enough about
you to know there is no one better fitted for the job,
and it gives me great personal pleasure to ask you to
become the new coxswain when Luke Fosdyck retires.
It's only for you to say yes or no."

There was a silence that was unexpectedly broken
by a giggle from Sally.

"You would look nice in a coxswain's cap, father.
Only wouldn't you have to grow a beard like old
Luke Fosdyck?"

"Hush, Sally," mother put in.

But the vicar turned and laughed.

"I'm sure that will be a point for Mrs. Lunn to
settle, eh?" He looked again at Henry, whose cheeks

were now definitely red, but whose expression was unaltered. "Well, Mr. Lunn, can we shake hands on it? Do you say yes?"

Henry Lunn at last moved, but it was only to lean slightly forward in his chair. He spoke very quietly, very deliberately, with an unconscious dignity.

"Well, sir, I reckon it's very kind of the committee to pick on me for cox, and I reckon it's very kind of you to come all the way down on a night like this to ask me about it. And I hope it won't give you any offence. But seeing you've asked for a straight answer —yes or no—then I've got to give it." He made just a perceptible pause, and then, without varying his quiet deliberate tone, he said, "I don't want to be cox. So I'll say no."

The vicar stared at Henry in astonishment.

"You don't really mean that, do you, Mr. Lunn? You don't really refuse?"

"Aye, sir," Henry answered just as quietly.

"But surely you know that you are the only one fitted to take the job?"

Henry smiled.

"Aye. I'm the oldest fisherman after Luke and Tindal, and Tindal would be no good with his weak eyes, and his health failing generally. There's John here, of course, and my other son, Marney. They could do it, and the committee's free to ask them. But I doubt if they'd take it on, any more than I would, as things stand."

It was the vicar's turn to go red in the face, and to show unmistakable signs of annoyance.

"But—I can hardly believe my ears. I'll admit I'm a landsman, and that I know very little about the lifeboat service, but I've always understood that you fishermen regard it—well—almost as a sacred duty to serve in the boat, in any position you're chosen to. I've always thought that the position of cox is looked upon as a very great honour. Surely there must be some very good reason why you should refuse."

Henry smiled.

"Aye," he answered. "There is a good reason. And if you'd like it put in a nutshell it's this: You don't want a new cox for Bramblewick lifeboat at all. Best thing that could happen when Luke Fosdyck retires—before, if you ask me—is for the Institution to close the station altogether and take the boat away."

There was a silence, in which the vicar regarded Henry Lunn as if he had uttered an appalling blasphemy. Then he glanced round at the rest of the family, and was encouraged to observe that to them, too, the statement had come apparently as a complete surprise.

"Close the station!" he echoed. "But Bramblewick has had a lifeboat almost since the first one was invented. Why, man, Bramblewick is famous for its lifeboat. Think of the number of lives you men have saved! Surely you don't mean it. It's almost like a famous old regiment dropping their arms and running away at the sight of the enemy. It's——"

The vicar stopped, suddenly conscious, perhaps, that he was letting his annoyance run away with him.

But if there was a vague irony in Henry's voice, there was no resentment in its quiet tones.

"Aye, sir. There's no doubt that Bramblewick lifeboat has done a lot of good in its time, and to any one who knows nowt about it, it might seem daftness taking it away, but not to those who man her. . . . Now, I don't want to cause any ill-feeling, one way or another, but a bit of plain speaking can do no harm if it's taken in the right way; and it's time someone spoke plain. You're the chairman of the lifeboat committee, sir, but you're a stranger. You've seen her launched for practice once or twice, but you've never seen her launched to a real job. What happens when there's a ship in distress? It's not only the lifeboat that has to go to her help. There's the rocket brigade. But the rocket brigade doesn't hold its practice same day as the lifeboat. Why? Because there isn't enough men left in Bramblewick to serve both. If I was cox of Bramblewick lifeboat I'd want twenty good men, besides my crew, to launch her. There's not a dozen you could depend upon in winter time. And if I had to take her out in anything like bad weather, I'd want a different crew to what there is at present: three of them drawing their old-age pensions, and none of them but us and the Fosdycks real fishermen. No, sir, it's time she went. And I wouldn't be doing the right thing if I told you I'd take on the job."

The vicar's annoyance had yielded to a patent embarrassment. Momentarily he seemed at a complete loss for argument. But he glanced round at the family, and again it seemed to him that he was not alone in his disappointment, that mother and John—and Sally in particular—were looking at Henry as though they were at least in some measure ashamed of what he had said, and certainly were not in complete agreement. He was encouraged, but his manner was less confident, almost contrite when he said:

"Well, Mr. Lunn, I'll admit I had no idea things were like this, and I'm surprised that the committee didn't let me know. It certainly seemed to me when I saw the boat launched that everything was done in a very efficient manner—although, of course, I noticed that some of the crew were elderly. . . . Yet I still can't believe that you'd like to see the boat taken away. Surely a boat with any sort of a crew is better than none. If a child or a woman is drowning, or screaming for help, a man doesn't stop to ask himself whether he can swim or whether he's too old or ill, does he? He just does his best. He can't help it. And I'll not believe that you, or any of your family or any other man in this place, wouldn't man the lifeboat if you heard a ship's signal of distress, or that you wouldn't find volunteers to help you. Why, even the women would help to launch. . . . Take a night like this. Suppose that at this very moment you heard the signal gun. Wouldn't you be the first man down?"

"Of course he would!" suddenly put in Sally. "I once saw father running down to the lifeboat in his shirt-sleeves and only carpet slippers on his feet—in winter, too. Mother and I had to run down after him with his coat and sea-boots, and we were only just in time."

"Eh—you wouldn't find any of our men lying in bed if the lifeboat gun was fired," mother was quick to add.

"It was us who had to wake the Fosdycks last time there was a ship ashore, sir," said John. "It was very thick weather. We'd been off all night, and we'd just got ashore when we heard her blowing. If you'll excuse me joining in the argument, I'll say that if father was the cox, you'd never have a better."

The vicar smiled genially.

"Ha—that's what I firmly believe. And I'm just as certain that if the lifeboat was taken away, no one would regret it more than your father. What would you feel like, Mr. Lunn, if you heard a signal of distress at this moment, and knew there was no boat—that you could do nothing to help?"

He looked challengingly at Henry, who, however, answered unperturbed:

"What would I feel like, sir? Why, that would depend on several things, but mainly I'd be glad that Bramblewick boat hadn't to be launched. For she'd be worse than useless. And I'd be glad, too, that a boat would be going to her assistance, quicker than our boat ever put out to a job—aye, with a better chance, too, of doing good. . . . You see, sir, there's been a big change in the lifeboat service since motors came into use. When every boat was either sailing or rowing, then there had to be a lot of them along the coast. But a motor-lifeboat can get away easier, and

C

steam almost into any weather, and be on a job in almost half the time it takes a rowing-boat like ours, even if it's further away. Maybe you've forgotten they've got a motor-lifeboat at Burnharbour. She hasn't got to be put down a dangerous slipway like ours, or need a score of men to do it. She's not weather-bound at high tide, like we are. Why, even with fifty men to help us, we couldn't put off to-night until the tide ebbed to the slipway bottom; and the chances are that we wouldn't be able to get to sea then. As for our doing nowt to help, we've got our own motor-coble. If the sea wasn't too bad for the lifeboat to go off, it wouldn't be too bad for us. And the chances are we'd be at the job in less time than it would take her to be in the water."

"But your coble is scarcely bigger than a small rowing boat! You don't mean you'd rather go out in her to the rescue of a ship than in the real lifeboat?"

"A hundred times over," Henry answered. "Not in very bad weather, of course, but in anything Bramble-wick lifeboat could put out in with her present crew."

Again there was an awkward silence. Again the vicar glanced round at the family, to measure the effect of this seemingly preposterous and arrogant statement. But if he was convinced that the effect was not one of complete approval, he saw nothing in the faces of mother, John or Sally to suggest a strong sympathy with his own point of view. He had set out on this mission with the pleasant sensations of a bearer of good news. Familiar with the shyness and modesty of working-class people, he had been prepared to find Henry Lunn embarrassed to the extent of an initial refusal of the honour that was being put upon him. But this would have been no more serious or difficult to overcome than the protestations of a poor woman to whom he might be taking a parcel of groceries. Instead, he had found himself confronted by a man who, despite his respectful manner, had cracked his own dignity, made himself feel ignorant and rather foolish. He was disappointed, disillusioned, angry, but he saw the futility of pursuing an argument in which his own technical ignorance must become more apparent, in which his dignity would suffer further shocks. He started to button up his coat.

"Well, Mr. Lunn, I'll confess you've taught me a lot about the local lifeboat, and I hope that you won't misunderstand anything I have said. Even if I could never agree with you about the station being closed, I shouldn't like you to think I don't see you have a very strong case. I'm not an expert on these matters, of course. I am in the hands of the committee, and I'll have to tell them that you refuse to take the post, and bring the whole question up again. But I'd like to say that I feel stronger than ever that you are the man for the job, and that if you change your mind it will give me very great pleasure to hear of it."

"There's no offence taken, and I hope none's been given, sir," said Henry. "I reckon you've only done your duty, and I've only done mine by telling you the plain truth as to how things stand."

The vicar shook hands with mother and Sally and John. Again he had a sense that they were not wholeheartedly on father's side; but he said nothing, and this time he avoided the direct glance of Sally's eyes. Henry moved with him to the door. The family waited in silence until he came back to his chair and picked up the rope he had been splicing; and still no one spoke. There was a new tension in the room. It was as though every one had something important to say, but that no one dare start. Yet to Sally that tension was exciting. All the constraint of her home-coming had gone. She felt that she was one of the family again, that things were happening, that father and mother and John had forgotten her existence as a lady, or anything else, in the disturbance of the vicar's visit.

She had herself experienced a variety of emotions. She could remember how in her childhood she had been passionately jealous of the part the Fosdycks had played in the lifeboat. In the earlier days, when the hostility between the foreigners and the Bramblewick fishermen had been at its height, her father had been debarred even from being one of the crew, and the village children had taunted her and her brothers with this. It had been a favourite day-dream of hers then to see the lifeboat called out on some desperate venture wherein for some reason Luke Fosdyck failed, and her father was called upon to take the coxswain's place, with such success that he was acclaimed. even by the Bramblewick fishermen, and persuaded to retain the position, to Luke's humiliation.

That dream had ever since been associated with her thoughts and her love for Henry, and she had been

thrilled when the vicar had disclosed the object of his
visit. She had been surprised, and at first deeply hurt,
by Henry's point-blank refusal. But she had listened
with growing conviction to his slow, deliberate argument. She had observed with a peculiarly feminine
satisfaction the pricking of the vicar's pomposity, in
which (despite that she was conscious of his attractiveness as a male) she detected the condescension of his
class towards her own. If her disappointment was
not completely gone, she had felt a new and intense
pride in her father. Yet she knew that mother and
John were upset by what had happened. They were
both ill at ease, staring at Henry as though in the
hope that he would break the silence, and give them a
chance of saying what was in their minds. Henry,
however, kept his attention fixed on the splice, and it
was John who at last spoke in a voice that betrayed that
he was repressing a strong emotion.

"Bye. You didn't half tell him off, father."

Henry glanced up sharply at his eldest son.

"Tell him off? I only told him the plain truth,
didn't I?"

"Aye, I know. But he didn't seem too pleased
about it."

"There's a lot of folks aren't pleased when they
hear the truth."

"Aye, the lifeboat committee included, and all
Bramblewick when they hear you told the vicar the
lifeboat ought to be taken away."

"And so it ought—oughtn't it?"

"*I* don't say it ought," John answered with sudden

courage. "She's no good for a real wreck, or for going out in wild weather, with a crew like she's got, but what about salvage? What if a steamer comes ashore in thick weather, and there's a job going to take out a kedge for her, like it's happened dozens of times before? Chances are a hundred to one it would be smooth water. We'd find her before the Burnharbour lifeboat did."

Henry was getting vexed.

"Is our coble as good as Bramblewick lifeboat, or isn't it?" he demanded.

"I won't say it isn't," John parried. "I won't say it wouldn't be better for actually doing a job, but that's not what I'm bothered about. What would the Fosdycks and the rest of Bramblewick folk say if we went out in her and made some brass? If you went as cox in the lifeboat, Luke and Tindal would still be in the crew, remember. They'd say we'd only argued for the lifebat being taken away so that we could have it all to ourselves and do them out of their share. Some of 'em hate us enough as it is."

"Eh—that's what I've been thinking all along, Henry," said mother. "I don't want to see us starting that all over again, just when it's beginning to look as though we'd all got nicely settled down in Bramble-wick, with no one left fishing but the Fosdycks, and them never interfering in anything, or trying to raise trouble like they used to do. We don't want any more quarrels with them. Why, think of young Tom Fosdyck. That shows how things have changed, him being so friendly with Marney, and as nice and quiet a spoken lad as you'll find anywhere."

"Is that the Tom Fosdyck who went to sea with Marney on his first voyage, mother?" asked Sally.

"Aye," mother said. "Luke's nephew. His father was blown up on a mine-sweeper in war time, you remember, and his mother died soon after of pneumonia. Tom lost his berth last back-end, when the ship he was sailing in was sold to the Greeks. Things are very bad for shipping now. Eddie and George are lucky not to have their ships sold or laid up. Well, as Tom couldn't get another berth, he came home and started fishing with his uncles. He lives with his Aunt Rachel. *You* know—the one that's religious. Tom's in the lifeboat, of course."

"We've got him in the band, too," said John. "Second bass. Only he's not got much ear for music. By the way, Sally, the vicar gave us five quid towards buying new instruments for the band. Say what you like about parsons, he's a decent chap all right. He'll help any one, doesn't matter what their religion is— Church, Wesleyan, or Congregational. I bet he's feeling pretty sick about the lifeboat, and father turning it down."

Sally remembered Tom Fosdyck as one of the roughest of the Bramblewick children; and best of all remembered hating him as the ringleader in the schoolboy gang who had made life so unpleasant for her own brothers, and the other foreigner boys. But she had never met him since he had gone to sea with Marney, and had heard nothing of his subsequent career, for after that first voyage he and Marney changed to different ships. She was surprised, not because it was Tom Fosdyck, but just because it was a Fosdyck, to hear of his friendliness with Marney. She did not, however, pursue her quest for information. She was enjoying this family battle, and was content to preserve a strict neutrality.

Father had started to work on his splice again, and his anger was well under control.

"Now, listen," he said, glancing up, but addressing no one in particular. "I've got nowt special against the Fosdycks. All the trouble there's been between us and them has been of their making. They didn't like us coming here. They hated our motor-coble. They did their best to drive us out, but Luke and Tindal have come at last to see they couldn't do without us. Lifeboat would have been taken away years ago if it hadn't been for us. I've got nowt against the vicar, either—or any one else in Bramblewick, so long as they'll mind their own business, and not interfere with mine. I've said all I've got to say about the lifeboat. She's no good as things stand, and that's an end to it. She ought to be condemned, and I'll bet the Institution thinks the same, and will be glad to save the expense of her. Motor-lifeboats have cut craft like her right out, and you all know they couldn't put a motor-lifeboat here. How often *is* there a ship in trouble round here, anyway? In sailing-ship days often enough, but in these days when nearly all ships have wireless, and there's lights or fog sirens at every dangerous spot, you might go years, and never have

owt happen. If owt does, our coble's handy. There's
three of us. There's six fishermen in this spot. Luke
and Tindal are getting on in years, but Tom's all
right. If there was a job to be done, they're free and
welcome to join us."

John looked at his father in astonishment.

"Do you think Luke and Tindal would ever set foot
in that coble? They'd as soon ask us all to join in a
game of kiss-in-the-ring. They hate that coble a damn
sight more than they've ever hated us."

"That's their lookout, then," Henry answered.
"They'd not be able to say we hadn't asked them."

"And what about Tom Fosdyck? What 'ud happen
to him if he came and they didn't? I bet they'd finish
with him. I bet"—John paused—"well, here's Marney
coming. We'll see what he's got to say about it. You
usually go more by his opinion than by mine."

"I don't go by any one's opinion in a concern like
this. I trust to my common sense."

The sound of steps outside was followed quickly by
the opening and slamming of the street door. The
inner door was opened, and Marney stepped into the
room. He was dressed, as Sally had expected, in his
ordinary fishing clothes, except that he wore shoes
instead of sea-boots. He was hatless, and his hair was
tousled with the wind, and full of hailstones, which
adhered, too, to his faded and muchly-darned guernsey.
Sally rushed towards him. Marney greeted her with
a broad grin.

"Now, Sally."

"Now, Marney."

He took her in his arms and kissed her.

"Bye, I'd hardly know you. Did John raise his hat when he met you at the station? You get more of a swank every time you land home."

"Don't talk so daft, Marney. I'm only wearing the clothes I've had given me, and I'd as soon have an apron on, only mother won't let me. How's Amy and the baby?"

"Champion. I've come to take you across, only you'll want to put summat different on to these togs. . . . Bye! It's a hell of a night. Hailing fit to tear the skin off your face, and seas are washing half-way up the dock already."

"Is the coble all right?" asked Henry.

"Aye, but she wouldn't have been if we hadn't pulled her right up."

"Sit yourself down by the fire, Marney," said mother. "It's a wonder you don't catch your death of cold coming out in such weather without a hat."

Marney moved—it was a lurch rather than a walk —across the room, but he picked up a tart as he passed the table, and then turned and stood with his back to the fire, grinning at Sally as she moved back to her chair.

"That's the worst of mother, Sally. She spoils you. If you'd come straight to our spot we'd have had you washing napkins by now."

"Did you pass the vicar as you came up through the dock?" John interrupted.

"No. If I had done, I'd have asked you all to come and pull the coble up another twenty yards. I've always said that meeting a parson's unluckier than meeting a black cat."

"Now, don't be disrespectful," mother admonished.

"He's been here to see father," John went on. Marney stopped grinning.

"What about—the lifeboat?"

"Aye. He offered him the job."

Marney turned on his father.

"Did you say yes, father?"

"I said no," Henry answered quietly.

"He told him straight out he wouldn't take the job, and that Bramblewick station ought to be closed," said John. "Aye, and then he said that our coble would be more use than the lifeboat. What's Bramblewick going to say to that?"

"It's going to make a lot of trouble, that's what I think," said mother. "What do *you* say, Marney? Don't you think father ought to take it?"

Marney reached over to the table for another tart.

"No, I don't," he answered. "I reckon he'd be daft if he did. If you want to know what I think about it, I'll tell you."

He stood again with his back to the fire, but shifting his balance continually from one foot to the other, as though balancing himself against the roll of a boat's deck. There was a strong likeness between him and Sally. They had the same clear blue eyes which expressed the abounding vitality they had inherited from mother. Their mouths were very much alike, particularly when they smiled. If Marney's hands were coarsened with sea-water, and the friction of ropes, they were small, the fingers supple and dexterous. He was of lighter build than father or John, quicker of action and speech. Yet when he was serious it was apparent than in character he was closer to father than John was—that he possessed a stronger sense of responsibility, that, next to father, he was the leader, John the follower. He was serious now, conscious that he held the undivided attention of his family.

"I'll tell you what I think about it," he repeated. Then, not so slowly as his father would have spoken, but with almost the same deliberate tones, "I'm sick to death of Bramblewick and everything and every one in it. I'm sick of the sight of the dock and the slipway —aye, and of Bramblewick Bay. I'm sick of old Luke and Tindal Fosdyck, eyeing us always as though we'd got no more right to be catching fish than looking under their beds for where they hide their savings. I'm sick of hauling our and their coble up and down every day, and of us not daring to shoot our lines far out to sea for fear of having to keep them waiting while we get back to shore. I tell you, I'm fed up with this spot. When the weather's fine we can't fish properly. When it's only middling bad we've got to stay ashore, because Luke won't risk it. How many days this winter have we stayed ashore and let the bait rot on our lines when if we'd been in a spot with a harbour we could have fished and done well? It wouldn't be so bad if Bramblewick itself was owt like a spot to live in. You might be on a desert island, for all there is going on at night, particularly in

winter time. It wouldn't be so bad if you could go
to the pictures "

"There's the pictures at Burnharbour, isn't there?"
interrupted John. "You can go to them on Saturday
when there's a late bus."

"*You* can," Marney retorted, "Seeing you've only
got yourself to think about. You've got no bairns,
either, to keep or look after. How often can Amy and I
go? Never, even if we had the brass."

"Eh—Marney's right about that, John," mother put
in. "Bairns are a tie and an expense. But all I can say
is a home's not a home without them."

John ignored this gentle jibe as to his own
unmarried state. Instinctively he was on the defence
on a more important issue. He had already guessed
what Marney was leading up to.

"Well, if you can't go to the pictures, you can't say
there's nowt to do in Bramblewick on a winter's night.
You could join the band if you wanted to. It's only
because you haven't the patience to learn an instrument."

"What the devil have bands and bairns got to do
with what we're talking about?" Henry interrupted
with a flash of anger. "What are you trying to get
at, Marney?"

Marney answered very quietly:

"I'm only trying to tell you I'm fed up with Bramblewick and the whole carry-on, and I think it's time
we all cleared out of it for good."

"Where to?"

"Burnharbour, of course."

It was a bombshell; and Marney himself seemed fearful of its effect, for he bent down to light a fag at the fire, and took a long time over it. When he looked up he observed through the cloud of smoke he exhaled that Henry's eyes were on his rope again, that John looked gloomy and very vexed, that Sally, if she smiled at him, seemed bewildered; and he was still afraid to look at mother even when she spoke:

"Eh—I don't want to leave Bramblewick."

"Neither do I," said John.

"If we left Bramblewick now," said Henry, "the Fosdycks would be able to say they'd beaten us at last."

"I thought you'd got nowt against the Fosdycks."

"Neither have I, really. It's always been them against us. But they tried their best to drive us out, same as they did the other chaps who came with us from Sledburgh. We've beaten them, and I'd not like to have 'em laughing up their sleeves, thinking they'd made us all pack off to Burnharbour."

"You wouldn't like us to have to leave this house, would you, Marney?" mother went on, with a sudden catch in her voice. "It's been a home for us for more than thirty years. *I* wouldn't like to start taking down the pictures and packing up all our belongings, and going off to live in a strange place where we know scarcely anybody and no one knows us—and a town, too. And think of leaving the hens. We'd never find a spot in Burnharbour where we could keep hens. . . . And just when everything quietened down. *I* don't want to leave Bramblewick. This is our home. What would Eddy and George and Steve think when they came back for their holidays and found us in a strange place, everything different. What would you feel, Sally?"

Sally caught Marney's eye. In its substance, his proposal had not taken her completely by surprise. Marney had frequently unburdened himself to her on the growing difficulties of making a living out of fishing in Bramblewick. The problem was less acute for the others. John, as Marney had said, had only himself to think about. Father, always of a careful, thrifty nature, had managed, in times when things were better, to save enough cash to tide over the periods of bad fishing. Marney had never been capable of saving. To him, money was something to be spent, not on himself, but on any one he liked, particularly his wife and kids; and, before the coming of his last-born, a week's run of good luck had always meant a Saturday afternoon at Burnharbour with Amy and the other two, intensive and (despite Amy's protests) often reckless shopping—and, of course, the pictures. He was a fine fisherman, as skilful as his father, and, because of his youth, perhaps, more daring. He chafed under the restraint implied by the necessary co-operation with the Fosdycks in the launching and hauling up of the boats. Time after time he would have put to sea in bad but not prohibitive conditions, when Henry, yielding (however grudgingly) to Luke's verdict, had said no. Instinctively Sally found herself on Marney's side. She had no roots in Bramblewick. She knew that Marney was right, and that the sooner the entire family packed off to a place where such restraint did not exist the better. But she was as quick to realise what a weight of opposition he would have to overcome, in the attitude of the rest of the family, particularly mother's. Her roots in Bramble-wick were strong—stronger because the soil had been so hard. She answered tactfully:

"Why, mother, it's you and father and the family I come to see, not Bramblewick. It wouldn't matter to me whether you were here or Burnharbour or Timbuctoo, it would always be home. But it's certainly a dead-alive place in winter time. It would be nice being in a place where there were plenty of shops, and being able to go to the pictures without having to go all that way in a bus."

"Eh, I don't hanker for things like that," said mother.

"I've only been to the pictures once, and it was nowt but a lot of daftness, and a waste of money."

"Aye, but it wasn't a talkie," said Marney. "And how long ago was it? Ages! There's good films and bad films, same as in everything else. If I could per-suade you and father to go to the Regal—only once—and there was summat decent on, I'd bet you'd change your minds. Like that thing Amy and I saw last time we went. It was champion. If we hadn't had the bairns with us, we'd have stayed in our seats and seen it twice."

"That was *Smiling Through*, wasn't it, Marney?" asked John.

"Aye."

"It was champion. I'd have liked to have seen it twice."

"If you'd been living in Burnharbour you could have seen it three times over with what you'd save on your bus fare."

"Aye, maybe. But that wouldn't make up for leaving Bramblewick. I tell you the idea's daft. We might only be jumping out of the frying pan into the fire. I say it would be better by half if father took the lifeboat and let things go on as they are. Vicar as much as said he'd leave it open in case he changed his mind."

"Now, look here," Henry suddenly put in, "hold your jaws about the whole business, because I'm about sick of it. I've made up my mind about the lifeboat. If Marney wants to go and live in Burnharbour, that's his affair. . . . Here's our Sally come home, and we've done nowt but squabble and argue since she set foot in the house."

Marney grinned.

"All right, father. You better ask John to play us 'Home, Sweet Home' on his cornet, and wle'll al sing. . . ." He looked at Sally. "Come on, Sal, get your coat on. Amy had nearly finished feeding Sam when I left her, and she won't let any one touch him once he's put to sleep. . . . I'll have another of those tarts before I go, mother."

Mother had stood up, and was putting her apron on again. Marney knew that she was very upset, and he moved towards her and put his hand affectionately on her shoulder.

"I'll put some in a bag for you and the bairns," she said. "I know Amy's hard put to it these days to

D

find time for baking. Wrap yourself up well, Sally.
You better take that shawl of mine to put over your
coat. And don't keep her over long, will you, Marney?
I've scarcely had a chance to say how-d'you-do to her
with all this upset about the lifeboat, and now you're
wanting us all to pack up and go. I hope there'll
be no more of that, anyway. I've never heard such
daftness."

Marney did not reply. He was watching Sally, who
had put mother's plaid shawl over her head and
shoulders, and was smiling at herself in the ornamental
mirror over the fireplace.

"Bye! That suits you better than those fancy togs
of yours, Sally. I wonder what Tom Fosdyck will
make of you."

Sally turned.

"Tom Fosdyck? I'm not going to meet him now,
am I?"

"Aye. He was warming a napkin at the fire when I
left home."

Sally was blushing.

"Well, if he thinks the same about me as I thought
about him last time I saw him it won't be much. I
hated him. He was always fighting you or John, or
getting some one else to fight you. I wish I hadn't
to meet him, Marney. Can't I come over later when
he's gone?"

"Garn. Tom's all right. A bit slow and quiet.
You can have Tom sitting in a room for hours, and
never know he was there but for him puffing at his
pipe."

"He's got a pair of ears, all the same," said Henry quietly. "So you can keep your mouths shut about what's been going on here to-night. We don't want it all round Bramblewick before morning."

"You can remind him there's a band practice to-night, too," said John. "Half-past seven."

"Come on, Sally," said Marney. "It sounds as though the squall's over. Let's hurry before another starts. You needn't get frightened about Tom Fosdyck. He wouldn't harm a mouse."

3

THE squall was over, stars gleamed overhead, but the wind was strong, and the fallen hail, too dry to lay, scurried along the ground, making drifts in the corners of the cottage walls, that were as quickly dissipated by the pursuing gusts. The cold took Sally's breath. She clung tightly to Marney's arm as they hurried down towards the dock. But there was a tonic quality in the cold, in the smell of brine, in the roar and thunder of the wind and sea. She could feel the coarseness of Marney's guernsey, the play of the hard muscles beneath, and she fell involuntarily into the rhythm of his sailor's lurching stride, and she was excited and happy. And Marney, free of the constraint of his family, aware instinctively of Sally's sympathy, let himself go.

"Fed up? By God, I'm fed up with this, all right. Off and on we've had this sort of weather ever since November. We haven't averaged more than one fishing day in a week. What we've got then scarcely paid for the cost of our bait, except once when we struck a big lot of haddocks, and made eight quid in one shot. That's what feeds me up, Sally. The fish are there all right, but they've got to be found; you've got to chase round after them to find where they're feeding. They may be close in one day, miles out the next. Way we've got to fish, it's one in a thousand

chance of us striking them. We ought to be out
fishing no matter what the weather, unless it's a
roaring gale. We ought to be able to stay out all
night if we want to."

"But doesn't father and John know that?"

"Aye, they know it all right. They know we'll
have to leave Bramblewick sooner or later, or give up
the game. I'm not troubled about John much. He'll
do what we do, even if he argues up to the last. And
I'm not so sure father wouldn't come round to the
idea, if he only had himself to think about. It's mother
who stands in his way. You saw how she took it. It
isn't that she's got fond of Bramblewick. But she's got
used to it, even to folks not liking us."

They'd reached the back of the old coastguard
lookout whose outer walls, flanking the south side of
the slipway, make a rampart against the full fury of
a north-easterly sea; and they had to stop in the lee
of it while the water from a spent wave swirled up
the dock in a spuming torrent, temporarily barring
their way across. The lifeboat house was close, and
behind it, under the light of a street lamp, they could
see the bows of the two cobles, the Lunns' painted
white with a blue upper strake and a dividing line of
red, the Fosdycks' a sombre and unrelieved grey.

"I'm glad, anyway, father turned the lifeboat job
down. If he'd taken that on we might have been
stuck here for ever, for, as you know, once he agrees
to a thing, nowt will shift him. It shows he's not
settled down to Bramblewick."

"Yes, but he says the coble would always be ready

to take the lifeboat's place. Would she really be as good as the lifeboat? She *is* a small boat."

"I'd as soon trust her as any lifeboat in this spot," Marney answered. "But if you want to know what I really think, I shouldn't be sorry if the coble was smashed up to-morrow. . . . Come on, now, before another sea rushes up."

They ran across the dock, and up to the opening of another alley opposite, reaching the shelter of it just in time to escape the spray from a terrific wave, which rose almost to the coastguard's roof before it broke.

"She's a good little boat," said Marney as they hurried on. "She'll stand up to almost any sort of weather. She's about the only sort you could use in Bramblewick. But the days of craft like her have gone. If you're going to earn a living out of fishing, you've got to have a craft big enough to sleep in, like those new keelers they've got in Burnharbour. *They* can earn brass all right. While we've been stuck ashore here, some of them have been earning anything up to fifty quid a week."

"But how could you ever get a boat like those, Marney? They cost a lot of money, don't they?"

"There's ways and means. If father could get his mind set on one, and set on leaving this damned spot, we'd manage it somehow."

They'd reached the top of the alley, and now turned up a shorter alley to their right.

"Well, we'd best shut up about it now. If you ask me, I don't think Tom's any fonder of Luke and Tindal than we are, but he's still in with them, and we don't want that lot knowing how things are with us. Here we are."

He pushed open the door of a small cottage and let Sally step in first.

"Here we are, Amy," he shouted as he latched the door. "Here's our Sally. A bigger swank than ever. John even raised his hat to her when he met her at the station."

For a moment Sally was confused, not by Marney's introduction, but by the fact that Amy had the child at her breast, and her natural instinct to rush forward and embrace her sister-in-law was frustrated. But Amy solved this problem by reaching up her disengaged hand and giving her a warm smile of welcome.

"Hallo, Sally. I *am* glad to see you. Come and sit down by the fire, and take no notice of Marney and his rudeness. You know Tom Fosdyck, don't you? I expect you remember him when you were all bairns together."

The room was no more than half the size of Henry's. It was lit by an oil lamp standing on the table, which, throwing a strong light on the table itself and on Amy, left the rest of the room in shadow, so that at first Sally had only been vaguely aware of Tom Fosdyck, sitting in an arm-chair drawn back in a corner by the fire. He had not moved when she came in. Now he stood up, and they faced each other. He was tall, a head taller than Marney. To Sally, the lowness of the room accentuated his height, and the impression he gave her of great physical strength. But she had expected this. She was not surprised, either, to find

him good-looking. He had the long, lean face of all
the male Fosdycks, the same high cheek-bones, and
deep, sunk eyes and swarthy complexion, the same
rather grim set of mouth. But his eyes had none of
that sneering arrogance which had so aroused her
fury in the past.

Her most vivid memory of Tom Fosdyck was seeing
him fighting Marney down on the shore by the old
coastguard station; Tom with his lips clenched tight
and his eyes flashing, raining blow after blow upon
Marney's bleeding face; of how she had rushed in
with a stick and tried to stop him. Unsuccessful, she
had run home to tell mother, and not the least bitter
part of that memory was the hiding she had got later
from Marney for telling tales. There was no trace of
the bully now. The eyes that met hers were meek,
instead of domineering. They were those of a man
who had suffered a vital setback, who temporarily at
least had lost faith in himself, and Sally's quick sense
of triumph over her childhood enemy yielded to an
easy sympathy. She smiled and reached out her hand.

"Hallo, Tom."

He grasped her hand firmly and said in a surprisingly
gentle voice:

"Hallo, Sally."

"I certainly wouldn't have known you if I'd met
you in the street."

"I wouldn't have known you, either. You've
changed, and no mistake."

"Give me those baby socks hanging on the line
before you sit down, Tom," said Amy. "Come and

sit by me, Sally. Bye! I do like that coat and skirt you're wearing. It does suit you. What do you think of this? Would you like to hold him a minute. I think he's had enough."

Sally was quick to notice the imperious way in which Amy had spoken to Tom, his meek compliance; but for the time she forgot Tom in the thrill of taking the baby in her arms. She gave a gasp of admiration.

"Oh—he's lovely! Isn't he like Marney? I thought Jeff and Alice were; but he's even got Marney's ears."

Tom, having handed down the socks, returned to his chair and began slowly and methodically to fill his pipe. Marney had picked up a cotton snood from a bunch lying on the table, and was now dexterously whipping a cod-hook to it, biting the fine whipping thread off with his strong teeth. Amy fastened up her blouse, and looked with a proud smile at her last-born.

"Yes, I think he's like Marney," she said. "But they do change, you know. Alice was just like me when she was born, and now she seems to take more after your mother than any one, and Jeff's like no one I know, except he's got all of Marney's devilment. Just fancy, he's only five, and only the other day I missed him; and, do you know, he'd got right down to the scaur ends by himself, waiting for the coble to come in! He was wet through, of course, having fallen into a big pool trying to catch a crab. Sam weighed exactly eight pounds when he was born. I expect you heard what a bad time I had. I thought it was going to be twins."

"I'd have had a bucket for one of them if it had been," put in Marney. "If not both."

"I bet you would," Amy retorted. "But you'd have seen that you got your ten quid insurance money from the *Daily Mail* first. . . . Do you know, Sally, I had the pains for nearly three days. I was in the wash-house when they first came on, skaning mussels, and Marney was off at sea, and I got such a fright, because I thought I'd have no one to send up for the nurse. I didn't like going out myself, of course, so I sent Jeff to tell your mother, and she must have thought it had happened by the way she came running across. She was white as a sheet. They fetched the nurse down, but by the time she came the pains had gone, and she said it was a false alarm; and I thought it was, too, and I went on skaning, but the pains came back in less than an hour, and this time I came indoors and made myself a cup of tea, and waited until I was certain, for I didn't want to make a fool of myself again. . . . Well, it was like that for three whole days off and on. Every one wanted me to go to bed, but how could I when there were so many things to do! Anyway, I knew when it was really starting, and I'll tell you when we're by ourselves all about that. . . . Bye! I shouldn't like to go through all that again. They had to give me chloroform. I didn't have chloroform for either of the others. Doctor said it was all because I'd gone on working too long. But I reckon myself it was just because it was winter time and very cold weather. He didn't *want* to be born. Both the others were born in summer."

Sally, as she listened, felt her cheeks tingling. She was not shocked by the subject of Amy's narrative. In her family there had never been any hush-hush about birth—very little about the other aspects of sex. At one time or another she had been given, by mother herself, fairly detailed accounts of every one of the family confinements, including her own. She had no dislike for the morbid details of maternity—for giving birth, after all, is adventure, and its perils and escapes as dramatic and worth telling as any that may befall a man. She was excited. She wanted Amy to go on with her story; but she knew, too, that her interest and excitement were deeply tinged with envy, an envy of which she was secretly ashamed and unhappy. She was jealous of her sister-in-law.

She could feel the warmth and the gentle stirring of the baby in her arms. It thrilled her, and at the same time made her more conscious of its mother's possessiveness, that really she was only helping Amy to show off. At home she had been resentful of every one regarding her as a lady. Here her clothes, her looks, her success meant nothing, while Amy with her baby held the stage; and she had to admit to herself, too, that despite the five years difference in their ages, that Amy's clothes were shabby, that she was careless of her appearance; she was even more attractive now than she had been when she had married Marney. There was not a line on her face. Her lips were red, her teeth dazzling white. Her hair which, as Sally knew, never got any other treatment than a Saturday night's wash with common soap, had the

golden wave and natural sheen of a little girl's. She
observed with what pride Marney was watching her ;
and glancing at Tom Fosdyck she imagined that she
had made a discovery which in a peculiar way
increased the uneasiness of her mind. Except to light
his pipe he had not moved since he had sat down, or
made a sound. But he was gazing at Amy, in the way
that a dozing dog gazes at its master. Tom, unless
Sally was very much mistaken, was in love with her
brother's wife, deeply, hopelessly in love.

Amy got up and moved over to the crib at the
farther end of the room, and started to rearrange the
bedding. Tom, Sally observed, watched her every
movement and his interest was not diverted when
Marney said :

"Aye, I wouldn't like to go through that again
either. When Jeff came it was bad enough. . . . Do
you know, Sally, every one laughs at me when I tell
'em, but when Amy gets bad I get bad too. Mind, I
don't say I go through one fraction of what she goes
through. But I get a splitting headache and I feel sick.
That night Sam was born, I thought my head was
going to split open, and it went on getting worse until
the very moment I heard him scream, and then,
damned if it didn't clear away and I felt as fit as a
fiddle."

Amy laughed.

"Listen to him, Sally ! What gave him a headache,
and made him feel sick was smoking too many fags
and going on eating anything he could lay hands to,
just because he'd got wind up about me. . . . Of

course, it's well known that there are folks who can take the pains of a labouring woman."

Amy came towards her chair again.

"I remember mother telling me about some one in Burnharbour who was always sent for if a woman was having a bad time. She wasn't a midwife herself, in fact she never had anything to do with that side of the business. They just let her sit down in the room and in a moment or two she'd start to writhe and groan and gasp and shout out how the pains had got her, and sure enough the woman who was really having them would start having an easier time and get the whole thing over without much trouble. . . . Shall I take him now?"

Sally let Amy take the baby, and again she observed how Tom Fosdyck watched her as she bent over the crib. She studied Tom herself more closely. She wondered if Amy was completely conscious of his devotion, to what extent she was interested in him. He *was* good-looking, she thought. She could hardly believe that it was the Tom Fosdyck she had known and hated as a boy. He was dressed, like her father, and John and Marney, in blue serge trousers and guernsey, but they had neither the uncomfortable smartness of father's or John's ' best,' nor the untidiness of Marney's. His guernsey was of a different pattern too. Theirs, which Sally could knit with her eyes closed, was a Sledburgh one which had been handed down for generations; and it identified a Sledburgh fisherman or sailor wherever he went. Vaguely she found herself trying to work out the pattern of Tom's, particularly where the sleeve joined the shoulder in a sort of ribbed epaulette, and at the same time she was growing more certain that he was in love and that Amy must know it, but it wasn't so easy to tell if she was really in love with him. It seemed to her that Marney was not too cordial towards him and that, in a way, he resented his presence in a room, but that might only be because he was thinking about what had happened at home and was impatient about having to keep quiet about it. Was it a hopeless love for Amy that had made such a change in Tom, that made him look so unhappy?

Sally felt a sudden wave of pity for him, that was sharply mingled with a new wave of jealousy against Amy. She had got everything. A good husband, three fine kids, and now she must have another man dangling on her string. Yet he was not the sort Sally herself could fall for, quite apart from him being a Fosdyck. He was a fine-looking man, and certainly very attractive, far more so than any of the young men she had met in London, but the thing he lacked was the very thing Marney had so much of—go. He looked slow, and gloomy. All the Fosdycks were like that. Besides, she had no hankerings to be a fisherman's wife. She had done well to cut herself away from that sort of thing. If it was nice to come home occasionally and pick up the threads of the old life again, she'd always been happy to get back to London. While she could envy Amy for a lot of things, she certainly didn't envy her skaning mussels in a cold, damp wash-house when she was far gone. If this room was more home-like than any in the house of her mistress, she did not relish the job of looking after it and a man and a family, doing all the cooking on an open fireplace, without water or gas laid on or any of the conveniences of a modern household and all in the shadow of poverty. . . .

Amy came back to her chair, then reached to the table for her work-basket, and took out some children's garments, and some stockings and a half-finished guernsey. Sally's eyes lit up.

"Is that guernsey for Marney?"

"Aye. I started it a month before Sam was born, and it looks as though I'll never get it finished with all the sewing and mending I've got to do for the bairns."

Sally took hold of the guernsey.

"Oh, by the way," she said, "I've got a few things I made for you and the bairns but Marney was in such a hurry I hadn't time to think of them. I'll bring them over in the morning. I do hope you'll let me have a peep at Jeff and Alice before I go back. I promise not to wake them up. . . . Shall I get on with this for you?"

Amy smiled.

"I wish you would. It is good of you to think about us all like that. We'll creep upstairs in a minute or two and have a look at them. Haven't you forgotten how to knit a fisherman's guernsey, Sally?"

Sally had already got the needles in her hand. She laughed confidently.

"You'd better by half help me to whip some of these hooks," Marney put in. "You used to be a good hand at that anyway. . . . What about you, Tom? Get

hold of a handful of hooks and snoods.   You'd better
be employed than sitting there doing nowt."

Tom grinned and suddenly got up from his chair.

"There's a band practice at half-past seven," he said.
"I'll have to be off."

"God—so there is. Last thing our John said to me
was remind you about it. But there's no hurry, is
there. Damn it, you've scarcely said a word to Sally."

Sally looked up at Tom, but he didn't look at her
when he said, with a rather surprising irony :

"I'd like to know when you and Amy have given me
a chance."

"Then you'd better take her for a walk along the
cliff tops to-night, when you've finished making the
dogs howl with that damned band of yours."

"There's no call for rudeness," Amy put in sharply.

"It would be a cold night for a walk, wouldn't it,
Tom?" laughed Sally.

Tom grinned again, but he still avoided her glance
as he moved towards the door.

"Aye, it would, Sally. I doubt we'll have to wait
for finer weather than this. . . . Well, so long,
everybody."

Sally joined in the general 'so-long, Tom,' but
Tom did not turn, and she felt her cheeks tingling
again when the outer door slammed, and deliberately
she kept her eyes on her knitting during the silence
which ensued, conscious that Amy was looking at her
and fearful that she should read her thoughts. But
Marney was quick to set the current of talk in a safe
direction.

"I'm glad we're by ourselves," he said eagerly. "What do you think's happened, Amy? Vicar's been up to see father to-night to ask him if he'll take the lifeboat on when Luke retires. I didn't like to say owt about it in front of Tom."

"Well, what happened?"

"He turned it down, thank God."

Amy was sewing.

"I don't see there's owt to thank God for in that," she said without looking up.

"Well, I do. It's a clear sign he's not got his heart set on staying in Bramblewick. I thought it was a good chance of telling them all it was time we all cleared off to Burnharbour."

"You could have saved your breath. You know that no one else wants to go but you."

"Well, *you* do, don't you?"

"I'm not that keen about it, not if it's just to go on fishing in that daft coble of yours. Things may be bad here as far as money goes, but I'll say this about Bramblewick, it's a far safer spot than Burnharbour. You *can't* fish here when it's very bad weather. The Fosdycks put a stop to it, even if the weather doesn't. And a good thing too! If it wasn't for them you'd all have drowned yourselves years ago. And *I* know how things will be if we went to Burnharbour. You're so daft and reckless you'd be out when it wasn't fit to put to sea, except in a big boat, and it would end in summat bad."

"Don't talk so daft. That coble of ours would stand anything a Burnharbour boat would; and, besides, we

E

wouldn't fish in a boat like her if we went there   We'd want summat bigger ourselves."

"Aye, a steam trawler, I suppose. We'd easily get a new one built with what *we've* got in the bank. . . . What did they say to the idea anyway? I bet John wasn't for it. I bet he wouldn't like to leave his precious brass band. And I bet your mother would take some persuading."

"I know all about that," said Marney quietly, as he pursued his task. "I didn't expect any of 'em to jump at it, but it's got to happen sooner or later or we'll have to give up fishing altogether. There's Luke Fosdyck already too old for the lifeboat. He'll soon be too old for fishing, and when he gives up Tindal will give up with him, *and* Tom ; and we can't haul our coble up ourselves."

"And what's going to happen to Tom?"

Marney bit a length off a bit of whipping cord, and answered thoughtfully.

"I don't know. But if we did get a bigger boat, and started working out of Burnharbour, we'd be a man short, and I reckon, if he was willing, we could take him on. Of course, it would be for father to say, but father's got nowt against Tom so far as I know, except that he's a Fosdyck."

"What did you make of Tom, Sally?" Amy remarked suddenly.

Sally laughed, but she avoided Amy's questioning glance.

"He's the strong, silent man all right, isn't he? He's certainly different to what I expected."

"He's a very decent chap is Tom," said Marney.
"And I'll tell you, I'm sorry for him. I know he's a
Fosdyck. I never had much reason to like him when we
were lads. I reckon I had more fights with him than
any other lad in Bramblewick, and even when we went
to sea together, we had a fight almost as soon as we
first left port. And then somehow or other we started
to get on better together. After all, we were the only
Bramblewick chaps on the ship, and whenever we got
to a port where there were letters waiting for us or
parcels, all with the Bramblewick postmark on 'em,
it was sort of natural we should pal on to each other,
and talk about what we'd heard in our letters. And
the rummest thing was that Tom quietened down so.
He'd always been a dunce at school, in fact, he hadn't
got beyond the sixth standard when he left. Well, he
started studying navigation, out of books the chief
mate lent him, and before we'd been at sea two months
he could use a sextant as well as the mate himself and
work out the ship's position. I always had a hell of a
job to persuade him to go ashore for a bit of fun when
we got into port, even in a spot like Rio. He liked to
spend all his spare time studying his books, and working
out sums, practising morse or nosing about the
ship to see how everything worked, and the mate said
once, that he reckoned Tom would get all his tickets,
and have a ship before some chaps had passed for
second."

"Meaning you, I suppose," put in Amy. "I bet you
spent a lot of time studying."

"I never had much use for books," Marney answered

frankly, "I liked messing on with ropes and sewing tarpaulins, but except when you were in port, it was all too slow. It wouldn't have been so bad in a sailing ship, for you could have put a line overboard occasionally and done a bit of fishing, particularly when you struck a calm, but in a steamer, you might as well be flying through the sky for all the use the sea is to you. . . . Anyway, I'm telling Sally about Tom. I didn't see much of him after he'd changed to a different ship, but I know that when he'd finished his apprenticeship there was nowt he didn't know about navigation, and the other subjects a chap has to pass in for his tickets. He went to a navigation school, of course, for two months, but they didn't put him through the doctor there. It wasn't until he went in for the actual examination they found out about his eyes and told him he could never be a ship's officer."

"But what was the matter with his eyes?" asked Sally.

"Colour blind," said Amy calmly, stealing the dramatic point of Marney's story. "You ask Tom to give you a ball of blue wool out of that work-basket and the chances are he'll give you a green one, if there happens to be a green one there."

"I bet if you did ask him, he'd get up and walk out of the house, for he'd think you were just making game of him. He's touchy about it, I can tell you."

"But hadn't he to pass a doctor before he went to sea at all?" Sally asked.

"Aye, we both went before the doctor at the same time, but it was at Burnharbour, you know, and although the chap put us through the tests with a lot of different wools he didn't notice anything wrong with Tom. There isn't much wrong with him anyway. His ordinary eyesight's as good as mine if not better. He can tell a port light from a starboard light, but the examination's very strict so they turned him down and Tom went back to sea before the mast. But his heart wasn't in it. It was no use him studying books any more. He'd set his heart on being a ship's captain and it must have been hell having to take his orders from young officers who didn't know as much about the job as he did himself. Anyway, the ship he was on was sold, and although I think he could have got another berth if he'd tried, he landed home last back end, and started fishing. Tindal Fosdyck had had a stroke or summat and although he'd got better, Luke and him were glad enough to take Tom on, in spite that it meant having to give him a share. Of course he'll never talk about it, but I reckon Tom never stops thinking about his bad luck. It's like a bad tooth that's always aching. And I bet it doesn't make him feel any better having to live with his Aunt Rachel, her being so gloomy and religious. And you'd hardly call Luke and Tindal cheerful company."

"Tom comes in here almost every night," said Amy. "I'm certain it would about finish him if we left Bramblewick and he had nowhere to spend his evenings. And he's so fond of the bairns."

"Aye. It's good to tell what would cure him too. What he wants is a wife and bairns of his own. Summat to get his mind off himself. Do you know, Sally,"

Marney went on after a moment's thoughtful pause, "It seems a pity to me that you ever left Bramblewick. If you'd stuck to the trade you were born to, you'd have made a champion wife for Tom. I'll not say it's too late yet!"

Amy turned on her husband with flashing eyes.

"Hold your mouth, Marney. If I was Sally I'd smack your face for talking so outspoken. What business is it of yours?"

Sally's cheeks were burning, yet she was thankful for Amy's violent outburst. It gave her breathing space. She had been deeply moved by Marney's story. She was filled with an intense pity for Tom, and that emotion was mingled with something else which at present she could not wholly comprehend, but it frightened her. She was shocked but she was not surprised by her brother's frankness. She was aware instinctively of what had really inspired Amy's anger. But her inward fear, the sense she had as of moving in the darkness, along the edge of a perilous cliff, became subordinate to the fear of Amy knowing it. She was aware that Amy was now staring at her as though trying with all her power to read what was in her mind, and she had the courage to meet her stare, to measure its antagonism, to accept its challenge and refute it. She laughed.

"Oh, I'm not vexed, Amy. I know Marney too well to take any notice of what he says, whether he means it or not. I *am* sorry for Tom. It must be awful for him. I should think Marney's right about him needing a wife to make him happy. But I think he'd need some one different from me, and who says I haven't got some one in my eye already?"

"*Have* you, Sally?" said Amy breathlessly.

"Well, I know a few young men in London," Sally answered easily. "I won't say there's any particular one, but then, I've never thought much about it."

Again the two women exchanged glances, and Sally had no doubt as to the relief in Amy's eyes as she suddenly got up, and reached for a candle on the mantelpiece, and for a spill of paper.

"Come on, Sally, shall we go up and have a peep at them now when they're dead asleep, it'll be safer than leaving it till later ? "

Sally got up eagerly.

"I'd just love," she said.

4

HENRY LUNN had been right about the official attitude
of the Lifeboat Institution. The paramount duty of
the service is saving life. Except where the men of a
fishing community expressly desired to retain their
rowing or sailing boat (chiefly to render assistance
among themselves) it had been the Institution's
growing policy to close such stations, and rely on
motor craft, stationed farther apart, yet with a much
wider range of action. Bramblewick lifeboat was
obsolete. A week after Luke Fosdyck's retirement, at the
end of January, she was bought and towed away by a
firm of yacht builders down coast for conversion into
a pleasure cabin cruiser.

Outwardly the passing of the lifeboat made no
difference to the relations between the Fosdycks and
the Lunns. Neither family could afford an open
quarrel with the other. Yet the Lunns were aware that
local feeling had grown strongly against them in the
matter. Tongues had wagged and would go on wag-
ging. It was said that Henry Lunn had refused the
coxswainship only to spite the Fosdycks and the rest
of the crew : that he could easily have taken it on,
and used his own judgment as to whether, if a call
came, conditions were too risky. The crew at least was
good enough for an ordinary salvage job, and anyway,
so long as there had been a boat there was a practice

launch every quarter, for which in summer the crew
got five shillings apiece, and launchers half a crown,
and double that rate in winter. The Lunns were still
at their game of taking the bread out of local folks'
mouths. As for what Henry Lunn had said about his
coble being more use than the lifeboat, well, let him
try! Chances were if he did, he'd drown himself and
any one else, daft enough to risk going out with him
to a job.

But neither Luke nor Tindal had been heard to
express their opinion on the matter. Even towards the
village folk they had always maintained an attitude
of reticence and aloofness. They were bachelors. They
lived in a cottage at the back end of the village, close
to the hill that was surmounted by the new coastguard
station. They had only to walk a few yards up this hill
for a commanding view of the bay which they had fished
since they could remember. Luke was slightly taller
than Tindal, but Tindal himself, despite his severe
illness of a year ago (caused, the doctor said, by over-
exertion in hauling up the boats) still had an erect
figure, and although the beards of both men were
nearly white and their faces deeply lined, neither of
them gave much sign of their advancing years. The
brothers were inseparable companions. When they
were not fishing or engaged ashore with their boats
or gear, they could be seen pacing up and down in
front of the lifeboat house, or if the tide was out,
walking along the beach: never out of speaking
distance of each other, but very rarely speaking. It
was known that Luke was Tindal's unquestioned boss.

Whenever there was anything to decide between them and the Lunns, he was always the spokesman, and if he appealed to Tindal occasionally for confirmation, that confirmation was automatically forthcoming. They were both hard men. Within their own memory more than a dozen ' fishermen ' Fosdycks had lost their lives in Bramblewick bay. But it was not the fear of being drowned that now made them cautious in putting to sea in bad weather, and avoiding the risks of fishing far from home.

The driving force of their lives had always been ' brass.' It was the same with all the Fosdycks ; but with the ' Up-Bankers,' the Fosdycks who long ago had deserted fishing for the Mercantile Marine, ' brass ' had come easier and quicker. At fishing every penny was hardly won, and hardly held, and there could be no sudden doubling and trebling of savings that were kept in solid cash, instead of in stocks and shares. Their ' brass ' may have been no more precious than the bank balances of their relations, but it was a more direct and tangible symbol of what they had won in their life-long struggle with the sea. And Luke, realising the growing physical handicap of his years, of Tindal's, was not going to risk a sudden diminution of that carefully-hoarded sum that was to be their chief support when they gave up fishing altogether. Part of that sum was the thirty odd pounds their coble should fetch when she was sold. They were still out to make ' brass,' but they were not going to risk having their coble smashed up, just to make a few extra shillings, and give the Lunns a chance of a bigger catch.

Rachel Fosdyck, who was four years younger than Luke, had many of the family characteristics. She was a hard, stern woman. There was little love lost between her and her brothers, for she was an ardent chapel-goer and they never set foot in a place of worship unless there was some special 'do,' and it didn't seem to matter to them then whether it was 'church' or 'chapel.' She detested smoking and drinking and bad language. Their drinking did not amount to more than an occasional pint in the Mariners, and they seldom swore. But the fact that they could sit in a public-house was enough, in her estimation, to put them amongst the damned. She lived in a larger cottage than theirs, nearer the dock, and she made a living by taking in summer visitors. This cottage was reputed to be the cleanest in Bramblewick. Every room in it was cleaned at least once a day, and if any one came to the door and set foot on the whitened step, Miss Fosdyck would have the mark washed off and the step re-whitened the minute her caller had gone. The walls of all the rooms, including the closet, were hung with texts and printed exhortations to the Holy Life, and in the best room there was a harmonium, on which, in very slow time, she could pick out the air of some of the most familiar and mournful of Moody and Sankey's hymns. Its lid, covered with an embroidered fabric not unlike an altar cloth, bore an alabaster bust of Charles Wesley, with vases and framed texts on either side of it.

Yet if there was no affection between her and her brothers, there was not a violent estrangement. When Tindal was taken ill, she had gone in and ' done ' for him, and when her nephew Tom had landed home from sea and Luke had offered him temporary work, during Tindal's disablement, she had given him ' hospitality,' on the condition that he would pay what he could towards his keep, and never smoke his filthy pipe inside the house. That employment had continued longer than Luke or Tindal had anticipated or wished for. It had meant giving up a third of what they earned, and that already was small enough. But the coble was a necessity in winter time, Tom a necessity if the coble was used, for Tindal had been warned that any violent exertion was likely to bring on a second and probably a fatal stroke, and, as winter was Rachel's slack time her qualified hospitality had been extended at least until next holiday season.

It was Mrs. Lunn who suffered from the consciousness of the village feeling most. She was, by instinct, social and neighbourly. In the early days of her life at Bramblewick when the antagonism of the villagers had at times reached violence, there had been the comradeship of the women of the other foreigners, who had come with the Lunns from Sledburgh. One by one these foreigners had drifted back, but her own family had been growing and she had found in her home a large measure of compensation. Now, with Marney married, and Sally and all her boys except John away, she was lonely, and the gradual softening of the old hostility had resulted in her finding companionship of sorts among the village women with whom in the early days she was not on speaking terms. There were not many. She did not imagine either that she had made any real friends among them, but it was nice to be able to have a chat, say with the wife of one of the elderly ex-sea-captains, who was a member of the lifeboat crew : to hear bits of local gossip: to give the latest news of her absent boys or Sally. Now, knowing what this woman and the others were thinking and saying behind her back, she avoided them and was lonelier than ever ; for when the boats were off there was no one in the house; and while she was passionately fond of Marney's children, Amy had some very pronounced ideas as to how they should be brought up, and was always going for her, because, she said, she spoiled them.

Mrs. Lunn was very unhappy. Her only distraction outside the house was looking after her hens. They had originally belonged to her youngest son, Steve, and they were kept in an old allotment on the cliff. She had a name for every hen, and would have starved rather than killed one for the pot. She knew it wasn't the hens, or even the connection they had with her last-born, Steve, that made her want to stay in Bramble-wick, but it was true that in spite of her being so unhappy she did want to stay. She was glad that since the night Sally had landed home, there had been no more talk about that. Sally, of course, was back in London. Things were looking better for her too, than ever. Recently she had written home with the news that her mistress was going to give her the chance to start a little dressmaking shop in partnership with another woman before the end of the year. But that meant, too, that there wasn't much chance of her getting home again until after next Christmas.

With the approach of spring, cod-fishing had yielded to lobstering. The season had started well. Lobsters had been plentiful, prices good, and now, towards the end of March, there had come a miraculous spell of fine, warm weather. With the wind off the land and the sea dead calm, there had been a respite from the toil of hauling up the boat when the days fishing was over. Moorings had been laid in the Landing (a channel of deep water formed by two prominent scaurs running seawards from the village front) and the boats could remain anchored all night. This, while the weather lasted, meant that the Lunns could fish when they liked.

But no one imagined that the weather would last for long, and Marney, while he was less discontented now that he was busy and making a bit of brass, had not changed his deep conviction about the future. Lobstering, at Bramblewick, was about the only sort of fishing that could be made to pay. But even in this the Burnharbour men had the advantage. With their big, modern boats (known as 'keelers') they could work three times the number of pots. They could stow them on board and carry them to deep water ground, quite inaccessible to a small boat, where no matter what the weather, the pots themselves were always safe. They could get to market quicker, without having to pay carriage on their catch, like the Bramblewick

men, and above all, except in the severest weather they
need never stop fishing. Here, the wind had only to
get round east or nor'east, to bring the seas rolling
across the Landing mouth. The boats would have to
be hastily hauled up again to the dock, pots left in the
sea to look after themselves, and once a swell had got
up it might last for weeks, even if there was no wind
at all. And how many times had they found, when at
last they had been able to go out again, that all their
pots had been washed away or smashed to pieces!

The break in the weather came, not suddenly, as the
season of the year might have justified, but with a
peculiar stealth, and it came at night, after a day of
bright sunshine and a boisterous west wind, which at
sunset had dropped completely and left the bay as
smooth as a mountain-locked lake. There had been a
chill in the evening air; a suspicion of frost. Just
before dark, a thin wisp of mist had wreathed the
summit of High Batts, the headland which marks the
southern limit of the bay. But this, if it gave warning
of a possible shift of wind, had shown no sign of
thickening to fog, which was the proof positive, and
Henry Lunn, taking his last look at the weather from
the cliff edge above his cottage before bedtime, was
satisfied that whatever change did come during the
night, it would not be a violent one; that the chances
were equal of to-morrow being another fine day, and
that anyway, the coble was safe at its moorings, for
the tide was ebbing, and nothing short of a gale from
the north-east could harm her or the Fosdycks' coble
between now and half-ebb, when both boats would be

in the lee of the bared scaurs of the Landing. Besides,
Luke Fosdyck would have seen to it by now if there
had been the slightest risk.

Yet Henry was aware of a peculiar uneasiness as he
sauntered slowly back to his cottage. Mother, who
usually enjoyed the best of health, had been out of
sorts all day. She'd looked pale and tired. She'd been
mangling some blankets, and she thought she'd
strained herself, because she kept getting a pain in her
side. It wasn't very bad. It hadn't, in spite of Henry's
protests, stopped her going up to the cliff to feed her
hens, and getting supper, and washing up, and laying
the table for breakfast before she went to bed, and
Henry didn't think for a moment it could be anything
serious. But he knew she was worrying a lot about the
lifeboat business, and what folks were saying, and
that, although she never complained she was very
unhappy.

He didn't know what to do about it. He was
unhappy himself. He knew what was in the minds of
Luke and Tindal Fosdyck, every time they looked at
him. They had never forgiven him for getting the
motor coble. Every time they helped to haul her up
he could feel their resentment, for (on account of the
engine) she was heavier than their own, and this
resentment was stronger now because of the lifeboat,
because, through his not agreeing to take the coxswainship, he had robbed them of their practice money,
and of any chance there might be of a salvage job. He
did not return that hate. But he resented it because
it was daft. In a spot like Bramblewick, with fishing

as it was at present, there was enough trouble in the job itself without all this jealousy and spite.

John, too, had gone to bed. The gas was out, and a candle stood on the table. Henry sat down by the dying fire and started to unlace his boots. Their bedroom was immediately above the living-room and he listened intently but he could hear no sound from mother. She had taken some hot milk with a drop of brandy in it last thing. It was late, and if the weather did hold, they would be off to their pots again before daybreak, but he thought that as mother was very likely going off to sleep, he'd better not disturb her, so he unloosened his belt, blew out the candle, and stretched himself on the sofa, where he had the habit of sleeping whenever there was a chance of being called out suddenly.

At first his mind was restless and he went on thinking. He knew in his heart that Marney was right, and that sooner or later they would have to leave Bramblewick. What he didn't like about it was that it would be as good as admitting he was beaten. The Fosdycks first had sneered at the idea of being able to use a motor coble at Bramblewick. They had been proved in the wrong a hundred times over. In every sort of fishing, cod, lobstering, salmoning, Henry had beaten them. He had never crowed about this. What he would have liked was for them too, to have gone in for a motor (they'd saved enough to afford it) and for them all to have shared in what was to be won out of fishing. It wasn't much, but it was a living if you went about it the right way. The Bramblewick grounds, to any one

F

who knew their tricks, were still as good as any on the coast. If the Fosdycks had only been young men, as young as Tom, and of the same mind, there would have been no need to think of going anywhere else, although that wouldn't have made any difference to the lifeboat being out of date.

Henry had been up since four that morning, mother was still quiet, the room was warm, and there was no sound except the ticking of the clock on the mantelpiece, and soon his thoughts became confused, and he went to sleep. When he awoke it was to an instant alertness, yet he did not know what had roused him until he heard the deep blast of the Burnharbour fog siren. He got up, lit the candle and looked at the clock. It was half-past one. In his stockinged feet he moved across the room, opened the street door, and looked out. The light of the candle threw his own shadow on what might have been a screen stretched in front of the doorway. The ground was almost invisible. A wind was blowing, not strong, but unmistakably from the sea. It brought with it, during the intermittent pauses of the fog siren, the sound of the sea itself, not louder than that of a gentle ground swell, but enough to confirm his impression that the fine spell had definitely ended, that bad weather lay ahead. He shut the door and without haste moved across the room to a corner where his seaboots lay. As he took hold of them he heard mother stirring. Then she called down to him :

"Is that you moving about, Henry ?"

He answered calmly :

"Aye. It's come on thick. Sea's smooth and there's not much wind yet but it'll most likely be a blow before morning. Fosdycks will want to launch up, anyway. How are you feeling?"

"I'm all right, except my head's aching a bit. Shall I come down and mash you a pot of tea?"

"You can stay where you are, lass, and keep yourself warm. It won't take us long to get the cobles up if we have to. Give John a shout, if you can't hear him stirring."

Mother shouted, and shortly there was a grumpy answer from the attic. "What's up?"

"Father's going down to see to the coble. It's come on thick. Can't you hear the foghorn. . . . You'd better mash yourself some tea then, Henry," she went on. "And have a bite of summat. You'll most likely be hours making up your minds whether to launch up or not, and it'll be cold down the scaurs."

Henry had already got his sea-boots on. He opened a cupboard and took out a storm lantern, and prepared to light it with an old matchstalk at the candle. But he stopped in the act of putting the match to the wick, stubbed it out, and took a quick stride towards the street door, which he flung open. He stood there in an attitude of intent alertness. Between the blasts of the stationary siren he could hear another siren, higher in its pitch and not so distant, and blowing continuously, the unmistakable signal of a vessel in distress. He strode back and flung open the staircase door.

"Look sharp, John," he shouted. "Can you hear that steamer blowing? She's ashore somewhere. Get down as sharp as you can and bring a lantern with you. It's thick as ink outside."

Quickly he lit the lantern. He heard the patter of mother's feet on the floor above him. He shouted up at her.

"Eh—you get back to bed. You'll do yourself no good getting up."

"Don't talk so daft, Henry," she shouted back. "I can't lie in bed when there's some one in trouble. Eh—I'm glad the sea's smooth. I'll get you summat to eat and put it in a tin and John can bring it with him. I reckon you'll need summat before to-night's done. I do hope those poor men aren't in danger of their lives. What a good thing the sea's smooth."

Henry swore under his breath, but he seized his hat and coat and without further argument stepped out, and moved fast as he could pick his way in the fog down the alley. The distress signal, which had stopped, was sounding again. Before he reached the dock there was a loud explosion from the new coastguard station above the village, the summoning gun for the life-saving brigade, and it was still reverberating when he saw ahead of him the haloed light of another lantern, and recognised the tall figures of Luke and Tindal Fosdyck. As he stopped they were joined by Tom Fosdyck and Marney, who was carrying a pocket flashlamp. Marney was the first to speak.

"It's a steamer aground, isn't it?"

"Aye," Luke Fosdyck said gruffly. "At High Batts, I reckon."

"Has it been thick for long?" said Henry.

"No. It came on only about an hour ago. I've been down all night, off and on. I had my doubts about it when it came in cold last thing. I said to Tindal, we'd have thick weather and an easterly breeze by morning. Tom had just gone up to give Marney a shout when that steamer started blowing. I'd made up my mind we'd be safer with the cobles up in the dock."

"There's no wind or sea to speak of yet," put in Marney.

Luke's voice was truculent.

"Maybe there's not, but there will be when the tide flows."

"Then what are you going to do?" Henry asked very quietly.

"Do? There's nowt we can do, now there's no lifeboat in the spot, bar going along with the rocket apparatus, and they'll have all the chaps they want. Coastguards will have telephoned the Burnharbour lifeboat. But it'll take them all their time to find her if it keeps as thick as this. Those Burnharbour chaps don't know High Batts like we do."

Henry could not have been insensitive to the ironic censure in Luke Fosdyck's voice, and it might have been that for the moment he felt a stern regret of his own decision in refusing the coxswainship of the lifeboat. It was a situation that he had not reckoned with, a vessel in distress and a fog so thick that here in the dock it was impossible to see a yard outside the circle of light thrown by the lanterns; with several hours to go before daylight, and then the promise of an easterly breeze and a heavy sea, without any certain hope that the fog would lift. It was not often that lives were actually in peril on this shallow coast, certainly never in smooth water, for all a ship could do was run aground, and as a rule her crew could walk out of her at low tide, if they wished. It had happened like that many times, but now Henry knew there might be danger, and that was the chief thought in his mind.

Other voices sounded in the fog, and hurrying footsteps, but the rocket apparatus was housed ' Up-bank,' close by the coastguard station, a more convenient position should a call for service come at high water, requiring a journey along the cliff tops, north or south. The fact that the tide was now down would make the present journey so much easier. The apparatus was packed in a special cart which could be drawn by horses along the shore almost to the foot of High Batts' cliff. There would be four coastguards with it, and the volunteer company was at full strength, now there was no lifeboat. For rescuing the crew of a wrecked vessel, the rocket apparatus was as efficient, perhaps more efficient, than a lifeboat, provided the vessel was close in to shore, and visibility was good. But at High Batts there were scaurs where a vessel might ground and be half a mile from the nearest firing point for the rocket, and the chances were that little help could be rendered from the shore unless the fog lifted.

John joined the group. For a short time all six men were silent. Then Henry said, quietly :

" Well, there's one thing we can do, and I'm for

doing it sharp. Tide will be low enough for us to wade
out to our coble. Are you chaps coming with us,
Luke? We can pull your coble up to the slipway first,
in case it does come on bad while we're out. She'll be
safe there till morning. Are you coming?"

There was a moment's silence, then Luke answered.

"No. I'm not. I would if I thought she'd be any
good. But she wouldn't be. It's a lifeboat job this or
nowt."

"And what about you, Tindal?"

"Nay—I agree with Luke. Wind's freshing every
minute. By the time you get to High Batts there'll
be too much sea for you to do any good, even if you
get as far."

There was a subdued anger, and a familiar hostility,
in the voices of both men, but Henry knew their
refusal was not prompted by cowardice, or spite, or
anything but the complete distrust of old men for what
was still, to them, something new-fangled. He turned
to Tom Fosdyck.

"And what about you, Tom?"

Tom seemed to glance hesitatingly at Luke.

"I'm willing," he said quietly. "But it's for others
to say first. I'm not my own boss, remember."

"You needn't think I mind," Luke burst in almost
savagely. "It's your own affair if you want to drown
yourself."

"Then you'll come?" said Henry.

"Aye. If it's like that."

"We'll want our coble safe first," said Tindal, in the

same, almost savage, tones as Luke. "We don't want her smashing up."

"We'll haul her up now," said Henry.

"You needn't trouble," said Luke. "We'll get her up somehow, if we've got to. I'll not have folks saying we stopped you getting to a job quick. Besides, there's a chance we'll need her to pull some of you chaps out of the sea before you're done."

Henry ignored this remark which, at any other time, would have stung him to real anger. He turned to John.

"Is there plenty of oil in the coble?"

"Aye. I filled the tanks full last night, and there's two spare tins."

"Then come on with you, sharp. We've wasted enough time talking."

5

THERE was, as yet, no great power in the wind. Had it been west it would have made scarcely more than a ripple on the bay. But it was east, and had already raised a short, choppy sea, with a long swell beneath it. The coble's course, once she had cleared the Landing scaur ends, and the treacherous bar, lay almost due south, so that she rolled violently and shipped more spray than if she had been meeting the wind and sea head on. Yet it made little difference to her speed.

She was an exceptionally fine sea boat. She had been built in Henry's native village of Sledburgh, by a craftsman whose cobles had always been held in high repute along the coast for their speed and seaworthiness under sail. She had been designed for sail and had been used for such for several years before Henry bought her, and had her converted. Her engine was a seven h.p. ' petrol-paraffin.' This, too, had been second-hand, but it was the product of a firm of marine engineers who understood the rigorous conditions under which fishing craft must serve, and although its rusted and salt-caked exterior had the looks of an assembly of scrap-iron; although its bearings were worn, and it exuded oil and fumes from many of its joints, although its vibration was such that at times it would seem that it must shake the boat to pieces, it had never seriously failed, and was capable at three-quarters throttle of pushing the boat along at a speed of five knots. As they cleared the scaur ends and turned to their course, Henry had shouted at John :

"Give her all she'll take."

John had sole charge of the engine. He crouched in the lee of its box, dodging the spray, carefully lifting the lid occasionally to make some adjustment to the controls, or to put his hand on the tell-tale water-cooling outlet pipe. Despite the confidence he had in his charge it was never without protest that he would give it full throttle. Already the coble was shaking from stem to stern and the racket of the engine, combined with the continuous crash of the waves on the weather side, made the sound of the fog siren and that of the distressed vessel almost inaudible. Marney and Tom were crouched in the bows. The fog was so dense that from there they could only vaguely distin-guish Henry's oilskinned figure by the haloed light of the lantern which, lashed to a thwart illuminated the compass. He stood with the long, curved tiller crutched under his right arm, his feet wide apart to steady himself against the rolling of the boat, his eyes fixed on the compass and the watch he had laid alongside it, by which, with the estimated speed of the boat and tide, he made his reckoning. His face was calm and resolute. Only when he shouted at John did he betray some of the excitement and anxiety he was feeling.

"Can't you get any more out of her than that?"

"No, I can't," John bawled back. "She's nearly shaking herself to pieces as it is. She's going faster than she's ever gone since we had her. She's doing six knots, I'll bet."

"How are you steering, father?" Marney shouted.

"Straight for High Batts point. We'll know soon which side she's on. We ought to be there in twenty minutes, if the weather gets no worse. We ought to do it in half an hour."

"Burnharbour lifeboat can do eight knots, can't she?"

"They say she can."

"We ought to beat them easy. I bet they're not much past the pier ends yet. If there's a job going it ought to be ours."

"I'm not thinking of any job, the way *you* mean. We don't know yet what sort of a ship it is. It may be a drifter or a trawler. If she's ashore on High Batts with the wind where it is, she's good enough to smash up when the tide flows. It's a wicked spot is that, with an easterly wind."

"Aye, but there's still no sea to speak of. We'll be all right if we get there first. For God's sake give her some more juice, John. She'll take it all right."

"Don't talk so daft," John retorted. "You'd be better employed keeping a sharp look-out ahead than giving me instructions."

"How far can you chaps see ahead?" said Henry. "I'm blinded with the lantern."

"Not the length of our noses. You can't even see what we're floating on. . . . Did you bring any fags with you, John? Damned if I've got even a fag end."

"I could have known that without telling," John

answered. "Day you remember to bring a packet of fags to sea with you, gulls'll start singing like blackbirds. You can get one out of my coat pocket. My fingers are too greasy."

Marney, despite the coble's roll, stepped easily from thwart to thwart to where his brother crouched, and groped in his pocket. He lit a fag and put it between John's lips; then lit one for himself and shouted to Tom :

"Do you want a fag?"

"Nay, I've got my pipe when I want it."

Since leaving shore Tom had maintained his customary silence. No one had commented on the fact that for the first time in the history of the feud between Bramblewick and the 'foreigner' fishermen a Fosdyck was sailing in a Lunn coble as a member of the crew. Indeed the others might have been oblivious to his presence. He was crouching on one knee with his head slightly higher than the coble's stern, his face turned into the impenetrable darkness. Marney rejoined him, but said nothing, and after a quick glance over the bow, settled himself down on a coil of rope with his back to the weather. Yet if Marney appeared outwardly calm the nervous way in which he drew at his cigarette betrayed his repressed excitement, and it wasn't long before he sprang up and took another look over the bow.

The steamer was still blowing intermittently and the sound was perceptibly louder, and it seemed, slightly on the lee bow. Their course was a line across the bay, so that as yet they were in deep water, and a long way from the actual shore. But every minute was bringing them nearer to the point where the bay sweeps outwards to terminate in the cliff and scaur of High Batts, and Henry suddenly yelled :

"Keep your ears and your eyes open now!"

"How long have we been?" asked Marney.

"Fifteen minutes. You ought to hear the swell on High Batts' scaur soon. Does she sound to you as though she's this side of the scaur or the other? I can scarcely hear anything above the engine."

Marney stood up and cupped his hands over his ears to drown the engine racket. But it was Tom Fosdyck who, in a few more minutes, first answered Henry's question.

"Aye. She's on this side of High Batts point. I can hear the swell roaring t'other side of her."

"Aye," Marney added quickly and excitedly. "She's this side all right. I reckon she's on Black Ledge, same place where that Italian went aground last year of the war."

"Come aft and hold the tiller," Henry shouted.

Marney leapt aft. Henry took his place in the bow, alongside Tom. The steamer temporarily was silent. Henry gave a shout to John.

"Throttle your engine down. Then maybe we can hear her."

The noise and racket of the engine died, and there was no more than steering way on the coble. Suddenly the steamer's horn sounded again, very loud and almost on the west quarter, and before it stopped, Henry moved back to the tiller.

"Let her go again, John. You keep forrard and get the sounding lead handy, Marney. She's on Black Ledge. Rocket can't be any use to her there, and we'll not be much use if she's far up. It's a nasty spot with a growing sea."

Although there was still no great increase in the wind, the swell was perceptibly growing longer and deeper, and as the coble forged ahead again, and Henry turned her to a slightly more westerly course, a sea struck her amidships and drenched him and John with spray.

"Look out for your magneto now," Henry shouted. "We'll get plenty like that. If the engine stops we'll be useless. Shout as soon as you hear anything to leeward of us, Marney. She's not far off."

Without waiting for Henry's orders, John throttled the engine down. The vessel was blowing immediately abeam, and when it stopped there came from the darkness the faint sound of voices just distinguishable above the rumble of broken water. At once Henry swung the coble round into the weather.

"Keep her throttled down yet. . . . Cast your lead, Marney, while we're slowed. I reckon we ought to be a cable out from the Ledge. You ought to get three fathoms and hard ground."

"Just over three," Marney shouted in a moment. "It's hard ground. What are you going to do? Creep in, stern first?"

"Aye, we'll take no risks. If she's just on the Ledge it'll be all right, but if she's far up, we'll not have room to go about. You chaps get your oars shipped

ready. . . . Go astern, John, and watch out for your
magneto. Give me the lead, Marney."

A coble is pre-eminently a surf boat. Her high and
narrow bows, her low draught aft when the rudder
is unshipped, make it possible for her to negotiate
waters which to anything but a lifeboat would be
impassable except at grave risk of disaster, but her
head must always be kept to the weather and without
a motor the practice in landing is to row her in stern
first, and at the approach of a particularly heavy sea,
to stop, and then start pulling ahead to avoid the peril
of the sea taking charge, and broaching her. To the
extent that a motor must be controlled by the rudder
(and that the rudder itself when shipped gives an extra
draught of six feet) it is a disadvantage; increased by
the fact that a boat is always slower to answer the
helm when going astern than ahead. Oars, therefore,
are always kept in readiness, and the helmsman must
be prepared to unship his rudder immediately there is
a chance of it fouling the bottom.

The oars were shipped, but laid in alongside the
gunwhale. Tom took the bow rowing thwart. Head-
on to the surf, and with the engine running dead slow
in reverse, the coble began to move astern, still
pitching, but for the time being taking no more water
on board. The vessel gave another loud and prolonged
blast. When it died, the voices rising above the surf
became more distinct, but still there was no visible
sign of the vessel herself. Henry, with the tiller now
under his left arm, made a cast with the lead.
Then, making a megaphone with his cupped hands,

he hailed. The voices stopped, shortly there came an answering :

"Ahoy!"

"We're not three cable lengths from her now," Henry muttered. "She must be just on the Ledge. Be ready to go ahead all of you. Seas may start breaking any minute." Again he cupped his hands and shouted. "Ahoy! Is there plenty of water where you are?"

The answer came in a gruff, unmistakably north-country voice.

"Aye. There's nearly two fathoms astern, but there's broken water close to our bows. Are you the lifeboat?"

"No, we're a motor coble from Bramblewick. Who are you?"

"Steam trawler *Fish Eagle* of Hull."

"Are you holed?"

"No, we're lying on smooth ground. Can you come alongside us?"

"We can when we can see you. Are you showing a light?"

"Switch the floodlight on, Jim," the voice shouted.

The coble, still pitching, continued to move in, and suddenly, above them and only a length ahead, the fog was pierced by a yellow light, pointing slightly downwards. It came from the powerful lamp used by a trawler when bringing her trawl alongside at night.

"Neutral with your engine now," Henry ordered. "Pull ahead with your oars, and swing her a bit nearer. *I'll* fend off."

He left go of the tiller and seized a boathook. Pulling ahead, but only strong enough to resist the driving force of the waves, Marney and Tom manœuvred the coble until she was almost under the floodlamp, and, looking up, they could distinguish vaguely the shape of several men leaning over the trawler's stern rails.

"Where are we?" the original speaker shouted.

"You're on Black Ledge, just inside High Batts Point. You'll be about half a mile from shore on a sort of island, with the tide as far down as this. You're safe until the tide rises. Our rocket apparatus is coming along the shore."

"We don't want any bloody rocket apparatus," the voice (which clearly belonged to the skipper) shouted down. "I've got two thousand boxes of prime fish on board, and we've got to get afloat somehow. I've wirelessed a S.O.S. for a tug, a trawler, or owt that can come and pull us off, but what's the use in this bloody fog? How much water is there seawards of us? Can we steam out if we get her afloat?"

"Aye. There's plenty of water, if you keep due east for half a mile, and then you've got a clear course south. You're lying fair on the scaur edge. You've only got to move a length, and you'll be all right."

"Can you chaps lay out a kedge for us? We've got one ready."

"We can if you look sharp and get it 'over to us. It's your only chance. It's about low tide now, and the flood will come in strong with this wind. You'll be afloat in under two hours. If you haven't a kedge out, or something towing you by then, you'll drive into the cliff foot."

"How much do you want for the job?"

"It's for you to say. If a tug did it, she'd claim into thousands. You know what it's worth if we get you safe on your course again and no harm done."

"I'll see you get a hundred quid."

It was not, in proportion to the probable value of the required service, and the risk, an unusual or an extravagant offer. It was true that a professional salvage boat would under such circumstances (provided that she was successful) make claim for a larger proportion of the vessel's value against total loss. Henry was shrewd. He saw that the predicament of the trawler, without his own assistance, would be desperate, that the skipper realised this fact, that without much argument the offer would be substantially increased. He knew, too, that if he left the matter of payment open and successfully carried out the salvage, he would be able to make a far bigger claim. Whatever sum was paid would come from the vessel's insurers, not from the skipper himself; but the skipper would suffer in that he would lose the favour of his owners (through the dis-favour of the insurers) if the payment was big, and would probably lose his berth. Henry was too kindly a man to profit at the expense of another's misfortune. He lowered his voice.

"Are you chaps willing? We could force him up

if we wanted to. But I reckon it's a fair price for the job."

"I'm willing if you are, father," said John.

"I'll not turn my nose up at it," said Marney, who with Tom was still straining at the oars. "It'll be twenty-five quid each. Let's get on with it sharp."

"What about you, Tom?"

"Nay, it's no affair of mine."

"It's as much yours as any one else's," Henry said quickly. "Whatever we get's shared—risk, too. What do you say?"

"Aye, of course," Tom answered.

Henry looked up and shouted:

"We'll do it."

"Do you want it in writing?"

"Nay, we'll take your word for it. Look sharp, and let's have your kedge before the sea grows any worse."

The figures on deck moved out of sight. There was a shouting of orders, followed by the screech and rattle of a winch; then, silhouetted by the floodlamp, an anchor rose above the trawler's rails, and slowly swung out clear of the side.

"Follow it with your lamp, Jim," the skipper shouted. And then, peering down over the side: "How will you take it?"

"We'll have to stow it aft," Henry shouted. "Lower away until you're about a fathom from the water. Then we'll come down astern. . . . Have your wire ready to lower over, soon as we've got the kedge.

We'll want three coils. Keep your light shining on the kedge. . . . Drive her up to windward, John, then put her neutral, and let Marney and Tom steer her down."

The coble was now slightly landwards of the kedge. Henry quickly unshipped the rudder, and while the coble forged ahead against the seas (steered by the oars) he laid the rudder across the gunwale so as to form a sort of deck. Then, forming a slipknot in a piece of stout rope, he stood with it in his hand and waited.

It would have been a ticklish and perilous job in daylight and clear weather. The seas, while not of themselves dangerous, were smashing under the trawler's stern and sweeping along her side, so that the crests of them would have brought the coble within a man's height of the rail, and the troughs lowered her well below the normal water line. In daylight the approach of each wave might have been seen and anticipated. Now there was nothing but the actual movement of the coble to say when one of them was sweeping in, and the kedge itself, one moment high and clear, the next with its flukes awash, was visible only as a vague silhouette in the yellow glare of the lamp of the invisible ship. To approach it dead on would have invited certain disaster, even if the coincidence of a wave had been favourable. Steering with the oars, pulling one moment, backing the next, Marney and Tom approached stern first so as to bring it within Henry's reach and yet clear of the coble gunwale, and twice they passed it and had to go ahead again and repeat the manœuvre before a comparative calm between two seas gave Henry his chance. For a moment the kedge was poised four feet above his head, and just within arm's length from the boat. He leapt up on to the rudder, and with only his stance to hold him, reached up and outwards and threw the loop of the slipknot over it. He had no time to draw it tight of his own volition. The bow of the coble reared to a big sea, the stern sank under him. In a desperate effort to keep his balance his feet skidded on the wet rudder, and he lurched forward and swayed over the coble side before the rising of the stern swung him back and brought him crashing from the rudder into the well of the boat. But as he fell he let the rope slip through his hands, without losing control of it; and, quick as a game pugilist, he was on his feet again, still letting the rope slip out as the coble swept past the now buried kedge.

"Go ahead," he shouted to John, who had come to his assistance with the rope. "I can manage this yet. Keep her head to the seas." And to the trawler: "Stand by to lower as soon as I shout. We're coming back to it now."

The shoreward movement of the coble was checked. She began to forge ahead again towards the kedge. The rope grew slack, and Henry coiled it in until he had a purchase on the kedge itself.

"Ship your oars, Marney, and give us a hand. Watch out, Tom, don't let her swing too close until we're fair under it."

Marney leapt aft. They were within a few feet of

the kedge once more, but this time going ahead, and
they had a check in the rope. They had to let it slip
when another big sea reared up and passed them, but
they tightened it immediately, and then as the kedge
appeared to rise clear, Henry shouted:

"*Now, Tom.* Swing her under."

Tom backed with his left oar. The stern of the coble
swung until it was immediately under the kedge.

"*Lower away*," Henry shouted to the trawler. "Get
hold of it, Marney. *Now!*"

Marney reached up and seized hold on a fluke with
his hands. Henry pulled at the rope, and as the kedge
was lowered, helped Marney to swing it over so that
it lay horizontally across the rudder, with its stock
projecting over the gunwale in a convenient position
to be let go.

"Slacken away," Henry shouted to the trawler.
"Let's have your wire as quick as you can."

Three coils of wire rope had to be lowered from the
trawler to the coble. That already fast to the anchor
and leading to the winch had to be unshackled,
shackled to one of the new coils, which in turn would
be shackled to each other, and finally to the anchor
itself. The operation was less difficult and perilous
than taking on the kedge, but even the task of unshackl-
ing and shackling the cables and handling the spring-
like coils required all of Henry's and Marney's skill,
for the ship's lamp was of little use to them, and
their own lantern had been knocked over when Henry
fell. There was no time to relight it. But at last
Henry shouted:

"We're all clear now. We'll drop it as far out as we can and give you a shout when it's down. It's good, hard ground out there, so you needn't fear of its not holding. Get a purchase on it soon as we shout. Tide's flowing already. You'll most likely be afloat in an hour."

"All right," the skipper answered. "I've just had a wireless that one of our own trawlers is steaming towards us, but she can't do it under four hours. Burnharbour lifeboat left an hour ago."

"You'll not need either of 'em," Henry shouted. "Pull at your oars as hard as you can go, and keep her to the seas."

The outward journey started. The kedge and the coils of wire rope had weighted the stern of the coble down and forced her bows well out of the water, so that instead of cleaving the seas, she breasted them, and their retarding force was doubled. Even with the engine full out, and Marney and Tom straining at the oars, it seemed for a while that she was making no headway at all. John, using the engine-box as a thwart, and facing the bows, added his weight to Marney's oars. Henry stood holding the wire, and it wasn't until another temporary calm came that he felt it tighten, and began carefully to pay it out. That calm, however, enabled the coble to gain a momentum that carried her over the next sea; and then slowly but certainly she began to move seawards. The trawler's lamp was eclipsed in the fog.

For a while no one spoke. Then Henry shouted:

"Is the lantern smashed, John? Light it if it isn't."

"Never mind that," said Marney. "There's a flash-light in my pocket. . . . Are we moving, father?"

"Aye. We're half a cable gone. But go on pulling hard; we've a long way to go yet."

Marney laughed.

"She'll pull herself off easy as smoke. It's money for nowt, this."

"Aye, but we've got to get home yet, remember," said John, who had found the pocket lamp, and had laid it so that it shone on the coils of wire. "There's twice as much sea as there was when we started."

"Hey—there's a horn blowing ahead of us," Tom suddenly interrupted. "Sounds like the life-boat."

"Give her a hail if she sounds close," said Henry. "We don't want her fouling the kedge."

Tom hailed, but it was a long time before the others heard, above the racket of the engine and the crashing of the seas, the sound of an electric horn in the darkness on the port side, and meanwhile two of the three cables had gone over.

"Can you hear 'em talking?" Henry shouted. "Give 'em another hail."

Tom hailed again, and suddenly from the port side came a voice:

"Is that Henry Lunn's coble?"

"That's Matt Coultas, Burnharbour cox," said John "I'd know his voice anywhere."

Henry answered:

"Aye. We're laying a kedge. It's a trawler fast on

Black Ledge. Her name's *Fish Eagle* of Hull, and she's got a big load of fish aboard."

"Has she taken any harm?"

"Nay. I reckon she'll come off easy when the tide gives her a lift."

"Is Luke and Tindal Fosdyck with you, Henry?"

There was a good-natured irony in the question, for the relations between the Lunns and Fosdycks were well known along the coast; and there was a sound of laughter from the invisible lifeboat before Henry answered:

"Nay, but young Tom is. It was him that hailed you just now."

"I bet old Luke will be waiting ashore for you with a gun, doing a job like this without him having a share in it. What are you making out of it? Will you all be coming to the pictures this week?"

"Aye," shouted Marney, still straining at the oars. "You can book us the whole front row of the one-and-sixpennies, when you get back. We'll treat you chaps, too. Get away home to bed. You've only come out to give yourselves an excuse for a go at the rum ration. Have you started on it yet?"

There was laughter from the lifeboat again, but the voice of the coxswain was serious when he shouted:

"There's an easterly gale forecast, Henry. We got it from the coastguards just as we left. You'd better look sharp getting home when this job's done. How much cable have you to lay yet? Can we give you a hand?"

"Nay, we've less than twenty fathoms left, Matt. We can manage all right, thanks. Are you going in to her?"

"Nay, we'll stand by out here until we see what happens. We'd only be in everybody's way. Give us a hail if you want any help, Henry. We'll not charge you."

The lifeboat sheered off out of speaking distance. With the dead weight of the cables nearly gone, despite the increasing sea, the coble was making better progress, and shortly, with only a few coils left, Henry ordered Marney to ship his oars and stand by in the stern.

"Keep her dead ahead, Tom," he shouted. "We've got to lay it clean or it'll be no use at all. Keep the light on the wire, John. Now, Marney, get hold of the end of the rudder, and as soon as the wire tightens heave it up."

The last coils were lying astern of the kedge. Henry lifted them up bodily and then, waiting while the coble recovered from a steep twisting dive, he heaved them over, and joined Marney at the clear end of the rudder. John sprang to his side and shone the light on the receding wire, and as Henry shouted, he too took hold of the rudder. They heaved it up, and as the wire grew tight, gave the flukes of the kedge a final shove that sent it crashing overboard. Immediately Henry lifted the rudder, leaned over the stern and shipped it. With the tiller hard over to starboard, he shouted:

"All right, Tom. Take a spell. We'll not go closer

in than hailing distance. Show the light on the compass."

The coble swung round and started shorewards. In less than a minute Henry's hail was answered from the trawler. Almost at once there came the rattle of her winch as she started to heave in the slack of the cable. Then Henry turned again into the weather, and they steamed out until, by Henry's judgment, they were slightly seawards of where the kedge had been laid, and clear of the wire, which, when it tightened, would be a dangerous thing to foul.

"Are we going to anchor?" said Marney.

"Aye," Henry answered. "We'll ride all right out here, and we'll be able to hear her better with the engine quiet. But if the wind gets really fresh, we'll not wait. We've done our job. Lifeboat's here in case she doesn't get off."

Steadily the wind had been freshening, and while it was still a long way from gale force, there was no doubt in Henry's mind that the forecast given by the lifeboat coxswain would prove true. But he knew the capabilities of his coble, that at present there was little risk of their not being able to make a safe return. Marney flung the anchor overboard. John put the engine into neutral and throttled it down until it was almost silent. Again the sound of the trawler's winch became audible, and a little to the north they heard faintly the sound of voices in the lifeboat. They listened intently to the winch. At first it was an almost steady rattling, but soon there were pauses, followed by sharper bursts of sound, and then at last by silence as the full strain was taken, and the kedge took a firm hold of the bottom.

"She's tight," said Henry. "It won't be our fault if she doesn't move off. It's lucky she's lying where she is—all smooth scaur—and deep water soon as she clears. She was lucky she didn't come ashore at high tide. They'd have found a different carry on then with their two thousand boxes of fish, and only the rocket brigade to help them."

"I wonder if the rocket cart's got on yet," said Marney, who was groping in John's pocket again for the packet of fags. "Bye! Think of it! Two thousand boxes! No wonder we chaps don't get a price for our fish, even when we do get a basket or two. That shows why our job's 's played out. How can a coble compete with that?"

"Aye. But those chaps don't get so much of it," said John. "Most of it goes to their owners. I'd sooner be my own boss and take a chance. Look at to-night! This'll be a nice little windfall, and only four of us to share it."

"Aye," Marney said thoughtfully, "it will. More than we earned all last winter. . . . Did any of you think of bringing owt to eat?"

"There's a grub tin under the stern thwart. I don't know what there is in it, though. Mother shoved it into my hand as I ran out."

"She ought to have stayed in bed, as I told her to," Henry muttered. "Who's that hailing us now, the lifeboat or the trawler?"

They listened.

"It's Matt Coultas," said Marney. "Wants to know if we want a drop of rum."

Henry laughed.

"Tell him we'll come and help ourselves when the job's done. . . . They're a decent lot, those chaps. They can't help but be thinking we've beaten 'em to a job, and yet there's no ill-feeling about it."

"Burnharbour chaps are all like that," Marney said significantly. "They always were. Think of that time our salmon nets drifted round Low Batts. There were two Burnharbour boats lost hours of fishing helping us to find them. They'll help anybody."

John had found the tin. He shared out its contents. They ate in silence. John and Marney lit fags. Tom, still sitting on the bow thwart, lit his pipe. Henry, who did not smoke, stood with one foot on the stern thwart, the other wedged against one of the coble timbers, the swaying tiller under his arm, silent and ceaselessly alert. The minutes dragged on. The fog remained dense as ever, but perceptibly the wind was veering to the south-east and blowing stronger, and, while the coble rode the seas head-on and shipped little spray, she pitched and rolled so violently that even John had to wedge himself against the engine-box, and Marney and Tom against the gunwales, to maintain a comfortable balance. From the shore the sound of surf grew louder as the tide flowed. When at last the trawler's winch started again it was only faintly audible, but it brought all of them into an instant alertness. It went on for a short spell, then stopped.

They waited for a long time in silence. Then Marney said excitedly:

"I bet she's not far from afloat now. Why the hell aren't they heaving?"

"She'll be all right so long as the seas aren't pushing her stern round," said Henry. "That's the only thing that can stop 'em getting off. It's this south-east wind I don't like. We ought to have laid the kedge a bit more to southward. There she goes again, anyway."

The winch had re-started, and this time it continued for a full minute before stopping.

"She took in some cable then, *I* know," said Marney excitedly.

"Aye, but it might have been the kedge dragging," said John. "We don't know."

"Don't talk so daft," said Henry, betraying his own excitement. "A battleship wouldn't shift that kedge once it got hold on that bottom. . . . There, she's heaving again. Stand by to haul the anchor, Tom. We don't want to be run down. . . . Get it up now."

The winch went on. It stopped, but only for a brief spell, like a man taking a breath from a strenuous task, and its speed after that spell suddenly increased.

"*She's afloat*," shouted Marney. "She *must* be. She must have heaved at least her own length of cable."

"We don't know yet," said John. "It may be the kedge dragging. She'll blow when she's moving."

As he spoke, there came a blast from the trawler's horn, short, and followed quickly by a second and a third, and then, in addition to the continued sound of the winch, the throb of her engine.

"Look sharp, Tom. Go ahead with your engine, John, and take the weight off the anchor."

"She's up," Tom shouted.

Henry swung the coble round to the north, and moved in a wide semi-circle before turning to the weather again, to a course which he judged was parallel to that of the moving trawler. She was invisible. But she had evidently cast off the kedge cable for her winch was silent, and was steaming slowly astern out to deep water. She blew again. Soon, although still invisible, she was close enough for Henry to hail, and he was answered by the skipper, in a voice which showed his relief and delight.

"We're all right now, thank you."

"Aye, you're all right. You've got nowt but deep water if you keep due east."

"What's your name?"

"Henry Lunn of Bramblewick."

"Right. You'll hear from our owners. Will you get back home all right? It seems to be blowing up for a gale."

"We're all right. We're only half an hour's run, and the wind will help us. Good luck to you!"

"Good luck to you, and thank you all for what you've done."

The skipper's voice had faded almost out of hearing. Henry swung the coble round for home. He had scarcely done so when the lifeboat horn sounded close astern, and the coxswain shouted:

"Shall we give you a tow to Burnharbour, Henry? It'll be safer than trying to make Bramblewick in this muck."

"I reckon we can manage all right," Henry answered "Tide's just right for us, and we'd only have the coble to fetch back. I'm sorry we beat you to the job, Matt. We couldn't have done it if there'd been much more sea."

"Garn, it's nowt but luck, a job like this. I'm glad you've earned a bit of brass. . . . So-long, if you won't take a tow."

The lifeboat forged ahead and out of hearing. With the engine full out, and the wind and the sea astern, the coble, despite her pitch and roll, seemed to move without effort, and at great speed. Marney had stayed aft, and was shining the lamp on the compass and the watch. There was a jubilance in his voice as he shouted at John:

"Light me another fag, John. I know you've got two left, and I'll make you a present of a hundred to-morrow. . . . God—this is what I call a good night's work. Our luck must have changed, and no mistake."

"Aye," said John, lowering his voice. "But there's going to be some trouble about this carry on. Bramblewick's not going to be too pleased about it, particularly with the rocket brigade having gone on to High Batts for nowt. And what about Luke and Tindal? I reckon we'd better keep our mouths shut as to how much we've made."

"Garn! I don't care what any of 'em think. It's all the more reason why we should clear out of this spot.

If I had the say, I'd say let's put every penny we get into buying a Burnharbour keeler."

Although it was common knowledge that the relations between Tom and his two uncles were not consistently happy, that Luke (despite that he and Tindal could not have worked their heavy coble without him) resented having to pay Tom a share of their earnings, it had seemed from the first to be an implied condition of the peculiar friendship between Tom and Marney that a strict neutrality should be kept regarding the family feud. Thus, the matter of the lifeboat had never been discussed, although Tom's friendship with Marney and Amy had continued as before. It might have been the excitement of the moment, or the sudden realisation of the fact that Tom Fosdyck had come as a member of the crew, and had fitted himself in as though he had belonged, or it might have been the darkness that made easy the discarding of the old restraint; but Marney suddenly shouted to Tom:

"Hey, Tom. What do you say about putting all we've got for to-night's job towards a keeler? Would you join us when your Uncle Luke and Tindal gave up fishing?"

Tom laughed.

" *They'll* never give up fishing."

"They'll have to give up their coble when we leave Bramblewick. They'll not need a third man if they use their small boat."

"Who said we were leaving Bramblewick?" Henry interrupted sharply. "I didn't."

H

"Aye, but that doesn't mean it isn't in your mind."

"There's nowt in my mind except steering this coble home, and I'd do it better if you chaps didn't start arguing that again."

"Aye, but you've got to admit that Tom's been useful to us."

"Aye, he has. But there's as much chance of us getting a keeler as there is of us going in for an aeroplane. . . . If ever we did go in for a bigger boat, and Tom wanted a berth, I'd be willing, of course. It wouldn't be a bad thing to have some one on board who could do their job and not yap about it."

"Did you hear that, Tom?" said Marney. "Would you come with us if we got a bigger boat?"

Tom did not answer, for at that moment there came a peculiar thumping from the engine, a jolt that shook the coble, the screech of grinding metal—and then a dead silence.

"Show the lamp, quick," said John as he lifted the lid. It released a cloud of stenching fumes that made him choke, but, holding the lamp himself, he began a quick examination.

"Ship your oars," Henry shouted to Marney and Tom. "Keep her going as she is. What's up, John?"

"Damned if I know. Summat bad. It sounded like a cracked cylinder. Exhaust-pipe's red hot, but she's had plenty of oil."

He took hold of the starting handle and tried to give it a swing. It was immovable. He shone the light inside the box again, and then:

"She's smashed up," he said. "It might be a big

end, but I doubt it's worse than that. She's finished for now, anyway."

Henry betrayed no emotion. He said in a perfectly calm voice:

"Show that lamp on the compass again. It's lucky we've got a following sea; but I'll not be sure of our reckoning now within a cable's length. We'll need be closer than that to hit the Landing mouth in this fog and it still dark. Keep her going, but there's no need to break your backs at it. We'll have to ride outside until daybreak."

"What time's it got to now?" said Marney.

"Nearly a quarter past three. There'll be more than two hours to wait."

"Tide will be nearly up to the slipway foot by then. It'll be a close thing. What about making for Burnharbour?"

"We wouldn't stand a chance without our engine. If we can't land at daybreak, we'll have to ride offside until the tide ebbs again."

"Couldn't you tell there was summat going wrong?" Marney growled at John. "We might have taken the chance the lifeboat gave us, and been well on our way to port by now. You're a bloody fine engineer."

"No, I couldn't," John retorted angrily. "No more could any one else."

"You must have starved her of oil."

"She was flooding with oil. If you knew so much about it, why the hell didn't you tell us it was going to smash up, yourself?"

"Now, stop your damned arguing," Henry interrupted. "Engine's gone, so has the lifeboat. That's all there is to it. We're lucky it didn't go until we got that kedge laid. If it's a cylinder smashed we'll need a good lump of what we'll get to have it put right. Lucky if it doesn't need a new engine."

There was no more talking. With an uneerie quietness now that the engine was dead, propelled only by the easy strokes of the oars, the coble ran before the wind and sea, until at last, at a command from Henry, Marney and Tom stopped pulling. The coble lost way, and at once the power of the following wind became more manifest, and close on the port side they could hear the sound they had heard shorewards and southwards of the trawler. It was the sound of surf, but deeper in its pitch, more definite and familiar in its rhythm of break and pause.

"That's the east Landing scaur," said Henry. "We're not far off the Landing mouth.

"Can't we risk it?" said Marney.

"I would, if we hadn't lost the engine suddenly like that. It put me out of my reckoning. You can't trust your ears in fog, remember. Those seas might be breaking a cable's length nearer than what you might think. There's nowt for it but to wait while daybreak. Get your anchor over."

The anchor was dropped. The coble swung round with her head to the weather. Again a silence fell upon the four men. Each of them knew the peculiar perils of the situation. The wind and sea were still rising steadily. The fog was dense as ever. Between them and the shore lay a maze of scaurs with one narrow channel of deep water, which itself would cease to be a channel when the tide rose higher than the slipway, before this if the sea had a full gale behind it.

And the wind was not far short of gale force : the seas were roaring on the hidden scaurs to leeward when, at the first sign of approaching day, Henry prepared for action. The coble was pitching and rolling and tearing savagely at the anchor. He unshipped the rudder. Then he stood, balancing himself against the stern thwart, staring intently shorewards. The others, too, were watching and listening for some sign that would give an assurance of their exact whereabouts. The white of broken water was now visible close to the coble side; but it was not that of surf, for it gleamed and vanished, and made no distinguishable sound above the roar from the scaurs. Suddenly Henry swung round and said calmly:

"There's nowt to tell whether we're south or north of the scaur, and we'll be no better off when it's full day while it's thick as this. I reckon we're still to southward, but we'll have to chance it. Tide will be up to the slipway in a few more minutes, and then we'll never get ashore without smashing up. Get your sea-boots off. It will be each for himself if we get into trouble."

"What about the anchor?" said Marney. "Are we going to haul it or cast it off?"

"Put a cork on the end of the cable, and cast it off. There's no time to waste hauling, and the chances are it will be fast. Tom had better keep to the forrard oars. You and John take an oar apiece aft, and let's have no arguing when we're under way. Cast off soon as you're ready, and start backing a little to nor'ard."

Henry had slipped off his sea-boots, and had seized the boathook. Marney had tied a cork to the slack end of the anchor cable, and now he shouted to Tom to cast off the rope itself. The coble began to move in, stern first, and slightly aslant the wind and sea.

They were following the ordinary practice of landing a coble in surf. They were putting little power into the oars, using them chiefly as a control, yet ready to reverse, and pull ahead when the approach of a dangerous sea warranted it. They had not moved a couple of lengths before a shout from Henry caused them to do this, and to swing the bow round in time to meet head on a sea which otherwise might have swamped them. Soon as it passed they backed astern again and on the original slanting course, and for a minute or two their shoreward progress was uninterrupted. And then Henry gave another shout, for over the stern, and exactly in their course, he saw the long, white gleam of a breaking sea, and, turning swiftly, saw behind the coble another wave, just beginning to curve over. There was no time to go ahead to meet it. There was just time for the oarsmen to swing the bows slightly round so that the sea rose not behind but on the starboard quarter, lifted the coble up, and carried her on its crest for twice its length, broke, and left her, broadside on but unharmed, in its boiling wake. And before the next sea came Henry, thrusting the boathook over, pushed with all his might against the solid rock which was not less than two feet below, heaved the stern round, and with the oarsmen backing, got way on the coble again; and the sea, while it lifted her up, broke harmlessly away from her bows, and left her still moving shorewards in water which Henry could just fathom with his hook. And by the depth of water, by comparison with that on the rock, he knew where he was, that the rock was the west scaur of the Landing, that they were in the Landing channel itself.

"Back—hard as you can," he shouted. "We're not a cable's length from the slipway."

Sea after sea rolled in, but broke harmlessly on the scaurs. The depth of water diminished. Suddenly there was a slight bump under the coble's bottom, and Marney and John unshipped their oars. Tom kept backing, and Henry pushed with the boathook until at last she could move no farther. She was aground. And close by them now became visible the Fosdycks' coble, on its wheels, ready for launching, and the burly figure of Luke Fosdyck moving out of the fog towards them.

"Now for some trouble," growled John. "For God's sake don't say anything about the engine."

Henry pulled his sea-boots on, got out and faced Luke as he drew near. But he was surprised by his manner, which had none of its usual hostility.

"So you've got back, Henry," he said quietly. "You're only just in time. I've got some bad news for you. Your missus has been taken bad. Marney's wife went in to ask about you chaps about an hour ago, and found her groaning on the floor. Doctor's been and says she has to have an operation. They're waiting for you now."

For a moment Henry stared at Luke as though he suspected him of some trick.

"Is it true?" he said fiercely. "Or are you fooling me?"

"Get your ways up and see," Luke answered. "We'll get the cobles up. They've telephoned to Burnharbour for the ambulance."

6

THERE was no ceremony about Sally's second home-coming. John, unwashed and unchanged from his night's adventure, met her at the five o'clock train. During the seven hours' journey from London she had been tortured by the fear that the wire they had sent her, saying that mother was very ill, and was going to have an operation, and that she had to come at once, was only the usual formality to break the shock of the news of mother's death. But her first look at John's face, grave and anxious though it was, reassured her before he spoke.

"She's going on all right. She got through the operation, anyway, and it's been a success. Father phoned through to Bramblewick Post Office about an hour ago."

The fog was not quite so dense. The gale having blown all day and raised a terrific sea, had decreased slightly and veered south, and it was raining. John had fetched mother's mackintosh for Sally to put over her own. She was relieved, but she had heard too much about the diseases of middle-aged women and operations not to dread hearing what the operation had been for, and it was not until they had passed the ticket barrier and turned along the station road that she had the courage to ask.

"It's appendicitis. Doctor said it was a very unusual

thing to find in a woman of her age, and one who'd
always been so healthy, and he wasn't quite certain
of it himself. But, from what father said on the
phone, there was nowt else, only it was very bad, as
she must have gone on working when it was getting
worse all the time. But you know what she is. She'll
never give in until she's forced."

They turned into the Bank road, and met the full
force of the wind. The fog siren was still blowing,
and now and again came the sound of distant ships,
safer now that the thunder of surf on the coast would
by itself give them warning. Again Sally's anxiety
was lessened. Appendicitis, after all, was not so
terrifying as some of the things she had imagined.
It wasn't often, these days, that you heard of any one
dying of it, unless the operation had been left too long.
And once the operation was over it could not happen
again. But she was sensitive and imaginative. She
knew what pain her mother must have endured before
giving in. She knew what she must be enduring now,
and what her mental sufferings must be like, at finding
herself in the strange surroundings of a hospital.
She had never spent so much as a night away from
home before.

John went on talking. From him the tension had
been more completely relieved by the news that the
operation was over, and he had begun to appreciate
the dramatic side of the events of the last twenty-four
hours.

"Aye, it's been a queer carry-on, and no mistake.
Of course, we couldn't tell you all that had happened

in a wire. A trawler went aground last night at High
Batts. We went off in the coble to her, and layed out
a kedge, and got her off. Last thing I saw of mother
was her running out to the door to shove a grub tin
into my hand. It came in pretty useful, too. We'd just
got about half-way back, with this gale blowing up
on us, when the engine smashed up. A hell of a mess.
I've only just now managed to get her to pieces. A
cylinder cracked about from top to bottom. Both
pistons smashed, and God knows what else. I doubt
whether she's repairable, so every farthing we get
from the trawler job will have to go into getting a
new one. Well, we had to ride outside the Landing
until daybreak. When we got in, there was Luke
Fosdyck waiting to tell us about mother. Luke was
as polite as could be to father; but, by God, he was
short enough with us and Tom when we were getting
the coble up!"

"Tom Fosdyck didn't go with you, did he?"

"Aye. And we wouldn't have been much use without him, either, with me having to look to the
engine, and father at the rudder most of the time.
But Luke and T ndal wouldn't come with us,
although father gave 'em the chance. Luke practically
told us to go to hell and drown ourselves. There's
some talking going on in this spot to-night, I bet.
We're not the popular heroes of the hour. Rocket
brigade was out all night, and they never so much
as got the apparatus out of the cart. I passed a chap
belonging to it when I was coming up to the
station, and he didn't half look sniffy. **Ted**

Sayers, who works for Sam Turnbull the joiner. He's in our band, too."

They reached the bank top. The roar of the sea was louder, the wind and rain blew stronger in their faces. A premature dusk was drawing in, and already there were lights in some of the cottages they passed.

"Amy wants you to go to their place for tea. Everything's in a hell of a mess at home. I've been working at the engine all day. Father and Marney's been at Burnharbour. Father said he'd be back on the six o'clock bus. But I don't know whether Marney's back or not. He went in on a bike he borrowed. I don't think I even remembered to make the fire up when I came out."

"All the more reason why I should go straight home, then," said Sally quickly. "I can guess what it'll be like. Poor mother! Did father say if she'd had a lot of pain?"

"She had plenty before she went. Amy says when she found her she was moaning and the sweat pouring off her face, and yet she played hell when Amy said she was going to get the doctor. But the doctor gave her summat, I believe, so that she be half asleep when they got her there. I don't think father's seen her since the operation. All he said was she'd come through all right, and that it had been a success."

The fire was out. The remains of a meal were on the table, which on the occasion of Sally's last homecoming had been resplendent with the best table-cloth and the best tea-service and so many dishes of cakes and tarts and jellies. Every cupboard in the room was open. There were boots and clothes scattered every-where; and even the teapot stood on the mantelpiece, alongside mother's most precious ornamental vases. Yet, but for the anxiety which still gnawed her, Sally felt more instantly at home than she had ever done since she had first gone away. Briskly she took her suitcase from John and, lighting the candle, which was still on the table where Henry had left it when he had rushed out, she went upstairs, and was down again quickly, with a handkerchief over her head and an apron on.

John had got some kindling and had started to rake at the fire.

"You'd better get across to Amy, and tell her not to make tea," she said. "I can manage the fire, and I can do everything quicker if I've got it to myself. Father won't want to get back to this mess. Is there plenty to eat in the house?"

Sally went to the pantry, and made a quick survey of its shelves.

"Mother baked only yesterday, so there ought to be plenty," said John.

"You'd better get a pound of butter, and there's not much tea. What time does Thompson's shut?"

"Half-past six; but I can get owt at the back door."

"All right, then, and remember to wipe your feet on the mat when you come in again. I know your habits."

John grinned.

"You're starting bossing us about pretty quick, aren't you, Sally?"

"No quicker than's necessary, if I'm to have the spot tidy for father to come back to. What would you like for supper? What's that fish in the pantry?"

"It's a codling we got in our pots day before yesterday. That would be all right, fried. I could get some chips from the fish shop. I think they'll be frying to-night."

"You needn't bother. There's plenty of potatoes here. Mother wouldn't buy chips when she could cook them herself. Now, hurry up and let me have the place to myself for a few minutes."

John went. Sally knelt down to the fireplace, dexterously finished the laying of the fire and put a match to it. She cleaned and tidied the hearth, then took hold of the kettle and, finding it empty, moved across to the pantry to the water bucket. But that too was empty. No water was laid on to the cottage. All supplies had to be fetched from the public tap, twenty yards down the alley. Sally slipped her mother's old mackintosh on and picked up the empty bucket. But as she did so the street door opened and Tom Fosdyck, his hands still on the latch, leaned his head inside. For a moment he did not see Sally, for she was partly behind the pantry door, and he was startled when she said:

"Hallo, Tom."

He stared at her uncomfortably.

"Hallo, Sally. I didn't know you'd got here. I came to see if there'd been any fresh news about your mother."

He was still standing with his hand on the latch. Sally smiled at him.

"Can't you come inside?" she said easily. "You're not a stranger, are you?"

He stepped inside, but only half closed the door and stood there still uncomfortable. He was washed and shaved and wore a short reefer jacket over his guernsey. It glistened with rain.

"Haven't you heard that father rang up to say she'd got through all right?"

"Aye, but I thought perhaps your father had got back, and he might have summat more to say. I was on my way over to Marney's, and I thought I'd just pop in and see. I'm glad she's going on all right. I'd better be going along."

He put his hand on the door again. Sally said quickly, "You needn't be in such a great hurry, Tom. What's this I hear about you going off in our coble? That's something new for a Fosdyck."

Tom grinned.

"Aye I suppose it is."

"John said they wouldn't have been much use without you."

"Garn, I did nowt but pull an oar. Any one could have done that."

"What's your Uncle Luke say about it?"

Sally was looking at Tom very intently, and she saw that her question had pricked him.

"Well, you wouldn't expect him to be too pleased, would you? But I haven't asked him his real opinion, and I don't suppose I ever shall.

Did John say what time your father was expected back?"

"He's coming on the six bus."

"Well, I'll be getting on, then."

Again he moved to the door, but again Sally frustrated him. She moved towards him with the bucket.

"Any one might think there was another ship ashore the way you're anxious to be off. Get me a pail of water, Tom. I want some for the kettle, and John's gone off without leaving me a drop. I want to get this spot tidied up before father gets back."

Tom took the bucket and grinned.

"You're about as good as Amy for ordering folks about. But I'll get it for you. It's raining hard now, and no mistake."

He went out, and Sally set about her job again. She felt pleased with herself. It was the first chance she had had of encountering Tom alone. He had disturbed her during her recent holiday. Despite his quietness, his gloom, she had realised that, next to Marney, he was the most attractive man she had ever met. She had been irritated and vexed by the seemingly deliberate way he had avoided her subsequent to the night of their first meeting. That might have been due to Amy's clever management, of course, but there couldn't have been much doubt that he had avoided her, and that he was in love with Amy, and allowed her to dominate him completely.

But she had been too busy in London, her life there was too full of other interests for her to think very much about him. Now it seemed he was neither so quiet nor so gloomy as she had thought, or some change had come over him. And it gave her a curious satisfaction that he was fetching her the water. She had swept the floor, piled up the dirty crocks, and got the washing-up bowl on the table before he was back. He was still grinning.

"Where do you want it?"

"It goes on the pantry floor. Kettle's there, too, so you may as well fill it and put it on the fire."

She cleared the garments that were lying on various chairs, hung them behind the door, and put all the boots away. Tom had put the kettle on the fire, and was lighting his pipe.

"Any more orders?" he said ironically.

"Is there plenty of coal in the scuttle?"

"It's nearly empty."

She smiled at him.

"Well, you know where it's kept, don't you, Tom?"

"No, I don't."

"You know where Amy keeps hers, though."

"Aye, of course."

"Well, it's not in a very different place. Just outside the back door near the wash-house. . . . But don't you trouble, Tom. There'll be enough to go on with. John can fill it when he gets back. I'm only having a joke with you."

She was satisfied with her little triumph. She had no wish to pursue it; and anyway she did not wish to be a second Amy, ordering a man like Tom about as though he was a kid. She was not certain, either,

I

whether she was pleased to find him less gloomy and more attractive than before. There was still something about him that frightened her. But Tom had got hold of the scuttle.

"I'll fill it for you," he said. "Then I'll be off."

He moved to the door and opened it just as Amy appeared, and he stood aside to let her pass in. For a second she hesitated, and Sally saw the quick glance she gave at Tom and the scuttle. But she said nothing to him, and came straight forward to Sally. Tom went out.

"Eh, I am glad you got here all right, Sally. I do hope the wire didn't give you a fright."

Sally knew she was blushing, but Amy didn't wait for her to speak, but went on quickly:

"Isn't it a good job the operation's over and it's been a success? Weren't you relieved when John told you at the station? I cried when I heard. She'll get over it now all right, I know. . . . I thought I'd come over and give you a help with the house, Sally. I'd have been over before, but Marney's only just got back from Burnharbour, and I couldn't leave the bairns. Eh, what a time we've had ever since last night, when they went off to that trawler. Has John told you about it all?"

Sally was very fond of Amy. She did not feel the same jealousy now that she was in her own home, doing things, instead of being a sort of guest. Most of her deep anxiety about mother was allayed. She felt queerly excited and interested in what Amy had to say. She got the fish and the potatoes out of the pantry, and, without waiting to be asked, Amy started to fillet the fish while she herself peeled the potatoes.

"John told me about the trawler being ashore," she said, "and how you came in and found mother."

"Aye, wasn't it a mercy I came in? You see, I thought maybe they'd got ashore, and that Marney had come in here with them for summat to eat. He's like that, is Marney! It never enters his head that any one might be anxious about him, although if you'd seen the way he went on about mother you'd have thought he was going to have an operation himself. Aye, and all that mother could talk about, when she could get her breath from the pain, was who was to get father and John their breakfast, and who was to feed her hens if she was too poorly. She wouldn't let the doctor come near her at first, it made me feel awful having got him out of bed at that hour and telling him it was urgent. He hadn't even stopped to put on a collar and tie. But the pain beat her in the end. She had to give up, although I'm certain she wouldn't have let the ambulance men touch her if the doctor hadn't given her summat and father hadn't been there."

Tom came in with the coal.

Again Amy gave him a quick, inquiring look. But she seemed too engrossed in her narrative to show any resentment, even if she felt any, and all she said was:

"I'm glad you're making yourself useful, Tom. Marney's got back, and he's wanting to have a talk to you. Tell him I'll be back in a few minutes, and if Sam's crying not to pick him up."

Tom put the scuttle down by the fireside and went out again without a word. As soon as the door was closed, Amy went on:

"Did John tell you Tom was with them last night?"

"Yes, and that Luke and Tindal refused."

"Eh, it has caused some trouble. All Bramblewick's talking about it and about the engine being broken and then mother being taken ill. I expect most of 'em are delighted about the engine. I went into the post office this afternoon, and there were two women there with their backs towards me, so they didn't know I was there for a minute, and I just heard two sentences of what they were saying, and one of them was, ' Well, I say it's a judgment on them,' and the other was: ' It serves 'em right.' They didn't half go red when they saw me, but I just ignored them; only I let them see I'd heard. Do you know, Sally, I'm beginning to come round to Marney's idea that it's time we all left Bramblewick. I haven't told him so, and I won't, but I'd leave to-morrow if we could find a nice spot to live in in Burnharbour. Do you know what his latest idea is? He's come back full of it. Apparently, while waiting to go up to the hospital, he's been mucking about the harbour, and he's found an old motor mule that's laid up and for sale cheap, and he says it would be just right for us, with a bit of money spent on it. He says that there'd be no real need for your father and mother to leave Bramblewick unless they wanted to, because father and John could sleep on board during the week and come home for Sundays. But some one would have to be there all the time to look after it, and that would be us. You see, if we got a cottage and it had a spare room we might even have Tom with us, then there'd be two men always there."

Sally's eyes were fixed on her job.

"Why?" she said quietly. "Is it all settled that Tom's going to join you if you do get a bigger boat?"

"As good as," Amy answered. "After last night. Tom hasn't said anything, but old Luke's naturally mad about him going in the coble. He and Tindal have been busy all day getting that small boat of theirs ready, which means they're going to lay their coble up so they'll not want Tom. Besides, Tom would be like a lost sheep without us. Of course, he'd have to come with us as an ordinary lodger and pay for his keep. It would help him and it would help us. But I don't know what father will say to it. Marney's going to tackle him to-night, although I said leave it until he's less upset about mother."

Amy had done the fish.

"Shall I help you chip the taties, Sally? There'll be the beds to make, too. You'll feel a bit lost having a spot like this to look after, after what you've been used to."

Sally was doing her best to hide the fact that she was jealous of Amy again and angry. She hated the calm way Amy was arranging Tom Fosdyck's life for him, the suggestion that he could not possibly be happy unless he could come in and see her every night;

and now, that Sally herself could not look after a
house without her assistance.

"Oh, don't you bother, Amy. You've got enough
to do with the bairns. I'll soon get into the swing of
things. It isn't as though I hadn't been used to it
before. How are the bairns? I'm dying to see them
again. I'll come across as soon as we've had supper.
Is this father coming now?"

It was John who opened the door and came in and
put the packets of tea and butter on the table. He
did not speak. He looked gloomy and bad-tempered.
Amy put on her shawl.

"Well, let's know if there's owt you want doing,
Sally, won't you, or if you're short of anything. I'll
expect you after supper."

"All right, Amy. Thank you for filleting the fish."

"Is Tom over at our place, John?" Amy remarked as
she moved to the door.

"Aye. Marney's yapping to him now about that
mule. I left 'em to it. I reckon it's about the daftest
notion I've heard yet, and I bet father thinks the
same when he hears. It's time he got here. I hope
mother's not any worse."

Amy went. John sat down by the fire and lapsed
into a gloomy silence. Sally finished the potatoes and
put them in the pan, and started to wash the dirty
crockery. Shortly there were footsteps outside again.
The door opened and Henry came in. Sally rushed
towards him. She was frightened again by the haggard
expression of his face, but at once he smiled, and she
was reassured.

"Hallo, Sally. So you've got here! I knew you'd come if you got the wire in time for you to catch the train."

"How is she, father?"

"She's sleeping. I went up about half-past five, and that's what they told me. She's going on all right. They say there's nowt to worry about, but it was a close thing, and she'll have to be a long time in bed; but if she takes care, she'll be even in better health than she was before."

Henry was still in his fishing clothes and wearing sea-boots. He gave a deep sigh that was half-yawn as he sat down in his chair. Quickly Sally got a pair of carpet slippers out of the cupboard and took down some socks that were on the line. She helped him off with his boots.

"Have you had anything to eat, father? I bet you haven't."

Henry smiled.

"Why, I went in and had a cup of tea with Matt Coultas, but I didn't feel much like eating until the job was over, and then I scarcely felt like asking. I hope it hasn't put you out, Sally, coming sudden like this? We don't want you to lose your job."

"You needn't bother about that, father. There's only one of the children at home now, and you know how kind they've always been to me. Anyway, you don't think I could have stayed in London, knowing mother was ill? Poor mother. How soon can we go and see her?"

"Doctor said maybe in two or three days if she goes on all right."

"It does feel queer in this house without her," put in John mournfully. "It's not so bad now Sally's here, but I can tell you when I was here by myself I kept hearing her shout as though she was just out in the wash-house. It didn't half frighten me once or twice."

"What about the engine?" Henry said quietly. "Did you get it to bits?"

"Aye, and it's worse than I thought. A cylinder's cracked, and everything's chewed up inside. I reckon what happened was that the water pump jammed, and then started again sudden with everything almost red hot, and the jacket dry. That would cause it."

"It doesn't matter much what caused it," Henry said dryly. "Can it be mended?"

"It can, but I reckon it would cost half as much as a new engine, and even then I doubt if she'd be as good as she was. I reckon we'd best try and get another second hand. It 'ud pay us."

"And we'd be lucky if we got one under sixty quid. Have the Fosdycks said owt?"

"No, but they've looked black as thunder all day. They've been fettling their small boat. That means they'll lay their coble up, and expect us to do the same, and use our small one whether we get another engine or we don't. It's just about what I expected would happen when we let the lifeboat go. I still think it was a mistake. It's put every one against us."

"For God's sake hold your jaw about the lifeboat,"

Henry returned with sudden heat. "If we'd had her, the Burnharbour boat would have beaten us to the job, and we'd have had a night's work for nowt. We did make summat, anyway."

John was silent. Henry's anger passed. He stared into the fire. He looked tired and dejected. Sally started cooking the fish, and between whiles laying the table. No one spoke again until the door opened and Marney came in. His face was unusually serious. He greeted Sally with a smile, however, and then looked questioningly at his father.

"She's still going on all right," Henry said. "They say there's nowt much to worry about. She was fast asleep when I left."

Marney's face showed his relief, but it was still serious as he swung a chair round from the table and straddled it with his folded arms on its back.

"Well, that's a damned good job," he said. "Mind, I never did doubt but what she'd get through it all right. Appendicitis, after all's, common enough. Think of the folks from this spot who've had it, and got through it and been on their feet again in less than a month. They say you can get it from swallowing a bramble seed or an apple pip. Some one was telling me in Burnharbour to-day they knew some one who'd got it from swallowing a fish-bone."

"You needn't tell us that," put in John. "Sally's frying us some fish for supper. . . . Anyway, it's a good thing she's got it over."

Marney was silent for a while, then, looking at his father, he said quietly:

"Has John told you about the engine?"

Henry continued to stare into the fire.

"Aye."

"Has he told you Luke and Tindal's getting their small boat fettled?"

"Aye, he told me that, too; but I could have told both of you that without being here to see them at it. I've been expecting them to do it for long enough. You can't blame them. Their coble's too big, even with Tom to help 'em."

"What are we going to do, then?"

"I expect we'll have to put our small boat down, soon as the sea calms. . . . We'll have to use her. anyway, until the coble's put right."

"We can't fish all the pots we've got in her."

"Then we'll have to bring some of them ashore."

"We're scarcely making a living as we are, without using less pots!"

"There'll be salmon fishing soon."

"Aye, but it only takes two of us at that. Last year we went on lobstering with the coble, remember, with you and Steve working her in fine weather."

Henry swung round. He was showing signs of anger.

"Well, what are you driving at, then?"

Marney lit a fag, then, exhaling the smoke, he said very deliberately:

"Do you know a Burnharbour mule called *Lucky Boy*?"

"Do you mean that tub of old Monk Patterson's?"

"You can call her an old tub, but she's earned him plenty of brass in her time. And I can tell you he's not

short of it now. There's not many chaps have been
able to retire on what they've earned from fishing."

Henry grinned ironically.

"Monk made his brass during the war, when every
boat belonging Burnharbour except his and another
were sunk by a German submarine. The captain only
spared her because she was the worst looking boat in
the fleet, and because he hadn't the heart to let everybody drown. He made them all get on board her, and
put a shell into every other boat. That's how Monk
made his brass. There was no one fishing out of
Burnharbour for nearly six months but him and
Christopher Coultas, Matt's brother, who'd been held
up with engine trouble that morning. . . . You can't
tell me much about *Lucky Boy*. She's about the ugliest
and wettest and slowest mule that ever fished along this
coast. She was like that from the day she was built.
And nothing could cure her."

"Everybody knows about her," put in John. "Monk
had to give her up because he couldn't get a crew to go
with him after his brother died. They say she rolls so
much in anything like a sea that you can't move
along her decks without a lifeline. I've heard that
even Monk used to be sea-sick in her if he hadn't been
in her for several days."

"You're telling me nowt I don't know myself," said
Marney. "But it's a queer thing that, with all her
faults, she's always paid her way until she had to
compete with those new keelers. It's a queer thing
she's never drowned anybody. It's a queer thing that
in that big gale five years ago, when other boats were

breaking adrift even in the harbour, she was out at sea for three whole days, and no one the worse for it."

"And why was she at sea?" said Henry sarcastically. "Only because she was too slow to get to port, and there was nowt else for Monk to do but ride it out. They were battened down the whole time, riding to a sea-anchor. Any boat with a deck and a good hull could do that if she had plenty of sea-room."

"Aye, but it proves she had a good hull, doesn't it? That boat's as sound now as the day she was built. And it's a lucky name too. Engine wants a bit of brass spending on it but less than what it would cost us to fix our engine up again, and anyway, our coble's going to be no use to us here if the Fosdycks are giving up theirs. We'll not be able to fish at all next winter."

Sally had made the tea, and now she was taking the pan off the fire, but she did not interrupt. She was listening eagerly to the argument.

"Well, what's it all leading to?" said Henry, still staring into the fire.

"He's at his old argument," said John. "He wants us all to pack up and leave Bramblewick. What better off would we be? Even if we could fish in a boat like *Lucky Boy* we'd be up against the keelers. He said himself that's why Monk had to give her up. There's no competition in Bramblewick anyway. You can't call the Fosdycks competition."

Marney made a gesture of impatience, but he looked towards his father and he went on in an unruffled voice:

"There's no need for any of you to leave Bramble-wick unless you want to. My argument is that we've got to do summat, and that *Lucky Boy*'s better than nowt. Those Burnharbour keelers never fish Bramble-wick grounds same way as we could fish them. They don't know them like we do for one thing. With *Lucky Boy* we could go on fishing here, even if we had to work her from Burnharbour. She's got five good bunks. We could sleep on board her and get back home for week-ends. And we could fish Bramblewick grounds just as we liked, without troubling about the Fosdycks. What's to stop us doing a bit of trawling?"

Henry turned.

"Trawling?"

"Aye—trawling. She's got a trawl and it goes in with what Monk's asking for the boat. Now take that narrow strip of soft ground just south of Low Batts point. That ground's lousy with soles in warm weather. How many times have I heard you say you'd like to try that spot with a trawl, only our coble was too small to drag one?"

"Do you mean Church Steeples?"

"Aye, and that's only one spot."

"By God," put in John. "Luke Fosdyck would have summat to say if he saw us trawling Church Steeples. That's their best plaice ground."

"So it is," said Marney quietly. "And how often have they fished it this last four years? Not once that I know of. They've always been salmoning in the right sort of weather. So have we, or lobstering. And what the hell have they got to do with it anyway? Bramblewick bay's not private. Besides the point about soles is, that you can only get 'em on lines once in a blue moon, and then you want special sole lines. But with a trawl you can get 'em any time the weather's fine."

"You seem to know a lot about soles and trawling," Henry said sarcastically. "When did you pick it all up—when you were out foreign? You don't want it over fine, let me tell you. And you want mucky water, too, unless there's not much sea-fire. Best time is when the sea's calming after a swell. What sort of a trawl is it, a beam or an otter?"

"It's a twenty-foot beam, and the nets almost brand new, Monk says. He didn't say whether a warp went with it, but that's only a quid at the outside. He'll take a hundred and fifty for the whole carry-on as she stands. And I think he might come down from that with a bit of persuasion, if we don't let him see that we're too keen to do a deal."

"That ought to be easy enough," John growled. "Who the hell's going to get our grub ready for us if we're living aboard a thing like that all week?"

"We can do it ourselves," said Marney. "There's a galley-stove and anyway, we can always hot up what we get from home. What do deep-sea boats do? I don't say it would be like living aboard a yacht."

"No, it wouldn't. I reckon the idea's completely daft. We'd better try and get a new engine and forget about it. What did Tom Fosdyck say?"

"Tom's willing, of course."

"So you've even got your crew picked," said Henry dryly. "You haven't wasted much time, have you?"

"We don't want to waste any time if we're going to get her and get on with fishing. You've already as much as said you'd have Tom when we got a big boat, so there's no point in arguing that again."

Henry grinned.

"I'd like to know what point there is in arguing anything where you're concerned. It looks as though you've already made up your mind about *Lucky Boy*, and that you're only asking me out of politeness."

Marney grinned too, but he was still in deadly earnest.

"Don't talk daft. All I do is to help you to make up your own mind, father. Your boss. It's for you to say. But we're in a hole, and you know it. I don't say *Lucky Boy*'s exactly what we want. I don't pretend she's anything different to what she is. But I say she's better than messing on here, and I say, have a look at her when you get to Burnharbour. Have a look at her to-morrow."

"And what about mother? Have you thought about that. She wouldn't like the idea of us being away all week?"

"She'd like it better than if we all went to Burnharbour to live, wouldn't she? That's why I say *Lucky Boy*'s our best chance. If we had a keeler we'd have to go for good. We couldn't afford to waste time coming back here even for week-ends."

Sally had poured out the tea. The fish was served and was cooling. Her mind was in a whirl. She couldn't stop thinking about her mother, about Tom Fosdyck, and the eager way Amy had talked of having

him live with her at Burnharbour. She saw the
subtlety of Marney's argument, the clever way he had
disguised his real plan for pulling up the family roots
in Bramblewick. She saw clearer than before how wise
it was that they should move, and yet how difficult
it would be. And all the time she was aware of a queer
excitement inside her, a half-pleasurable sense of
danger at the prospect of going over to Marney's, and
meeting Tom Fosdyck again. Henry was staring into
the fire. John was watching him gloomily. Marney
was lighting another fag, and appeared to be concen-
trating his whole attention on the job, but suddenly
he glanced at Sally, and smiled, and Sally understood
that smile. She saw that he had pushed his argument
as far as he dared at present, that he was unwilling
to risk a definite decision from his father, that he was
engaged in a strategical retirement. Sally took her cue.

"Come on now, and get your tea. Everything's
getting cold. You can think and talk about all this
better when you've had something to eat. Will you
stay and have something, Marney?"

Marney got up as Henry and John took their seats
at the table.

"Nay, I've just had my tea. I'd better be going across
or Amy will be thinking father's brought some bad
news. . . . What about to-morrow, father? It doesn't
look as though there'll be a chance of getting to our
pots. Will you be going in to see mother?"

"Doctor says no one can see her for a day or two, but
I reckon I'll be going in, if it's not fine enough for us
to fish."

Marney had already got to the door.

"Well, *Lucky Boy*'s lying up by Lawson's old ship-yard if you want to have a look at her. I'll very likely be going on myself if I can borrow a bike again. Maybe I'll see you."

Henry said nothing. Marney, with another smile at Sally, went out. The meal began.

7

THE sinking of the Burnharbour fishing fleet had a
curious and far-reaching effect upon the economic
life of the port. It happened during the third year of
the war, when the German food blockade was at it
height. By then (although fishing was an industry
exempt from the conscription acts) a large number of
local men were serving in the navy or the auxiliary
fleet. Those left were chiefly the old men, and the very
young, and their boats were mules.

They were comparatively small craft, the biggest
of them thirty feet. They were double-ended, decked
and with rude sleeping accommodation for a crew of
five. They had no wheelhouse. The helmsman sat
flush with the deck, with his feet in a narrow cockpit,
and to all intents and purposes exposed to the weather.
The engines were petrol-paraffin of a similar type used
in the cobles, only more powerful. They carried a
short mast and sail in case of an emergency. They were
safe, with plenty of sea room, and, battened down, could
ride out almost any sort of weather. But they were
slow, uncomfortable, and uneconomic. A rot was
falling on the port when war broke out. The employment of a large number of trawlers for war service, a
consequent scarcity of fish, and a rise in prices, saved
the rot, and up to the time of the disaster, maintained
a boom, which in the case of the two mules left and

the smaller craft, continued into the first year of the peace. Those who had lost their boats, however, found it impossible to replace them, for all boat-yards were engaged with other work, and there was a dearth of skilled labour. The old men were forced into retirement, or into munition works. The young, as they came of military age, joined the navy or mine-sweeping fleet or mercantile marine. Many of them were killed or drowned on active service; many were satisfied with their new profession and had no desire even to return to the precarious one of fishing, so that for long after the end of hostilities, the actual fishing population of the port was only a fraction of what it had been in pre-war days.

But among those who came back were several men, who, fishermen by every instinct and desire, saw that there was still a decent living to be made if they set about it the right way. They were young, and their war service had widened their experience of mechanically-propelled craft. They saw that the old mule had been beaten chiefly by the steam trawler, that where the moderate-sized boat might still score was in the freshness and better quality of its catch, and also in lobster and crab fishing, but that it would be necessary to employ bigger and faster and more powerful craft than the mule. They found local financial backing. The craft decided on were a modified form of Scotch 'keeler' with a diesel engine, that gave them a speed of seven and a half knots. They had a wheelhouse and full navigational equipment; electric light, a power winch for hauling gear, broad decks for stowing pots and comfortable sleeping accommodation. From the first the venture was successful, particularly with lobster fishing. The local financiers were eager to help towards the building up of a fleet, and any man of experience and proved ability, with a little money of his own and a potential crew, was encouraged to join. Men were scarce, but less so when demobilisation came. The young men were drawn back, the rising generation was attracted to what had nearly been a dying profession, and the port authorities, impressed by the growing amount of the invested capital, by the value of the landings, had provided a new fish quay and new facilities for the speedy landing, sale and despatch of fish. The fleet now numbered fifteen, giving direct employment to seventy-five men.

· · · · · · ·

There was no message from the hospital that night. The sea had fallen considerably by next morning, but when Henry first looked out there was still broken seas across the Landing mouth and he knew that fishing was impossible. After breakfast he set out to walk the seven hilly miles to Burnharbour. He was not altogether surprised to find, on arriving at the hospital, that Marney had already called. He saw the matron. She told him that his wife had passed a very good night, and was progressing favourably, but that it was unlikely he would be able to see her for at least another two days, and even then she must not be excited or troubled in any way. She was not a very good patient, the matron said, she seemed to be worrying a good deal already about her family and her home, and that was bad for a woman of her age who had just undergone a very serious operation. Henry sent a message to mother, that there was nothing at all to worry about, that Sally had arrived and was looking after the house and also the hens. Then, far from easy in his own mind, he made his way down to the harbour side.

Henry liked Burnharbour. Long before he had emigrated to Bramblewick, he had been familiar with the place and its people, for the Sledburgh fishermen were then engaged in herring fishing during the summer months. Henry was working with his father, old Marney Lunn, in a big sailing boat, which, like the mules, had a crew of five. Burnharbour men had never shown any resentment towards them, as the Bramblewick men had done. They were good-natured, light-hearted, always ready and eager to give a helping hand to a stranger. Henry had often thought that he and the other Sledburgh men would have done better if they'd come here instead of Bramblewick, but at the time of their emigration there had been a slump in herrings, a boom in shell-fish, and Bramblewick, in spite of many drawbacks, had offered better prospects, particularly as there were plenty of cottages empty, and available at low rent.

The old part of Burnharbour resembled Bramblewick the way its stone-walled, red-roofed cottages were thickly clustered on the slopes of a cliff, with cobbled alleys wandering in between them. The new part likewise was on higher ground, and clearly separated from the old, but it was more extensive, and as the place had become a very popular seaside resort, there were many hotels, boarding-houses and a spa. The harbour, of course, was the big advantage in Henry's eyes. In sailing ship days, Burnharbour had been a prosperous port. It had been one of the chief bases for the Arctic whaling industry, and its own shipyards were famous. There were no shipyards now, and little shipping. The upper harbour was silted, but the lower harbour, with its twin piers extending over a quarter of a mile seawards, had plenty of water, and the piers afforded safe access even in the wildest weather. This morning, for example, all the keelers and most of the small cobles were at sea, and the harbour side was deserted but for a few old men, mending lobster pots, and one middle-aged man in a blue serge suit and a bowler hat who recognised Henry and accosted him with a cheerful, "Now, Henry."

Henry knew the man, but he had never had any dealings with him. His name was Mowbray, and he was a retired sea-captain who, by the skilful investment of his savings in shipping shares, had acquired a small fortune which he had re-invested chiefly in Burnharbour keelers. He owned the major share in four of the latest additions to the fleet, and he was, too, an extensive property owner. He had a lean, swarthy face and very clear, blue eyes. He was reputed to be a hard business man, but straight in all his dealings. Henry returned his greeting with a smile and a quick, "Now, captain."

They both stopped out of hearing distance of the

nearest of the old fishermen, and the captain leaned his backside against the quay rails in a manner which suggested that the meeting had more than a casual interest to him.

"How's the missus, Henry?" he said.

Henry showed no surprise that Captain Mowbray was familiar with events.

"Going on as well as can be expected, thank you. I've just come down from the hospital."

"I'm glad to hear that," the captain answered. "You must had had an anxious time, one way and another. I hear you did a smart bit of work night before last, getting that trawler off the rocks in a fog thick as it was."

Henry smiled.

"Why, we were lucky. It just happened she was lying in the right spot for us to get her kedge on board, and the tide favoured us."

"But what about your engine? You smashed it up getting back, didn't you?"

"Aye, that was unlucky. A cylinder cracked and she got chewed up."

"Did you agree anything with the trawler's skipper about damages to your own boat?"

"Nay, we never dreamt of owt like that happening, of course."

"Still, you'll have made a tidy bit of brass out of the job?"

Henry did not answer. The captain did not press the point. He was eyeing Henry shrewdly.

"It was a bit of bad luck anyway," he said. "Can

you get it fixed up again, or are you looking round for another engine?"

"I reckon we'll need another engine. You don't happen to know of one that would suit our coble, do you, captain?"

"She's a twin-cylinder six, isn't she?"

"Aye."

"I know there isn't one here, second hand. A new one would cost you a hundred and fifty pounds! It wouldn't be worth it, fishing in a spot like yours. Why don't you come to Burnharbour and go in for a keeler? Have you ever thought about it? You'd do a damned sight better here than in a god-forsaken spot like Bramblewick." The captain grinned ironically. "Are you as matey with the Fosdycks as ever?"

There was a suspicion of resentment in Henry's voice when he answered.

"Young Tom Fosdyck was with us on that trawler job."

The captain stopped grinning.

"That's the one who couldn't get his tickets because he was colour blind, isn't it?"

"Aye, but no one would know there was owt wrong with him. He's a very decent young chap."

"So I've heard. In that case you wouldn't have far to look for a crew, if you went in for a keeler. You've got two smart lads in John and Marney. I saw Marney a few minutes ago, going up towards Lawson's ship-yard with old Monk Patterson. I've heard he's trying to persuade you to go in for *Lucky Boy*."

"It looks to me as though Burnharbour's as good a spot as Bramblewick for things getting about!" Henry said dryly.

The captain laughed, but he was quickly serious again.

"Look here, Henry," he said. "I don't want you to think I'm trying to pry into your affairs. But I've been meaning to have a talk with you for a long time. I know a lot about you and your sons, and what's been going on at Bramblewick the last few years. You're too good a fisherman to be stuck in a spot like yon, when there's good money to be earned here, all the year round and no bother about hauling your boat up and down a slipway, and not being able to go to sea when the weather's only middling bad. These keelers are averaging at least four quid a week a man, and that clear of oil and bait and everything. You'll not do that in a boat like *Lucky Boy*. You'll not be any better off than you are at present. What I want to say is, if you're thinking about getting another boat, then think about a keeler, and if you're short of a few hundred pounds, say the word. Have you ever had a good look at one of those boats?"

"Aye. I went all over the *Jane Mowbray* the day they brought her down from Scotland. They're fine boats, and no mistake."

"Then why not go in for one? It would be better than mucking about with a thing like *Lucky Boy*. You can get one built in three months."

Henry's cheeks had reddened. He felt uncomfortable

and vexed. He resented the fact that a comparative
stranger like Captain Mowbray should know so much
about his personal affairs; that without being asked,
he should start offering him advice as to where and
how he should live. What did he know about Bramblewick anyway? What did he know about its fishing
grounds? Who was he to say that by getting a boat
like *Lucky Boy* they would be worse off than they were
at present? As though he could not judge for himself
whether the boat was worth having. As though Monk
Patterson could fool him into getting it against his
own judgment. There was no doubt that the keelers
were fine boats, that there was good money to be made
out of them, and that with his two sons and perhaps
Tom Fosdyck, he would have as good a crew as any
working out of Burnharbour; but it would be a big
responsibility, it would mean the laying down of
every farthing of his savings (the only provision he
had been able to make for himself and his wife in
their old age), it would mean, above everything,
leaving Bramblewick and he had only to think of
mother, and the way she was pining to be home, to
know he would never do that against her wishes.
But he hid his resentment.

"Why, it's very kind of you, captain, to offer to help
us, but as things stand I can't see us taking on a keeler.
It would mean us flitting from Bramblewick, and
there's a lot against that. If we went in for another
boat, it would have to be one we could work Bramblewick grounds with, and have a shallow enough
draught to let us go ashore in fine weather. A keeler

would be no use for that and no use for fishing our grounds either."

"But you'd still have to spend most of your nights in Burnharbour unless you walked home!"

"Aye, we would if we got a mule, but I didn't say we were getting one. There's nowt wrong with our coble if we can get another engine."

"Well, if you ever do think of coming here, I've got a nice cottage that would suit you and your missus very well. It's close by the quay-side and it'll be empty soon. There's an allotment goes with it, too. Only you needn't take that on unless you like. The garden's up above the old rope works. I can show you the cottage now if you've a minute to spare. The man who's in it is moving to a council house in about a month "

"Nay, I'll not trouble you," Henry said quickly. "I've got one or two things to buy before I go home, and I'd better be off, thank you very much all the same."

The captain grinned.

"You're a queer chap, Henry, but I'm glad I've had the chance of a word with you. Think it over anyway. You've only got to say the word and I'll put down half the price, and you can pay it off, or let it stand as a paying share as you like."

They parted, and Henry found himself walking down the quay side towards the old men, who, Henry suddenly realised, must have been watching, and would be full of curiosity as to what he and the captain had been talking about. He turned abruptly into an alley leading between some warehouses on his left, and, reaching a narrow back street, he turned so that he was moving in the direction of the upper harbour, which came in sight when the street slanted to his left again and ended near the town railway station. There was a wooden quay and an old wooden capstan (a relic of sailing ship days) and beyond this a coal depot, and a derelict shed on the harbour shore which marked the site of Lawson's shipyard. The tide was ebbing. Henry took a path along the shore. He still felt uncomfortable and vexed from his interview with Captain Mowbray. He had a peculiar sense of guiltiness when he thought of his sick wife. Never in the long years of their married life had he made any big decision without her being in his full confidence. Not that he had always waited for her approval. Not that he hadn't sometimes gone against her wishes. But she had always known what he was going to do, she had always been free to express an opinion, and now, with one of the biggest decisions of his life to make, she was lying helpless in bed, and under doctor's orders that she was not to be upset or worried in any way. What would she feel like if she knew what Captain Mowbray had proposed? If she knew that he was now actually on his way to have a look at *Lucky Boy*?

Not until he reached the shed, did Henry see the mule, for she was lying dry at highwater mark, close behind the shed itself, and at once he saw Marney in conversation with a stoutish, elderly man in serge trousers and fisherman's guernsey, and a very faded

bowler hat jammed down on to his head. Henry knew
Monk Patterson. He owed his nickname to the fact
that his head from a very early age had been entirely
bald, and his figure, his fat cheeks and rubicund
complexion, his customary joviality, helped to make
the name fit. He had never jibbed at it, nor had his
personal appearance troubled him, but the lack of hair
on his skull made it very sensitive to heat or cold, and
he had found that a bowler hat was the best means of
protection, ashore or afloat, in all seasons and weathers.
He had been a good fisherman. Fate had been kind to
him in that war-time disaster, but it had not been fate
alone that had helped him to a modest financial
independence in his retirement. In the last period of
the war, when the German U-boats had orders to sink
every British vessel at sight, when the shallow waters
of the coast had been thickly sown with German and
British mines, every fishing trip had its exceptional
perils, and on many occasions *Lucky Boy* had closely
missed joining the rest of the fleet at the bottom of the
sea. Henry respected and liked Monk as much as he
did any of the Burnharbour chaps, but the sight of him
now, standing there with Marney, both clearly
expecting him, did not ease his resentful state of
mind. He had the feeling he was being enticed
into a trap, and Monk's genial smile increased this
feeling.

"Now, Henry," he said. "I'm very glad to hear your
missus is going on all right."

Although Monk and Marney were standing close
to the bows of the mule and Henry had to walk her

length to reach them, he did not glance at her, and when he stopped it was as though he were deliberately keeping her out of sight.

"Thanks," he said. "How are you keeping, Monk?"

The older man seemed a little puzzled by the perceptible lack of cordiality in Henry's manner.

"I'm not so bad, Henry," he said. "I'm not so bad. It's bad luck about that engine of yours."

"Aye," Henry answered. "It is. Very."

There was a prolonged silence during which Henry appeared to be interested in a locomotive that was shunting in the sidings close by the shore. In which the usually jovial Monk seemed gravely interested in the general view of the upper harbour, and Marney, who from the first had avoided his father's direct glance, carefully lit a fag. Then Monk said:

"Well, Henry, I hear you're looking for another boat."

Henry grinned ironically.

"Everybody in Burnharbour seems to have got hold of that idea, Monk. We've got two boats, you know, so we're not stuck for another, even if our coble is out of use for the time. We'll be out to our pots in our small boat, soon as the sea's calm enough. And we can get another engine somehow."

Monk glanced at Marney who, however, kept his eyes averted. He looked at Henry again, and then, with a jocularity that seemed forced, he said:

"All right, Henry, you needn't think I'm trying to sell you summat you don't want, but you haven't just walked along here to see that engine shunting, and

seeing you've got this far, you might as well look at
the old boat. There she is. She cost me and my brother
Fred five hundred quid the day she was bought. I don't
say she's as good now as she was then, any more than
I am. She's had her wear and she's had her knocks.
There's that time we got her piled up on the west scaur
and put a hole in her bottom. She was under water
two days, and bad weather, too. Most boats would
have smashed up, the knocking about she got, but she
was none the worse when we got her mended. I won't
say she won't leak a bit with her having been laid up
so long, but she'll tighten, and I reckon her hull's sound.
She wants some paint on her, of course, but she's going
cheap and I reckon she'll suit you chaps for working
a shallow spot like Bramblewick Bay, better than
anything. Have a look at her anyway."

Henry turned and looked at *Lucky Boy*. He had
always had an eye for a boat. His own coble had produced in him an intense excitement when he had viewed
her first. Without much technical knowledge of boat
design, he had felt that her shape was just right for the
service that would be demanded of her. The graceful
sweep of her bow reminded him of a curving wave.
Instinctively he felt she belonged to the sea. But
Lucky Boy seemed to him to have no shape. Her broad,
squat hull bulged rather than curved. Her graceless
bow was vertical from stern to water line. Her stern
was like that of a lighter, and seemed to be merely the
end of her, something to hold the rudder. The paint
on her top sides was blistered and cracked, or entirely
gone. Her tarred bottom was encrusted with barnacles

and weed, but it did not entirely hide the timbered patch where she had been holed. To Henry she looked scarcely like a boat, but something which would float, and unwillingly move, and his expression was eloquent of the sensation she aroused in him. Monk observed that expression.

"She's not pretty," he remarked with an apologetic air.

"Nay, she's not," said Henry. "I've never seen a boat I liked less by looks."

"But looks aren't everything, and she'd look different with a coat of paint, and the muck scraped off her bottom. . . ."

"Aye, maybe she would, but paint and scraping's not going to alter her shape, and that's what I've got against her, Monk."

The owner of *Lucky Boy* made no immediate retort to the remark, but suddenly he shrugged his shoulders and said:

"Well, there she is, Henry. As I said before, I don't want to sell you summat you don't want. You know what you want, and you know what you can afford. There's nowt fancy about her. She's not a keeler, and she's not a keeler price either. She's got a good engine anyway. We've had it running just now and you can try it for yourself. It only wants new metal on its bearings and cleaning up. What I say is, have a look at her, and take your time about it. I'll leave you to make up your mind, and if you don't want her, there's no harm done one way or another. You'll find me down on the fish quay if you want me, or in the Dolphin."

With another shrug of his shoulders, which seemed to indicate relief, Monk turned and started off along the shore. Without a backward glance he moved round the end of the shed, out of sight, and still Henry continued to stare at the mule, immobile and silent, while Marney, watching him out of the corner of his eye, lit another fag. Then at last Marney broke a tension which for him had grown unbearable.

"Well, aren't you going to have a look at her, father?"

Still Henry did not move, but he said in ironic tones: "What for?"

"Why—to see if she's any use, of course."

"I know whether she's any use or not, without bothering to look at her. I know she's the ugliest craft I've ever set eyes on in my life. I know she's a damned bad sea boat. I know how she rolls. I know how fast she can go, or rather, how slow. I know what use she'd be to us."

"Then you'll admit she'd be some use."

"She might be. She could carry as many pots as we could fish. She'd be all right for summer lining. If that trawl you were talking about is any use, she'd do for Bramblewick grounds."

"Then what are you just staring at her for? What are you thinking about?"

Henry turned angrily on his son.

"What am I thinking about? I'm thinking about mother, of course. Didn't the woman at the hospital tell you she hadn't to be upset about anything, or it might make her worse? What would mother think

L

if she knew we were standing here thinking about getting a craft like this? And you needn't think I don't know what you're plotting and planning for. Have you been saying owt about us to Captain Mowbray?"

Marney looked at his father with unfeigned surprise.

"Captain Mowbray? Do you mean him that owns shares in those last four keelers?"

"Aye, there's only one Captain Mowbray I know of."

"I've never seen, let alone spoken to him. Why? You don't mean to say he's offered to help us get a keeler?"

"I only asked you if you'd been saying owt to him. If you haven't it doesn't matter what he said. But I'll tell you this, you can get the idea of a keeler out of your head, if it's there. I'll tell you that we're not leaving Bramblewick, until mother says she wants to. That's what a keeler would mean. I'm not going against mother."

Marney looked completely puzzled.

"I wish you'd tell me what you're really thinking about instead of going off the deep end like this. You say you won't have a keeler. You come along here, but you won't even trouble to go aboard *Lucky Boy* and see what's she like. And yet you say she'll do for us. I say that if there's a chance of a keeler, then it would be a waste of time and brass getting this. If there isn't, *Lucky Boy* would do. With no other boats fishing close in this summer, we might easily make her cost in a couple of months. Monk has fetched that trawl across. It's lying on her deck if you want to have a look at it. Wait a minute, I'll heave it down."

Marney pulled himself up on to the deck of the mule, and threw down on to the shore near Henry's feet a bundle tied up in sacking. He leapt down after it, and swiftly unfastened its lashings. Henry's anger had gone. His expression changed to a growing interest when Marney pulled out a length of net.

"It's a brand new net," said Marney. "Never been in the sea. Monk got it just before his brother died, and you know he had to lay *Lucky Boy* up after that. God— I reckon we'd do well with this on Church Steeples, and that other ground just off High Batts. One or two good hauls of soles would almost pay for the mule by themselves, never mind lobsters and lining."

Henry bent down and examined the net closely.

"It wouldn't be any use until we got some fine weather," he remarked. "Summer's the best time for trawling."

"Aye, of course. But we might get some good weather early on, and the best of a trawl is, it's always ready in case you did get a fine spell suddenly. If we got *Lucky Boy* we could go lobstering for the time being, and do a bit of lining too. That would give us our pot bait if nowt else, but I say we might easily get a few haddocks. I've often heard you say that if it wasn't for having to get in because of the Fosdycks, you'd like to go on lining this time of the year, and I've heard you talk about some good shots of haddocks you've had when we were kids."

"Haddocks? When we first came to Bramblewick we

often filled the boat bottom with them with a couple
of lines. I've known us cut 'em up for pot bait. But
you could never rely on finding 'em like cod. There's
no fish shifts about so much."

"That's no reason why we shouldn't strike them with
a bit of luck. There's one good thing about *Lucky Boy*.
We'd never need to come ashore unless we wanted to.
We'd be free of the Fosdycks for ever. Shall we spread
the net right out and have a look at it?"

"Nay, we'll not bother. We'd likely as not get some
meshes cut on this rough ground. It's a middling
good net. Where's the beam? Is it on board?"

"Aye. Do you want to have a look at it?"

Henry did not answer. He was staring at the mule
and once more he looked gloomy and perplexed.
Marney tied up the net and threw it on board. Then
he lit another fag, and eyed his father nervously.
Suddenly Henry turned on him but not with anger.

"You needn't think I don't know what you're
plotting and planning for. You think that if we get
Lucky Boy and you and Amy come to live in Burnharbour, that it'll be the thin edge of the wedge."

"What do you mean?"

"You know what I mean well enough. You know
that mother's fond of your bairns. You know she'll
pine for the sight of them. You know that even if we
do most of our fishing in Bramblewick and get ashore
when the sea's calm, she'll not like us sleeping here
when it isn't, and that'll be all of winter time. She's
used to getting all our meals ready. She'll be lost and
lonely, having next to nowt to do. You think that in

the end she'll get so sick of it she'll want to leave
Bramblewick. Who's going to tell her if we get
Lucky Boy? Who's going to break that to her? She
doesn't know yet that the coble engine's smashed up."

"No, and she doesn't know we're making a hundred
quid out of that trawler," Marney said quickly.
"There's no need to tell her, not until she's fit again,
and anyway, it's not going to break her heart. It isn't
as though she's got to be told we'd all been drowned.
I don't think mother's so daft about leaving Bramblewick as you think."

"She's not daft. She's got so that she likes Bramblewick, and that's all there is to it. Say what you like,
there's worse spots to live in. I tell you, if there were
a few more fishermen there, and they were matey,
like Burnharbour chaps, I wouldn't think of leaving
it. You can't beat it for all-round fishing."

"I know you can't," Marney said simply. "So what
about *Lucky Boy*?"

Henry was silent for a while, then very quietly he
said:

"Did that woman at the hospital tell you whether
mother was eating owt or not?"

"Nay. All she said was she'd had a good night."

"Do you think she *would* be eating owt so soon after
an operation?"

"Damned if I know. When folks are bad they
usually give them only slops, or nowt at all."

Henry was thoughtful for a time, then:

"I've heard of them having grapes, haven't you
I believe grapes aren't a food really, but they're very

refreshing. I wonder if I could get some in Burn-harbour, and take them up for her."

"There's a fruit shop along Eastgate. I've never been in myself, but I reckon they'd have them if anywhere. They'd be a hell of a price."

"I don't care what the price is, so long as I can get 'em. After all, the doctor would say whether she could have 'em or not. I think I'll have a walk on and see."

"And what about Monk? What about *Lucky Boy*? For God's sake, say straight out what you're going to do. Are you going to have her or not?"

"You've had a look at her, haven't you? You were there when the engine was running?"

"Aye."

"Well, you know as much about boats and engines as I do, more, the way you've always talked. Do you think she's ready to put to sea?"

"Nay, she's want a bit of fettling. Engine wants new bearings, and overhauling, but I reckon if John and us got going on her, she'd be ready under a week, and anyway it'll be that before we can get her off. It'll need a full spring tide, unless we took her ballast out."

"What did he say he wanted for her?"

"A hundred and fifty quid, with all gear."

"Then you'd best see Monk and offer him a hundred. That's what we'll get from the trawler, and that's about as much as we're likely to get her insured for. I'll come along again after I've been up to the hospital."

Marney stared at his father.

"Then you're going to have her?"

Henry looked at *Lucky Boy*, still with that expression of disgust upon his face.

"Aye," he answered. "As you say, she'll be better than nowt."

He turned and walked towards the town.

8

SALLY wasn't sure whether she was in love with Tom
Fosdyck or not. If she was, then love was a mixture of
pleasant and unpleasant emotions. The pleasant ones
were those she experienced when she was alone, doing
housework or knitting the guernsey she had started
(without daring to admit, even to herself, that it was
for Tom). Then she had a powerful sense of his nearness
so that she could see him and carry on an imaginary
encounter with him, not in the manner of love-
making, but as they had behaved and talked when he
had come in to ask about mother; and he had
fetched the water and coal, before Amy arrived and
shooed him off.

There was nothing gloomy about Tom in these
imaginary encounters. He talked slowly but freely
and there was an ironic humour in his eyes. She
pictured him standing in front of the fire, or sitting
down opposite to her, snooding hooks or sewing with
a palm and needle (like Marney did) while she knitted.
She could see every feature of his face, every gesture;
hear his deep slow voice, smell his tobacco. Deliberately
she held back her imagination at that. Yet there were
times when she felt her heart beating wildly, and she
would have to bring herself back sharply to reality and
an empty room.

Alone with Tom in this vivid dream existence,

Sally was happy, but when she saw him in the flesh, saw him watching Amy still with that expression of dog-like devotion in his eyes, and how Amy continued to dominate him, she was wretched. She hated Tom, hated Amy, she hated herself. As an escape, she made herself think of the life she lived in London, the life she was going back to when mother was quite well. She told herself that she loved nice clothes and going to the movies, and not having to worry about money, and that she could never be happy as a fisherman's wife, and that certainly she would never want to marry a man like Tom, no matter how attractive he was. It seemed to her that he was still deliberately avoiding her, or that Amy was taking special care that they should never be alone together. He had a good excuse (and plenty of chances too) of coming to the house now, if he wanted to, for Marney and John were away all day at Burnharbour and Bramblewick had been given a new topic for talk by Tom joining Henry in the small boat lobstering.

Sally herself was indifferent to the gossiping, to the coolness of the people she met in the village streets or the shops. She heard plenty about it from Amy, of course. According to Amy, every one was saying that the Lunns had gone out of their way to persuade Tom to join them, just to spite Luke and Tindal. Tom, Amy said, was furious about it, because what had happened was that Luke had given Tom more than a hint he wasn't wanted now they were using their small boat, and anyway, Luke, although he was scarcely on speaking terms with Tom since the trawler 'do,'

didn't appear to mind him joining Henry. Sally did
not care whether he minded or not, or what any one
thought about it. The fact that concerned her was that
Tom was now fishing with her father, that he was
joining the *Lucky Boy* as soon as she was ready for sea,
and that since the night she had arrived he had never
even set foot in the house. More important still, Tom,
according to Amy, had simply leapt at the suggestion
that he should go and live with them at Burnharbour.
Marney had found a cottage. He had given notice to
his Bramblewick landlord, and they were going to flit
as soon as possible after *Lucky Boy* was ready for sea.
And Tom was going to lodge with them.

On the whole Sally found her emotions relating to
Tom more unpleasant than pleasant, and although
mother continued to make a good physical recovery
from her operation, she was justifying the doctor's fears
that she was a bad patient. And the general situation
was full of difficulties and problems. So far only
Henry had been allowed to visit the hospital. He had
returned home gloomy and uncommunicative, and it
had taken all of Sally's patience and tact to glean from
him his impressions of that visit. He had been shocked
to find how thin mother had gone. She had looked as
though she hadn't an ounce of flesh left on her body, he
said, and her face was white as a sheet. She had told
him that every one had been very kind to her and that
the doctor had let her have a few of the grapes, but
she hadn't had one real meal and she was aching with
hunger. And she was worrying so. She wanted to
know everything about home, and if Sally was doing

everything all right, cooking and washing, and seeing that Henry's and John's sea boot stockings were dry when they went off in the morning, and if they'd lost any pots in the gale, and how many lobsters they were getting. She was fair crazed, Henry said, to know if her hens were all right, and if Sally was giving them enough to eat, and she said she didn't know how she could manage to go on lying in bed doing nowt. And Henry, of course, hadn't dared to say a word as to what was really happening about the mule, and Marney flitting to Burnharbour, and the talk that was going on in Bramblewick about the whole carry-on. He'd done nowt but tell her a pack of lies.

Henry was not good company in the house. Most of the time he was silent and preoccupied, and he never volunteered a word about the mule; and John when he got back from Burnharbour, his hands and his working clothes covered with paint and oil, was no better. Although in argument with Marney he had been obliged to admit they would have to go in for a bigger boat, and perhaps all leave Bramblewick for Burnharbour in the end, he had been very critical of the present venture, and every time he got back he brought information about some new fault he had discovered during his task of overhauling the engine, a worn bearing, a leaking joint or packing, something wrong with the pump or the magneto or the reversing gear; all of which he would recount to his father with an exasperating fullness of detail.

Sally felt sympathetic towards John. His heart was very much in his band. He had been the prime mover in its organisation, he had triumphed against all difficulties: financial, the apathy and in some cases the active ridicule of the local inhabitants: the shortage of men, the problem of a place to practice in, of finding an instructor. He had organised whist drives and dances and concerts, to produce funds. He had gone to outlying villages, to remote farms in his search for men and youths with a latent musical talent. He had found an instructor in Burnharbour, and overcome the prejudices of the trustees of a chapel hall for its use two nights a week, and his pride was immense now that the band had quite a wide repertoire of marches, polkas and selections which it could play with credit at concerts, benefit society walks or any public function. The buying of the mule itself did not necessarily mean the end of John's connection with the band, but it would mean the loss of one player in the person of Tom, and John wasn't so stupid he couldn't see it was the beginning of the end. He was morose, irritable, and Sally was always relieved when supper was over, and she could slip over to Marney's, where, if the atmosphere was potentially perilous, there was relief from the dead weight of Henry and John.

Amy already had started getting things ready for the move. It had been suggested that if a spell of fine weather came they could use the mule for this. She had gone down to Burnharbour one afternoon, leaving the bairns in charge of Sally (and, Sally had observed, taking good care to have Tom go with her). She had liked the cottage Marney had found. It wasn't much better off for conveniences than the present one, for there was no water or sink, and no proper kitchen range. But it was close to the waterfront, and it had a very large attic, divided into two rooms, one of which would be just the place for Tom. The other rooms were bigger too, and Amy's chief anxiety was that she wouldn't have enough things to furnish it all 'proper.' She certainly couldn't afford to buy anything new like floor canvas or carpet, seeing that all the salvage money when it came would have to go into the mule, and that there would be a lot of other expenses like painting and papering. She had measured all the windows and had discovered that none of her old blinds and curtains would fit. Sally helped her with the altering of these and making new ones, and sewing on rings, but if Tom was there, and he usually was, she couldn't get it out of her mind that she was in a way helping to make his home, and it made her even more jealous. Yet she hid her feelings. Apart from Amy's attitude to Tom she liked and admired her sister-in-law as much as she had ever done. She was glad they were going to Burnharbour. She could see that even for mother it would be the best thing if they all went in the end; and the sense she had that she was in a conspiracy, that she was aiding and abetting Marney, secretly thrilled her.

Curiously, it was now Marney who was the least cheerful member of his own family. Usually he came back later than John, for he was working at the cottage after they had finished their day's work on the boat. He was tired, of course, and hungry, but that did not account for his quietness, his air of preoccupation, his

obvious lack of enthusiasm whenever the mule was
discussed. Sally wondered if it was just that he was
worried about mother, and how she was going to take
it when at last she was told. She wondered whether
it was the feeling that the responsibility of buying the
mule was being laid too heavily on him, and that he
and John were finding her in a much worse condition
than they had anticipated. She wondered sometimes if
he was altogether pleased at the idea of Tom living
with them, if he was secretly jealous and alarmed. One
night when he came back late, and Tom was not
present, he said to Sally with that nonchalance
which she knew he always assumed when he was
worried.

"Has father ever said owt to you about a Captain
Mowbray of Burnharbour?"

To Sally the name was quite unfamiliar.

"You've never heard him and John saying owt
about a keeler then, have you? Or owt to show that
father's keen on ever getting one?"

"No. Father scarcely opens his mouth except
to tell John to stop finding fault with the boat.
Why?"

It was Amy who answered that question.

"I'll tell you why. Captain Mowbray's the chap
that's helped several Burnharbour chaps to go in for
keelers, and that day after mother had her operation
and father went to Burnharbour, he told Marney
Captain Mowbray had been speaking to him, but he
wouldn't let on to Marney what it was about. Marney
thinks he offered to help father get a keeler, for father

as much as accused Marney of putting him up to it.
I've told Marney he's daft to go on worrying about it.
I'm not too pleased about the mule, from all I've heard
about it, but I say it's a step in the right direction. The
main thing is getting some of us to Burnharbour.
I think myself that everything's working out
champion."

Sally glanced sharply at Amy. Yes, she thought,
everything was working out champion, from her point
of view. She remembered that Amy hadn't seemed a
bit keen on going to Burnharbour when Marney had
spoken about it that winter's night after the vicar's
visit to Henry. That was before any one could have
guessed that Tom Fosdyck would be fishing with the
Lunns, and going to live in the same house as Marney
and Amy. It would have meant then an end to Tom
dropping in every night, an end to Amy having some
one at her beck and call. Was Amy really in love with
Tom? Did Marney think she was? Was it just the
feeling that they might have had a keeler instead of the
second-hand mule that was bothering him? Marney
had said nothing, but had started to wash before
sitting down to his supper, and a little later when Tom
came in his greeting was friendly as ever. But Sally
observed that Tom's first glance was towards Amy
and that although Amy didn't trouble to look at
him when she spoke, her manner had changed and
had become subtly yet aggressively possessive. She
might not be in love with Tom, but she claimed him.
Subtly, but with all her power, she was warning Sally
off.

It was not until the middle of the following week that a chance came for Sally to see mother. She was still making good progress, but the doctor had been firm in not allowing her to be excited and even Henry had only been allowed one further visit of short duration. The mule was ready for sea. They were waiting for the biggest of the spring tides to float her off. Marney had worked hard at the cottage. Tom had gone down and helped him once or twice, but the buses were awkward and he couldn't ride a bike, and anyway there had been plenty for him to do at Bramblewick. He and Henry rarely finished their work before dusk.

The cottage hospital stood on a wooded hill above the upper harbour. Originally it had been the home of one of Burnharbour's wealthy shipowners, and while there was one fair-sized general ward, Mrs. Lunn as a surgical case had a room to herself. Sally had been warned by her father not to say a word that would give her an inkling of what was going on, and the matron gave her a further warning not to excite her.

Her first impression was one of agreeable surprise, for mother was sitting propped up on her pillows and while her face was very thin there was a faint colour in her cheeks, and her eyes were bright and clear as ever. Her hair was down, and Sally thought that she had never seen her look so lovely as when she smiled and raised her head for Sally to kiss her.

"Eh—I'm glad to see you, Sally," she said. "I *am* glad to see you. How are you keeping, love? You do look nice. Sit yourself down. Have one of those grapes. They're what father fetched me last time he came. Eh—I daren't think what he paid for them."

Sally sat down by the bedside. She had no need to think of the matron's warning to realise how careful she must be. She had bought a big bunch of daffodils (and some more grapes) on her way through the town. Tactfully she kept flowers and grapes out of mother's sight and helped herself to one of Henry's.

"Now, you're not to get excited, mother, or talk too much, or the doctor won't let me come any more."

Mother gave a quick, indignant look.

"Now don't *you* start telling me that, Sally. I've heard nowt except how quiet I've got to be ever since I came to this spot, and I've *been* quiet too. Never mind about me. I'm getting well all right, and I'll be out of here as soon as I can stand on my two legs. Tell me how everything's getting on. Your father might be dumb for all I can get out of him. Are you giving him and John plenty to eat? What about the washing. Are you giving the hens hot mash as I asked father to tell you to. I'm all right! I'll not get excited."

Sally had a feeling of intense pity for her mother. She thought of all the physical and mental pain she must have suffered, of her loneliness, and she had an impulse to put her arms round her neck and comfort her as though she had been a child. But something warned her off. She sensed a resentment, a subtle yet

M

powerful antagonism towards herself. It was not, for Sally, a new sensation. She had felt it in the days before she had left home, when she was taking an increasing share in the household jobs. It was jealousy, and the harder and better she worked, the more she felt it. Then it made her very miserable, for she had a great love and admiration for her mother, and she could not understand why, having taught her to do things, mother should be so resentful that she did them well, and not show her own love and gratitude in even greater measure. Now Sally did understand and she wasn't hurt. It was only natural that mother should resent her presence at home, doing her jobs, looking after her men folk. The knowledge, while it held her back physically, made her more compassionate. She recognised the need for continued tact.

"I'm doing my best, mother," she said. "But you can't expect me to run everything like you would if you were there, can you? I'm not such a good cook as you are, and never will be. I never could manage that oven like you do for baking."

Mother smiled.

"Nay, it takes a lot of knowing. You want to get everything well-raked out before you start, and then put a handful of kindling right under it, and see there's a good lot of wood-ash left. That keeps it right for bread, but you've got to have it different for pastry or a joint . . . Eh—I wish I was back, I'd soon show you how to do it proper. What about their porridge? Father likes his with salt, you know: but John likes sugar and milk, and plenty of it."

"Yes, I'd forgotten that—but they soon reminded me."

"Aye, John would, but father wouldn't. He's like that with any one he's a bit strange to."

Suddenly mother reached out her hand and clutched Sally's arm.

"What is it father's got on his mind, Sally?" she said quickly, "I know there's summat. He's brooding —that's what he's doing. What is it?"

Sally was taken by surprise. She was preparing herself for a discreet account of such domestic happenings as she thought would interest mother, and not excite her; the doings of Marney's kids, the job she had one night getting all the hens fastened up, how she had forgotten to put any baking powder in some pastry she had made. She was alarmed by the excitement in mother's eyes. She felt herself blushing when she answered.

"Father's not got anything on his mind that I know of, except you, mother. And that's been enough to make him worry, hasn't it? Wouldn't you be anxious and worried if any of us was taken to hospital for an operation?"

"Aye, I would. But I wouldn't be brooding. When your father's brooding, it means he's keeping summat back. I haven't lived with him all these years without knowing that. What happened that night I was taken bad? Was there trouble with the Fosdycks about them going off to that trawler? All he'd tell me was they'd got her off, and made a hundred pounds for the job, and I only got that out of him by a lot of asking.

Did the Fosdycks make trouble? Is there any trouble going on with them now? You needn't tell me any lies, Sally."

"Of course there isn't any trouble," Sally answered, a little more self-possessed. "Things are going on just as usual, as far as I know. Of course Bramblewick folk were not pleased about our boat doing the job, but they can only talk, and talking won't break bones . . . Now you stop worrying about it, mother! All that father's got on his mind is you being ill, and away from home. He wants you back more than anything, I should think, and you won't get back quickly if you worry. You know what the doctor says. Now just lie back on your pillows, and don't bother."

Mother gave Sally a quick, disbelieving glance, but she lay back and gave a tired sigh.

"Eh—I do wish I was back home, Sally. I shouldn't feel so bad even if I had to lie still on the sofa. I would know what was going on, anyway. All right—I won't ask any more about father. I know he's holding summat back and I'll get it out of him somehow or other—I usually do, for he was never a great hand at keeping secrets. How's Sam getting on? Has he started teething yet?"

"I don't think so. He's going on fine."

"He'd go on better if it wasn't for this daft idea his mother's got of feeding him every four hours, instead of when he wants it. I'll say this for Amy, she's made Marney a good wife, and she does keep her bairns nice, but she's got some very daft ideas about them. Why—what did mothers do before there were any books

or newspapers to tell them how to bring their bairns
up? They got on all right, didn't they, or we wouldn't
be here. Have the hens been laying well? There ought
to be at least eight eggs a day now, if they're getting
their hot mash. There's that black hen with a lame foot
often lays in the brambles at the far end of the run.
She never did like an ordinary nest."

Sally was relieved that mother's appetite for news
had become more general, but while she answered
most of her questions and successfully avoided any of a
leading nature (and mother herself seemed less excited)
she was aware all the time of that subtle antagonism.
Mother told her how thankful she was that she had
been able to come and look after the home; and she did
so hope her mistress was not badly put out by it, and
that there wasn't any fear of her losing her job, but
Sally noticed the special eagerness with which she at
once spoke of being well again and getting back home,
so that Sally herself could return to London.

"It's no place for you, Sally, a fisherman's house,"
she said. "It's been a great load off my mind, your
coming like this, but I don't like to think of you getting
back into our rough ways through me. You're a lady
now, remember. You're among the quality, and you'll
be more among them when you get this shop of yours.
I hope you're writing to your mistress and telling
her how things are going on. Don't you lose her
favour. You tell her you'll be back the very day I
get home."

Sally was glad when the matron came in to tell her
she must go. She kissed her mother and promised she

would come again next visiting day, and she put the
flowers into her hands and hurried out before she had a
chance to say anything else. As she walked down the
hospital drive, she felt very wretched. While her
reason told her it was a perfectly natural thing for
mother to resent her being at home, to wish her back
in London, it did hurt. No one seemed to want her
really, she thought. She was happy looking after the
house, cleaning and cooking and doing her best for
every one, but, when she thought of it now, even father
and John seemed to regard her as a very poor substitute
for mother. Tom appeared to be completely indifferent
to her existence. Last night when she had told Amy
that she was coming into Burnharbour to-day Tom had
never moved an eyelid, although there had been a
general discussion about the new house, and there had
been a vague suggestion that Tom might go down in
the afternoon and give Marney a hand with the white-
washing of the bedroom and the attics. If Tom had
been interested in Sally, Sally's announcement should
have interested him unless he was too daft even to add
two ideas together. Clearly it hadn't, nor had he been
concerned one way or another, when Amy with her
usual cleverness had at once found a good excuse for
Tom not going to Burnharbour. He had just meekly
assented; and yet Amy had had the coolness to ask
Sally to do several jobs for her, to go to the house and
take some floor measurements and try the curtains in
the living-room. No, Tom wasn't in love with her.
So long as Amy was on the scene, she had no existence
in his eyes; and she told herself that she couldn't be in

love with him, that she didn't want to be anyway, and that the sooner she got back to London the better. There, she felt, she was appreciated.

But when she reached the end of the drive, which ran through a belt of gloomy pines, Sally felt less wretched. It was a lovely afternoon. The wind was south, and strong, with big white clouds flying across a very blue sky, and as she cleared the last of the pines, it was as though a window had suddenly been flung open, for the harbour came in sight, and with it the roofs of the old town, so red in the sun they might have been on fire. The wind was boisterous, but it was warm. There was a touch of spring in the air. Sally saw a young fisherman approaching, dressed in his best and carrying a parcel, and evidently bound on a visit to the hospital. He was tall and good-looking and at once Sally was aware that he was staring at her. She returned his stare, and as he drew near to passing, she gave him a look which was just sufficiently short of a smile to deny him confidence and oblige him to avert his own eyes at the actual moment of passing.

But as she walked on, Sally knew, as though she had an eye in the back of her head, that he was staring after her, and she felt very pleased with herself. Her self-confidence was restored. She knew that she had a good face and a good figure, and that she knew how to dress. She knew she had plenty of sense and was capable of doing most things she gave her mind to. She knew that when she gave her love to a man, it would be something worth having. She began to think of Tom again and she felt suddenly that she only needed a chance to get him by himself to find out all she wanted to know about him and Amy, and also that she could make him love her if she wanted to, although what she would have to find out first was whether she was really in love with him, and wanted to marry him, and settle down as a fisherman's wife.

Sally too, had always liked Burnharbour. As a child she could think of no more thrilling treat than to go in a train with mother on a shopping expedition. To her it had all the advantages of Bramblewick with none of its drawbacks. There was the harbour and the sea, and if the town itself wasn't very big, there were plenty of shops, and there was always something to look at. And of course there was the Regal, Burnharbour's cinema.

The Regal wasn't much of a place, compared with those she knew in London. It was very small, and there was no luxury about it. The films were those you could see in London months before, but the machine for showing them was good, and if the seats were hard, they were cheap. Sally thought she would have a look at the Regal before she went home, and see what was on, but it was at the back of the town, and her present route took her down to the west quay and along the harbour side, towards the bridge connecting the east and west towns, down by the fish-market.

The tide was nearly up. The fishing fleet was in, and Sally walked on past the bridge towards the busy market, and suddenly she was hailed, and looking back saw Marney hurrying after her. They stopped at the rails which divided the market from the quay road. Sally gave a short, carefully optimistic account of her visit to the hospital, for she perceived that Marney was still bothered and unhappy. While she spoke she was aware that his interest was divided between what she said and what was going on in the fish-market, and the boats made fast alongside.

"You know, I reckon father's daft about mother," he said when she had finished. "I don't think she'd make half as much fuss as he imagines, if he told her straight out what we'd done. I don't think she'd object so strongly to coming here to live either, once she got used to the idea. I tell you there's no comparison between this spot and Bramblewick. Folks here can't do enough for you. You've only got to mention to any of these chaps you're short of a drop of tar or a bolt, or a bit of rope or canvas, and it's there. What troubles me is that we're spending all this brass and time on *Lucky Boy* when I'm certain as I can be that if it hadn't been for mother father would have gone in for a keeler straight away. I'll bet anything that Captain Mowbray *did* offer to help us. I've seen Captain Mowbray looking at me in a queer way once or twice, and it's been on the tip of my tongue to ask him straight out, and then I've thought it would only put father's back up more than ever: and now I've got that, when I see him coming, I look the other way. Look at that for a craft, Sally. Have you ever seen owt to beat it? Look what they're landing too, and this is nowt to what they get later on, when there's more fish about."

From where they stood, they had a clear view, not

only of the market, but on to the deck of one of the keelers, moored alongside the quay. Sally's knowledge of boats was confined to cobles and the smaller craft of Bramblewick, but she appreciated the lines of the craft she saw, the spacious deck, the neat wheelhouse, through whose windows she saw the gleam of a polished brass binnacle and the engine controls. Her ropes were still new and white. She carried a short sail (now furled) and her shining pitch-pine mast was surmounted by an electric navigation light. A wireless antennæ reached from the mast to the wheelhouse roof. Everything about her looked neat and shipshape, and efficient. Even the fish were lying in neat cribs and it was being off-loaded with a derrick and a small power winch. Chiefly it was skate and cod and conger-eel, but there was a very large halibut which formed one load by itself.

"That's the *Jane Mowbray*," said Marney. "Her skipper's Patsy Stevens, but of course it was Captain Mowbray who put up most of the brass to have her built. Patsy's ashore, I think, but that young chap working the winch is Ted Stevens, his son. Bye— they've made some brass since they started. They were lobstering first, and they averaged nearly fifteen quid a day for the first fortnight. They'll not be doing so well at present, but I bet they clear a good eight quid with that lot."

The fisherman working the winch suddenly glanced up and caught sight of Marney, and grinned. He was short, about Marney's own size, but he was dark, and he had magnificent teeth.

"Now, Marney," he shouted. "Have you got *Lucky Boy* afloat yet?"

"We're going to see if she'll move to-morrow, at high water," Marney answered.

"Have you asked the lifeboat to stand by? She's good enough to sink you before you get her through the bridge."

The fishermen who were standing on the quay, receiving the fish, all grinned at Marney, who however took the ragging in good part.

"Don't talk so daft. We'll be showing you chaps how to catch fish in a day or two. She's a lucky boat, remember. Where have you been for that lot, Ted?"

"Four hours east nor' east of Burnharbour light."

Sally was aware that Ted was staring at her very hard, and she blushed when he suddenly said:

"Eh—who's the lass you've got with you, Marney? I've always understood you were a married man, and she's not your missus. You Bramblewick chaps never had any manners. Aren't you going to give us an introduction?"

Ted grinned, and Sally grinned too, a little self-consciously, but she rose quickly to the occasion and shouted down in a mocking voice.

"I'm Miss Lunn, Mr. Lunn's sister. Am I speaking to Mr. Ted Stevens? How do you do? I'm sorry I can't shake hands."

"You wait till I'm washed and changed, then you can!" Ted retorted. "What are you doing to-night. Would you like to go to the pictures?"

"Perhaps I would, perhaps I wouldn't. It just depends

how you look when you *are* washed and changed. You might look worse than you do now, instead of better."

The men on the quay laughed, and Ted found it convenient to turn his attention to the winch. Marney clutched Sally's arm.

"Come on," he said, "I'm going over to the house. Do you want to have a look at it?"

Ted had made a quick recovery from his discomfiture, and he gave Sally a parting smile, which she returned, for she liked him and had not misunderstood his line of talk.

"He's a very decent young chap is Ted Stevens," Marney remarked as they walked towards the bridge. "He's always full of fun like that, only I'm glad you gave him it back quick. Do you know, that chap holds I don't know how many certificates and medals for saving life. He can swim and dive like a cormorant, and somehow or other he always happens to be at hand when any one falls into the harbour. It's bairns as a rule. There was a day last summer when he rescued no less than three, and one of them had gone under altogether and there was nowt but some bubbles to tell Ted where it was. He's a good fisherman too. When old Patsy retires, I reckon Ted will be skipper of the *Jane Mowbray*. I wish *we* had her."

"But there's nothing very wrong about the mule, is there?" Sally asked.

They had reached the bridge, from which there was a view of both harbours, and Marney pointed towards the old shipyard where the stern of the mule was just visible, jutting out from the end of the shed. Her hull had been tarred, and her top strakes painted blue, but she was too far away for them to see anything else.

"There she is," Marney said without enthusiasm. "I'll take you up and show you round later if you've got time. John's there mending the paraffin tank. She's no worse and she's no better than I thought she'd be. As a matter of fact I think she's still a damned good boat, and that she'd suit us a treat for fishing Bramblewick grounds, but I can't get excited about her when father's like he is. Damn it—he'll scarcely say a word about her. When I told him we might get her off to-morrow evening he didn't seem any more interested than if I'd told him his bootlace was undone. His heart's not in her. That's what's wrong. I've got him to agree to us going lineing in her to-morrow night if we can get her off, but it's been left to me to wire for a box of herrings so that we can get baited in time."

"And what about Tom? Isn't he a bit excited?"

Marney laughed.

"Tom? Tom excited? I don't think Tom could get excited if some one left him a million quid. Do you know, him and me were once ashore in a spot on the coast of Chile and there was a row going on between a lot of dagoes. We couldn't find out what it was all about, because we didn't know what they were saying, but they'd got a little chap down on the ground, and they were knocking hell out of him. Well, Tom never said a word, but he just walked in, and signed to the chaps who were holding the little 'un to leave go of him, and suddenly one of 'em out with a knife and snarled at

Tom like a tiger, and Tom just let him have it right on the jaw, and flattened him. I tell you I was scared stiff, as we were only lads, but Tom thought no more of it than if he'd just swatted a bed bug. You ought to have seen the way that poor little dago went on, when the others cleared off. He tried to kiss Tom's boots."

They moved on. Sally's heart was beating fast. She would have liked to have heard more of that story, for it had created for her a vivid and very pleasant picture of Tom, but her interest was more topical and she said:

"He must be queer. Wasn't he a bit excited even when you asked him to join the mule, and come and live in Burnharbour?"

"Garn. I don't think Tom cares a damn what happens to him one way or another. Mind, I think he'll be happier working with us than with his uncles; and I don't think he'll mind saying good-bye to his Aunt Rachel, but you'd never get him to show it. I tell you, Tom's never got over not being able to get his tickets; and he never will. He just thinks he's a failure."

They had crossed the bridge, and had turned along a narrow street with alleys leading from it, some actually ending at the harbour side, and wherever there was any space between the cottages there were piles of lobster pots, and fish boxes and baskets, cables and anchors and oars, and everywhere was the strong smell of fish and tar and brine. There was no wind here, for it was broken by the town cliff, but the sun poured into the alleys, and in front of many of the cottages bare-armed women were cleaning the lines which had already been fetched across from the returned keelers.

Bramblewick once had been like this, Sally thought, but how different it was now. Here everything was alive. Many of the women were young and good-looking, and all of them seemed happy, and Sally herself felt happy and excited. The women stared at her, but not in an unfriendly way. Most of them spoke and smiled at Marney.

They turned at last into an alley that shortly opened into a sunlit yard open to the harbour, and Marney pointed to a cottage whose end wall rose up actually from the harbour side.

"That's our spot." he said.

He opened the door and signed to Sally to enter. But he didn't follow.

"Go in and have a look round. I won't be a minute. I've got to get some more whitening to finish the staircase walls. Mind your head when you go upstairs. There's a low beam just where it turns. And the paint on the bedroom door isn't quite set too. I won't be a minute."

Sally stepped inside, and as Marney had already turned to go, she shut the door behind her. The sound of it made a peculiar echo in the empty house, and the echo was repeated eerily as she took a couple of steps across the bare wood floor. She stopped, as though afraid of making another sound. The room was square, with a low ceiling whose rafters were thick and hand-hewn. There were two windows, one looking out on to the yard and the other commanding a view of the lower harbour and the fish quay on the opposite side. An open staircase, twisting like that of a light-

house had its beginning in a recess in a wall opposite
the street door, and there were cupboards on each side,
and another next to the fireplace, which was of an old
type like that at home. The ceiling was newly white-
washed, and so were the insides of all the cupboards.
The sun streamed through the yard window on to the
floor, and the light from the other window reflected
from the sunlit harbour was very strong. Despite the
odour of paint, the air smelt sweet and Sally thought
she had never been in a room she liked so much. It
thrilled her and at the same time gave her a sharp pang
of jealousy against Amy. She had a sudden picture of
the room as it would be in a few days' time, full of
Amy's things, full of Amy herself. She saw Tom sitting
by the fireplace, gazing at her, ready to attend to her
wishes, and she had a violent desire to dash out of the
house, and never come near it again. And then slowly
she began to move into that dream-state again. She
walked across to the harbour window, and sat down on
its wide ledge, and she imagined it was her room she
was in. She saw it as it might be on a winter's night
with the lamp lit and the fire bright and everything
snug and cosy.

There would be lino on the floor, of course, because
it was a working room, but there would be a large rug
in front of the fire, with a lot of red in it, and this she
and Tom would most likely have made together. The
curtains would be chintz—not lace—and they'd be
modern, but not too modern in design. There would
not be room for an upholstered suite (she didn't like
them anyway) but there would be a narrow divan,

covered in something to match the curtains; and there would be at least one easy chair, preferably wood. The paper Marney had put on the walls would look all right with Amy's things, but it wouldn't suit hers. She'd have distemper, and she'd have all the woodwork painted ivory; and she'd have plain brass handles on the doors, and keep them polished.

A winter's night, with perhaps a storm blowing, but the boats safe in harbour. She would be knitting or sewing. Tom, wearing the guernsey she had made for him, would be in his chair, perhaps making a sailor's rope mat. And Tom himself would be different. He might be quiet, but he wouldn't be gloomy. His glance might be soft, but there'd be nothing of the devoted dog about it, and less still of the failure; for he'd be boss, and being boss of a woman, living with her, making a success of it, wasn't such a poor substitute for being boss of a ship. A winter's night, and before another winter she might have a kid of her own. Sally started to tremble; then her heart gave a violent jolt as she heard footsteps outside and then the handle of the door. She stood up, terrified that it might be Tom himself, but it was only Marney. He came in, slamming the door behind him. He had a paper bag in his hand, and he came over and put it down on the ledge where Sally had been sitting.

"Well, what do you think of this for a spot, eh— Sally? I think this room's a bit on the big side, but it won't look half so big and bare when we get all our things in. Do you like it? It's going to be handy for the pictures anyway. Just fancy, only having to walk to the other end of the town to be there."

Sally did not look direct at her brother when she answered. She thought she was going to cry, and turned towards the stairs and said:

"I think this room's lovely. And isn't it sunny. I'm just dying to look upstairs. Shall I go?"

"Aye—but mind that beam. I bet Tom wishes he was a smaller man before he's been living here a week."

9

THE wind was still south the next day, and fairly strong; but there was every sign that the evening tide would be high enough to float the mule. Henry and Tom had returned early from the lobster pots (which had been left in the sea), and the small boat had been hauled up into the dock alongside the disabled coble. After dinner they had both gone to Burnharbour to join Marney and John in the baiting of the long lines and the final preparations for the proposed fishing trip. The plan in which (to Marney's idea) Henry continued to show an exasperating lack of enthusiasm, was to carry on with the lobstering for the present and use the long lines chiefly for getting bait. Lobsters weren't so plentiful now as they were at the height of the season and they weren't bringing a very high price, but if the heavy item of bait was cut out, they were still worth catching, and there was a chance that the lines might produce something directly marketable.

According to Henry, this was a very slender chance. The keelers were all working a long way out to sea, and even then they weren't doing too well. John's typically pessimistic opinion was that they'd be lucky even if they caught enough fish to bait a fleet of pots and Marney's optimism was heavily taxed during the course of the afternoon, for Henry, having paid a short visit to the hospital, was in a worse mood than ever. Apart from saying that mother was going on all right, he did not give any information about his visit. He found fault with the boat. He criticised Marney's painting, the new rigging of the mizzen mast and sail. He roused John's ire by being equally critical in the engine-room; and having poked his head into the cabin he said that it wasn't fit for pigs to sleep in; that if it came to sleeping, he'd prefer to stay out on deck. There was some justification for this, for the place had no ventilation except the hatch, which would have to be closed at sea if the weather was at all bad; and the stove, which Marney had lit to boil a kettle for the tea, had an imperfect draught and smoked rather badly. The herrings which had come from a distant northern port were stale. Henry said they were next to useless for bait; and that they'd have done better if they'd got a couple of bags of whelks; a remark which produced from Marney the heated retort that if he wanted whelks, why the hell hadn't he said so, and anyway there wouldn't have been any bait at all if he hadn't acted on his own and sent a wire.

Thus the actual floating of the mule, an occasion which, seeing that it was almost the equivalent of a launch, might have been exciting, and justified at least a mild celebration, passed off in an atmosphere of apparent apathy and gloom. She was hauled off, without much effort on the part of Marney and Tom, by her stern moorings. John had already started the engine. Marney held the cable short, until she swung round with the tide and her head was pointing to deep water. He cast off, and John at a gruff order from Henry put the engine into gear, and as she began slowly to gather way, Henry swung the tiller round and *Lucky Boy* was heading down harbour towards the sea.

Night had fallen. The wind, though still strong overhead, scarcely ruffled the water, which reflected the bright lights of the harbour side and the bridge. They passed under the bridge to the lower harbour, keeping well into the fairway. Even here, although there were puffs of wind, and the reflected lights were rippled into corkscrews, the water was smooth, and but for the passing lights it might have seemed that the boat was making no headway at all, for the engine was very quiet and its vibration was scarcely noticeable in the bows where Marney remained with Tom. That quietness, the lack of vibration, had already impressed Marney, for the engine was at least as old as the coble's and he had expected a far greater racket. Shortly he walked aft and looked through the hatch of the engine room, lit by a hurricane lamp. John was cleaning his hands with a rag, and was regarding the engine with a more cheerful expression than Marney had seen for many days.

"Bye," Marney said. "She's running sweet."

John actually grinned.

"Aye, I reckon it's those new bearings. The coble engine would have run almost as sweet if we'd had her overhauled. And that might have saved it from going west too."

Father was in hearing, but he remained silent, **and**

they were half-way down the harbour before Marney had the courage to speak to him.

"What are we going to do. Steam straight out, or give her a proper try inside the harbour?"

"We'll take one turn back to the bridge," Henry answered. "Try the pump and see if she's making much water."

The pump, an old-fashioned type with a two-handed beam, was amidships. Marney primed it with some sea water and pumped vigorously. In less than a minute it was dry. He walked aft.

"She's scarcely making a drop," he said. "It wouldn't have surprised me if she'd made a barrelful by now, years she's been laid up."

Henry answered quietly:

"I've always heard she was dry underneath. It's on top she's wet—and we'll know it before long."

Marney wasn't quite sure, but it seemed to him that his father sounded better-tempered. He waited until the mule swung round and was heading up-harbour again. Then he remarked:

"Well, the engine's running sweeter than I thought it would. There's nowt much wrong with that, is there?"

"Nay. It's sweet enough," Henry answered. "But it always was a good engine from all accounts. Trouble with *Lucky Boy* never was the engine, but the boat herself. She's not a boat, I tell you. She's just a lump of wood. Look at her now. She ought to be travelling twice as fast as she is."

John had poked his head out of the hatchway.

"I haven't got her full out," he put in with a sudden vigour. "Throttle's only three-quarters, and she'll not get more until her bearings are run in, if I have owt to say about it. She's going champion, I reckon, for her age."

There was no doubt that John's attitude towards the mule was undergoing a change; and if there was still an irony in Henry's voice, there was no sting when he retorted:

"Giving her full throttle won't make that much difference to her speed. You ought to know that the shape of the boat's got more to do with how fast she goes than what drives her, whether it's sail or engine. If you put one of those keeler engines in this you wouldn't get more than another knot out of her. You'd only drive her harder against the sea, instead of over it. It would be like trying to bore a hole in a lump of wood with a bit of square iron."

John dived into the engine-room again. Marney was content to leave his father's statement unchallenged, and he walked forrard. Tom, imperturbable as ever, was making a neat stow of the mooring ropes and the anchor. Marney did not speak to him, but there was an approval and a friendliness in the glance he gave at Tom's broad back, as he swung round again and lit a fag. They were moving closer to the fish quay side of the harbour and had nearly reached the bridge. The keelers had already put to sea, and the only craft visible were a few cobles which (engaged in lobstering) would not be out till daybreak. The town shops were closed, but the light from the electric street lamps was

strong enough to make everything clear on the deck of
the mule, and Marney's face began to show signs of
pleasurable excitement.

Everything had gone off so much better than he had
expected. The engine had altogether surprised him.
It had surprised him to hear John talking about it
almost with pride, to find father not half so sarcastic
as he had been before. She wasn't such a bad boat
anyway. In this light the new paint, the new ropes,
made her look not far from new herself, and the
best thing about the whole job was that they
were starting to fish from Burnharbour. How
different it was to the start of a fishing trip at
Bramblewick.

Henry swung the mule round and once more she
was heading seawards. Shortly he said:

"Hey, Tom. Will you hand me my oilskin and
sou'wester. They're down in the cabin, I think. You
chaps had better get your oilskins on too, if you want
to keep your shirts dry."

There was a matter-of-fact calmness in Henry's voice.
Marney sprang forward and took the oilskins from
Tom as he handed them up through the cabin hatch.
He came aft again and held the tiller while Henry put
on his smock and sou'wester; then, as the mule moved
slowly down the harbour, he and Tom put on their
oilskins. The quays began to narrow into the outer
piers, where there were no visible lights. They were
leaving the shelter of the cliff and the town, and the
wind became more noticeable, but the piers were high,
and the water was still smooth.

"See that there's nowt loose anywhere," Henry said. "Have you fastened the anchor?"

"Aye," Tom answered.

"You'd better have the cabin hatch shut too. Are the lights all right?"

The mule carried a white lantern at the top of her short mast, and, just above the deck another with red and green panes showing port and starboard.

"Everything's correct," Marney answered cheerfully.

"Then watch out for yourselves when we get round the pier head. This isn't an ordinary boat, remember."

They ran close into the east pier. Suddenly above them they caught the beam of the fixed green light which marked its end, and the next moment they were clear of its protecting wall. For a couple of lengths nothing exceptional happened. Like the forces of an ambush which withhold their fire until the victim has moved irrevocably into the trap, the waves might have been lurking in the shadow of the pier wall, for the first came not ahead or abeam, but from the rear, a dark, smoothly rolling wave that did not break, but lifted the mule up stern first and then rolled her over so that her lee rail was awash. There was a crash from the engine-room, a rattle of cans as the mule reared and swung over to the other side. Henry had steadied himself with the tiller and he saw that Marney and Tom had both got hold of the wire forestay of the mast. He shouted into the engine-room.

"Didn't I tell you to make everything fast. What's that damned thing clattering about?"

"It's a paraffin tin, if you're so anxious to know,"

John retorted indignantly. "It was lying on the floor and it hit the bloody ceiling, as well as nearly breaking my jaw on the way."

"Then get it lashed to summat," Henry answered unsympathetically. "I tell you this boat's a bad 'un for rolling. If she'll do this with a bit of southerly jowl, what will she do in bad weather?"

"I should think she'll loop the bloody loop," John shouted back.

"Hold your jaw . . . Look out, there's another coming."

Henry had to steady himself as another wave, this time directly abeam, sent the mule over on to her side, and then twisted her, so that she seemed to recover, not from a roll but from a steep pitch, which quickly developed into still another roll. It was not bad weather. The wind was slightly west of south and only moderately strong. The coble would have made easy going of it, but *Lucky Boy* seemed to translate and exaggerate every movement of the sea into an uncomfortable movement of her own. The wind and the general direction of the waves was abeam for the first half-mile from port. But even when Henry turned into the weather to a southerly course, when by rights all rolling should have ceased, the only noticeable difference was that her progress was slower. At times it appeared she was making no progress at all, but merely wallowing.

Henry's face, which caught a beam of light from the engine-room, had become impassive. He did not move a muscle of it when John suddenly lifted his head and shoulders out of the hatch and took a deep breath.

"God, it's fit to suffocate you in there," he said. "I'm as near sea-sick as makes no matter—what with the stink and the heat and everything heaving up and down. It's a thousand per cent worse than crossing the Bay of Biscay in ballast. Where's Marney and Tom. Have they gone below?"

Henry ignored the question, but he gave a shout to Marney.

"Hey—try the pump again."

The deck was almost continually swept with spray, and Marney and Tom had found shelter of sorts hard up in the bow, their backs against the low bulwarks. Hanging on to what they could, they lurched amidships and started to pump, using both handles. The operation took appreciably longer than the first trial, but it wasn't so very long before they stopped and Marney lurched aft.

"She's made next to nowt," he said to Henry, quietly, almost apologetically. "She was bound to make a drop more when she started burying her top-sides."

"Aye," Henry answered laconically. "Of course."

Marney waited, hanging on to the mizzen boom, while the mule indulged in a violent roll. Then:

"Have you any idea yet about where we're going to shoot?"

"I've got plenty of ideas," Henry answered. "But I don't know that this craft's going to let us carry any of 'em out. I've never been in a slower boat in my life, or a worser one."

"Then why the hell did you make us buy the bloody thing?" put in John, who still had his head out of the hatch. "We'd have done better if we'd stuck to what we'd got."

"What's up with you," Marney said sharply. "The engine's all right, isn't it?"

"I'm going to be sick any minute, if you want to know," his brother answered. "And I'll tell you summat else. There's a chap in Burnharbour who ought to have a statue built to him, aye, before he's dead too. And that's Monk Patterson. A man who could go on fishing in a boat like this all his life is a bigger hero than Nelson!"

Henry turned to his elder son.

"If you want to be sick, be sick," he said. "And don't make such a song about it . . . I don't know where we're going to shoot our lines yet," he said to Marney. "If we can't go faster than this it's no good trying for Muddy Dooks. We'll maybe shoot out from Low Batts point. Then we'll be close enough to our pots to haul and bait 'em at daylight."

"We might easily pick up a few haddocks off Low Batts, this time of year."

"Not with that bait," Henry answered. "If we get a few congers or ling I'll be satisfied. Why don't you chaps go below. You might as well get practised to it. There's no need for a look-out a night like this."

Despite the wind the night was fine and clear. They were moving not more than half a mile from the coast, whose tall cliffs were easily distinguishable to starboard. The lights of Burnharbour itself had been eclipsed, but almost due west, surmounting the most prominent point of the cliff, the Burnharbour High Light (whose fog siren had awakened Henry the night the trawler went ashore) shone brilliantly. From this point it was five miles in a straight line to Low Batts, the south extremity of Bramblewick Bay, yet nearly two hours had passed before the coast line began to recede to the west into Bramblewick Bay, and a solitary light above Bramblewick village came in sight and the familiar headland of Low Batts lay immediately abeam. Throughout this time Henry had maintained an impassive silence. John having been sick (it was not an unusual thing to happen to a fishernan in a boat he was not used to) had so far recovered that he was smoking a fag, but he had stood for the most part with his head out of the hatch, and he too, had not spoken. Marney and Tom had gone below. The odour of fresh coal smoke, blowing aft from the galley chimney, suggested that they at least had stronger stomachs against the combined effects of the heat, bad ventilation and the movement of the boat: but Marney occasionally had poked his head out of the hatch, and now he came on deck, and made his way aft to Henry's side. The boat was pitching and rolling as wild as ever.

"That's Bramblewick coastguard light, isn't it, father?"

"Aye, of course it is," Henry answered testily. "There'll be no one else in Bramblewick with a light burning at this time of night."

"You bet there isn't," growled John. "Even old Luke and Tindal will be fast asleep in bed. And I wouldn't mind if I was there too. Even if we had to launch the coble in a gale in the morning."

"Are you still feeling sick?" asked Marney not unsympathetically.

"I've *been* sick," John snapped.

"Have you? Well, I'll tell you, I thought I was going to be a few minutes ago, when I laid down in one of those bunks. I felt sort of dizzy and my head started aching, but I felt all right as soon as I stood up. It must be the queer way she rolls. Anyway, I've been thinking about mashing some tea. That galley stove works champion when there's plenty of draught. Kettle's boiling its head off. There's nowt like a sup of tea when you've been sick, or when you're fighting it off. And I don't think it does you much harm to have a bit of food too, if you feel you can keep it down."

"In that case you'd better make some tea, and we can have a picnic out on deck," said John. "We'd only need chinese lanterns and somebody to play a banjo and we could think we were at Burnharbour regatta."

"For God's sake hold your jaws," put in Henry. "I'm not so far from being sick myself. Smoke from that damned galley's enough to turn anybody up. I don't know what you wanted to light it for. It isn't winter. What's Tom doing?"

"He's in a bunk, sleeping like a bairn in a cradle."

"Then wake him up. If we're going to do owt with those lines it's time we made a start. We're fair off Low Batts now. Get your flares and your lines ready. By the time we've shot and hauled it'll be daybreak, and we've our pots to haul then."

Marney lurched forward again, but Tom Fosdyck was already out of the cabin hatch.

"We're going to start shooting, Tom," Marney said to him. "Light the flares before you come up. They're under the bottom bunk. Two of 'em."

Marney stood by the hatch until Tom handed up to him a large paraffin flare and followed on to the deck, himself carrying another. They were tin canisters. with spouts stuffed with tow, and the flames from them, if spluttering and mingled with thick and noxious-smelling smoke, gave an efficient illumination of the mule's deck. Marney lashed his half-way up the mast. The other was lashed to a short post secured to the starboard rail amidships, and close by this and slightly astern, Marney put a fish box bottom up, so that he had a table flush with the rail. Tom, meanwhile, and without a word from Marney had fetched a buoy and a small anchor (to which was attached a coil of rope), from below. The lines were piled near the foot of the mast, each coiled on a wicker 'skep,' that was like an African war shield. He took hold of the topmost one, waited for the mule to recover from a roll that brought the bulwark rails almost level with the sea, then heaved it up and laid it squarely on the fish box and unfastened its lashings. Marney had got hold of the anchor. He bent it on to the loose end of the line, hoisted the anchor over the bulwark rail and picked up the buoy. The whole operation had taken less than two minutes, and not a word had been exchanged between the two men.

"We're all ready when you are, father," Marney

shouted. "Where are you going? Straight out to sea? We ought to hit that patch of sand with our third line if we keep a bit to southard. If there are any haddocks about they'll be there."

"There won't be any haddocks about," Henry answered. "Our only chance is conger or maybe a ling or two. We want to be on rough ground all the way. I'll bring her round now. Look out—she'll roll worse than ever with the wind abeam."

"Shall I slow down for you?" John asked.

"No," Marney shouted. "We can shoot as fast as you can drive her."

The mule swung round so that she was heading out to sea, and almost at once Henry gave the order to start shooting.

In the coble, shooting had always been done by Marney. It was an operation that called for great manual skill. The lines were coiled on the oval skeps so that the baited hooks (each on a snood a yard in length) lay in a separate pile. There was a hook for every two fathoms of line, and the art lay in lifting and throwing each two fathom coil so that the hooks were lifted and not dragged overboard, and sank clear of the line itself. But no matter how skilful the shooter, there was always a possibility of two hooks fouling, with a consequent fouling of the line. This in a rowing coble would have merely meant delay, but in a power-boat whose momentum could not immediately be checked, there was the danger that unless the fouling could be cleared in seconds, the whole line might become tangled and the hooks catch in some one's arm.

Father and John, in the coble, had always been ready
to assist in case of any such accident, and in the changing
of the lines. But they were all in arm's reach of each
other. Here in the mule they were widely separated
and the co-operation of a fourth man was essential.
Without asking, without a word from any one, Tom
Fosdyck had assumed this responsibility. He stood
close to Marney, his feet apart, and one of them
jammed tight against the bulwark, hanging to the
bulwark rail with a hand whenever the boat rolled
over, but never for a second taking his eyes from the
line.

The light from the flares shone full on the faces of
both men like a spotlight on actors playing on a
darkened stage. There was a great contrast between
them, quite apart from the difference in their stature.
Every movement that Marney made was quick. His
hands fell and rose on the coils of line asthough it were
a savage musical instrument he was playing, and his
whole body seemed to respond to the rhythm of that
movement like a dancer's. Tom moved only to the
movement of the boat, slowly, ponderously. There was
an unconscious and a joyous swagger in everything
that Marney did, a perfect self-confidence. But Tom's
face had its habitual expression of lurking unhappiness,
of morose self-contemplation. Yet there was a curious
harmony between them, such as had never existed
between Marney and John. Despite that there were
several technical differences between the Lunns' and
the Fosdycks' methods of fishing (the Fosdycks' snoods
were closer together and their lines were thicker and

o

of an opposite lay), Tom seemed to anticipate Marney's instructions, and his hand had moved to clear two baits that looked like fouling a full second before Marney's warning shout.

They were shooting on the weather side. The pressure of the wind and the waves was giving the mule a drift to leeward and to shoot on the leeward side would have meant the line dragging under the boat at the risk of fouling the propeller. It meant that Marney had to work principally with his left hand. The rail was almost level with the sea with every roll to starboard, and time after time the mule would rise too late for the advance of a following wave, which would break and throw a torrent of spray in the faces of the shooters. The deck was slippery. When Marney got near to the end of the first line, Tom moved to the pile for the next one, and as he lifted it a sudden and unexpected pitch caused him to slide backwards and then spin completely round and crash into the mast with his shoulder; but he hung on to the line and half-slid, half-walked back to Marney's side, put the line on to the deck close by the fish box and expertly bent the new line to the end of the old, and stood ready to exchange the skeps when the precise minute came.

"Did you hurt yourself?" Henry shouted.

Tom grinned, but he did not take his eyes from the line.

"Nay, I'm all right."

"I bet this boat'll kill somebody before she's done," John shouted, his head and shoulders still out of the hatchway. "Watch out when you change lines, Tom. She's rolling worse now than ever."

"You get below and look after your engine," Marney shouted at his brother. "We can look after this side of the job . . . Now, Tom."

Marney had reached the last coil. He lifted it and flung it well up, and away from the boat side, the last bait travelling with it, and, as the line tightened, Tom whipped away the empty skep and lifted the new line on to the fish box so that the shooting went on without interruption.

There were eight lines, each about a third of a mile in length, and each took about a quarter of an hour to shoot, so that they were nearly three miles from the coast and it was long past midnight when the last coil went over, followed by the anchor, and then by a large buoy with an eight-foot pole to which was attached a lighted storm lantern. Apart from Tom's slight accident, the shooting had been carried out without mishap, and as soon as the lighted buoy was riding clear of the boat, Marney turned to Tom:

"Well, that's done, anyway. You go below and see if the fire's still on and if the kettle's boiling. I'm as hungry as hell."

Tom disappeared into the cabin. Marney moved aft.

"Have you got a fag handy?" he said to John. "My hands are too wet to light one."

John did not speak. Gloomily he produced a packet, lit a fag from his own, and put it between his brother's lips. Henry too remained silent. He had turned the mule into the weather again and the buoy was now slightly astern. Marney drew at his fag awhile, then he said diffidently:

"How long are we going to give 'em, father?"

"It'll be no use waiting longer than an hour," Henry answered. "Not with that bait! What hasn't washed off on the way down, I reckon will be cleared by starfish and crabs in less time than that."

"We might just as well have stopped at home," growled John. "That's my opinion."

"Garn, what you want is a good cup of tea and summat to eat. You two get below. Me and Tom can take charge while you have a spell. I'll take the tiller."

"You needn't trouble," Henry answered drily. "You better get below yourself if you're that keen on the idea."

"You can fetch me a mug of tea if you like, when you come up again," put in John. "But I don't want owt to eat."

A whiff of fresh coal smoke blew down the deck.

"Tom shapes well, doesn't he father?" Marney remarked as he swung round to go.

"I never doubted that he wouldn't. And the best thing about him is he does his job and doesn't argue the fat. If you're fetching John a mug of tea you might as well fetch me one too," he added. "But you can let that fire go out when the kettle's boiled. Coal's not that cheap we can afford to waste it."

There was too great a depth of water for the mule to anchor; and a sea-anchor, which, holding her head to the waves, would have given comfort to an ordinary boat, seemed to offer no advantages to a craft which

rolled as much head on as with the waves abeam; so
Henry merely kept her under way, with the engine
throttled, steering in a wide circle round the lighted
buoy. But the wind, as it so often did in the early
hours of approaching day, was failing, and when an
hour later Henry gave a shout that fetched Marney and
Tom on to the deck again, it had dropped to a comparative calm. The swell remained, the mule pitched
and rolled as badly as ever, but there was an advantage
in that hauling could be carried out on the lee side of
the boat, right-handed instead of left.

The hauling began in an atmosphere of pessimism,
which even Marney seemed to share. Again he and
Tom worked in partnership. The line had to be coiled
as it came on board, and laid on its skep, the buoy and
the anchoring gear unbent and stowed away, and Tom
had to be ready to assist with the gaff should anything
like a big fish come aboard. But the hooks came up in
a monotonous succession, most of them clean, a few
with a starfish or a crab clinging to the remains of a
bait, and not a single one with a fish. Hauling was
slower than shooting, and nearly half an hour passed
before the end of the first line (the last one to be shot)
came on board, and Tom having unbent it lifted it out
of the way and slipped a bare skep in its place on the
fish box. Throughout this time no one had spoken;
and as the hauling went on, and hook after hook came
in bare, the expression on Marney's face grew as gloomy
as John's. More than half the line was hauled, and still
there were no fish. Then suddenly Marney's expression
brightened.

"There's summat coming now, anyway. A big one too. Feels like a skate."

No one spoke, but Henry stood up, and John leaned out of the cockpit for a clear view. Tom got hold of the gaff. He waited a moment, then, as the mule rolled down to starboard he suddenly leaned over the side, thrust the gaff down, and using both hands, pulled a very large fish on board. But the landing of the first catch aroused no further excitement. It was a monk fish, a grotesque creature with an enormous head and mouth, and a short, thick tail. It was a species of practically no market value, and Marney's expression changed to disgust as he went on hauling. But John was grinning ironically as he watched Tom cut the hook out of the fish's mouth.

"It's a queer coincidence, isn't it?" he remarked, loud enough for every one to hear. "A line and a half empty and then the first fish a monk fish. I wonder if Monk Patterson is dreaming about his hundred quid?"

"You're funny, aren't you?" Marney retorted. "There's a dozen good pot baits in that if nowt else. We haven't finished hauling yet either, by a long way. I bet we'd have had a good few haddocks if father'd only taken my advice and shot over that bit of sandy ground . . . Here *is* a haddock anyway—by the looks of it. No, it isn't, it's a whiting."

There was no need for the gaff. Marney swung the fish on board and Tom unhooked it without comment. Marney went on hauling. He came to the end of the second line without another fish. The stars in the east were beginning to pale when the third line was hauled, and by then the catch had grown only by a couple of codlings and a small conger eel. Ahead of them the configuration of the coast was growing clearer, and below the solitary light in Bramblewick coastguard station one or two lights in the village itself had become visible. But no one looked shorewards. The hauling went on in silence. The fourth line yielded two more monks and a medium sized conger—the fifth line not a single fish, and day was actually breaking when, with a quarter of the sixth line in, Marney broke the silence.

"Here's summat heavy coming. I doubt it's another monk, but it might be a conger."

The strain on the line was obviously increasing. Suddenly Marney shouted.

"Hey—slow down your engine a bit, John. You're going too fast for me. It's either a damned big fish or we've fouled summat."

Henry had stood up again.

"No," Marney went on excitedly. "It's a fish all right. I can feel it now. It's pulling like a bloody whale. Hey—give us a hand, Tom."

Tom got hold of the line. They both heaved with all their strength, but the line came in scarcely more than a foot at a time, and several minutes passed before Marney said:

"Leave go, Tom, and get your gaff. It's here. I'll hold on."

Again Tom reached over the side. Marney held on tight to the line without attempting to haul. Tom jabbed with the gaff. He heaved and brought a fish over the rail. It was a ling, weighing only about fourteen pounds, and John shouted ironically:

"Are there any more whales like that?"

"There's one more, anyway," Marney retorted, as Tom without waiting to unhook the ling jabbed into the water again and jerked up another and slightly bigger one. Marney continued to haul at the line with all his strength. Tom took hold again; but they'hadn't hauled in more than two bare hooks when he had to leave go, and gaff another ling.

"Are there any more coming?" Henry shouted.

"Aye, there's a ton weight on this line."

"Give 'em a hand," Henry shouted at John. "I can nip down to the engine if it's got to be stopped."

John sprang to Marney's side.

"There's three coming together," Marney shouted. "And I won't say there's not a dozen more below them."

"Don't stop to unhook them. Break the snoods," Henry shouted. "Get them aboard and we can clear up the mess later."

There was no more talking. Marney and John heaved at the line. Tom swung fish after fish on to the deck and still the strain on the line showed no sign of decreasing. Apart from a solitary conger—itself weighing about forty pounds—they were all ling, averaging about twenty pounds apiece. There was no time to throw them into the fish crib. As they hit the deck, Tom gave the snood a sharp jerk which either disengaged the hook, or snapped the snood itself, and the fish simply slithered about the deck as the mule pitched and rolled. The flares were still burning, but there was enough daylight now to see the fish coming up through the water. There were gaps of bare hooks. But there was one period when more than a score of ling came in consecutively, and there were only three bare hooks between the last one and another batch of five. They reached the end of the sixth line. Ahead of them the precipitous cliff of Low Batts stood out clear in the growing twilight of dawn. A mile south, where the bay swept in, the red roofs of the village were becoming visible, but no one had time even to glance towards the shore, for the fish were coming up as thick as ever. Then, towards the middle of the seventh line, the break came. There were three fish on consecutive hooks, then a blank of several fathoms; another conger eel, another blank and then nothing but bare hooks until near the end of the eighth and last line, when Marney swung on board a solitary haddock, which he hailed with a jubilant shout.

"Just what I've been waiting for, for our supper to-night! Who said you couldn't catch haddock on rocky ground?"

"I didn't," Henry answered, glancing at the fish-strewn deck. "And I didn't say you couldn't catch ling either. But I'll tell you this carry-on's beaten me. Mind, we've never had a chance to fish this ground proper in the coble for years. But I didn't aim on striking them thick like this bang off."

There might have been a repressed excitement in Henry's voice, but for the time being there seemed to be a reluctance on the part of every one to comment freely on the stroke of fortune that had come their way. John had gone back to the engine. Tom had laid the gaff aside and had started heaving the fish into the crib, although there was obviously six times as much fish as the crib could hold. The end buoy of the line was in sight, and Marney hauled quicker, for there were no more big fish. Then suddenly, catching Henry's eye, he said:

"Well, what about it, father? What are we going to do now. Start hauling our pots?"

John had poked his head out of the hatch.

"Haul our pots when we've got a catch like this for market? Don't talk so daft, man. Let's get back to Burnharbour. We can come back to our pots later. Are you going to get the galley fire on again, Tom? I'd like a cup of tea and summat to eat."

Henry grinned.

"You've changed your tune. I thought you were sea-sick."

"I'm not sick now. You can get used to anything in time . . . You've changed your tune too. If every-thing had been so bad about the engine as you tried to make out yesterday, we wouldn't have got all this fish. And what did you tell Marney about the bait?"

Marney had got the anchor up and was hauling in the buoy. Henry ignored John's remark and said:

"What's ling been fetching at Burnharbour this week?"

"There's been next to no ling landed," Marney answered. "Only lot I saw fetched five bob a stone. If our lot's not worth fifteen quid, I'll be surprised."

He suddenly glanced shorewards.

"Bye—I shouldn't mind us going ashore at Bramblewick with them, just to show everybody."

"Aye," said John sharply. "And have to cart it all up to the station and pay carriage on it."

"As well as getting it in late for market," said Henry. "Nay, we'd better leave the pots. We might even get in before the keelers if we're lucky. Besides, I doubt if we could land at Bramblewick in this swell."

Marney grinned as he saw his father swing the tiller round so that *Lucky Boy* headed north for Burnharbour.

"Aye, of course," he said, "but I'll tell you what, father. I'd like to see mother's face, when she's told how we've got on—first trip in *Lucky Boy*."

Henry's face momentarily clouded.

"Aye, maybe—maybe," he muttered. "But *I* don't relish the job of telling her." He turned to John. "Give her a bit more throttle. She'll take no harm, and we've got to beat those keelers, if we want top price."

10

SALLY had nearly finished the guernsey she was knitting but she wasn't sure it was going to be for Tom, and she still wasn't sure that she was altogether in love with him. But she knew she was going to find out before long. She'd have to, for mother was now convalescent, and she'd very likely be home in another week, and although the doctor said she wouldn't be allowed to leave hospital unless there was some one at home to help her and to see she didn't overtax her strength, Sally knew her mother too well to imagine that the two of them could go on living under the same roof for longer than was absolutely necessary.

Besides, her mistress had written a very nice letter, saying that she must not think of coming back until her mother was quite well, but making it clear that she was expected (and wanted) back as soon as everything was all right, not only to take up her duties in the house, but to go into the matter of the dressmaking shop.

This letter had perturbed Sally very much. She did like London. She'd been very happy there, and the opportunity that was being offered to her was a wonderful one. She knew she could make a success of it too, that she'd like the work, that she could make money not only for herself, but to help her parents, perhaps even enough to make it possible for her father to get a keeler. They had discussed it before, more as a suggestion than a definite proposition. But in this letter it was clear that her mistress had been doing something more than talking, for she mentioned an actual shop that would be to let very soon and she said she was very anxious for Sally to see it. Her friend, the proposed partner, had given her strong approval. It was close to Baker Street, in one of those backwaters where many small but quite exclusive dressmakers had their premises. An ideal location! What would her mistress think of her if she just turned the idea down, and told that she was going to marry a fisherman.

Whenever she reread the letter, and she did this many times, Sally told herself what a fool she would be if she let the opportunity slip; what a fool she was even to imagine she was in love with Tom. But, whenever she sat down to write an answer to it, to tell her mistress she was returning at the earliest possible moment, that she was eagerly looking forward to seeing the shop and making a start on it, she found herself slipping back into that waking-dream in which she and Tom were now complete lovers, and all the problems and difficulties which had kept them apart from each other had no existence.

Actually, she seemed farther from solving the problem of Tom, and what she felt about him, than ever. A few days after the first successful fishing trip of *Lucky Boy*, the wind shifted to the west, and one afternoon *Lucky Boy* steamed into Bramblewick Landing and dropped anchor within wading distance of the scaurs.

The arrangements for Marney's flitting had been made the previous night. Almost everything was packed by morning, and Amy had caught the two o'clock bus to Burnharbour, taking the baby with her. She would leave him at a neighbour's house while she made the final preparations for the arrival of the things, got the curtains up and did the shopping. Jeff and Alice were left in Sally's care for the afternoon, and Sally could bring them down by the last bus, by which time their cots would be ready and they could go straight to bed. Sally might have been wrong, but it seemed to her that, even in this, Amy had thought of every possible way in which she and Tom might have been left alone together, and cunningly prevented it. There wasn't much chance of her saying what she wanted to say to Tom while she had two excited and boisterous children in her charge, even if the actual business of carrying the things down from the cottage to the boat had allowed.

Marney and Amy had taken particular care to keep the arrangements for flitting secret from the village. They didn't want to have everybody out of their houses, 'nosey-parking.' Indeed, Marney had suggested doing the thing in the dead of night, but this had been rejected by all as impracticable. The arrival of the mule in the Landing, however, by itself was a sufficiently noteworthy event to arouse the curiosity of certain watchers on shore, including of course Luke and Tindal Fosdyck, and the news that Marney Lunn was flitting had travelled round the village, and had drawn many people to their windows and doorsteps

and down to the dock and slipway before half the
flitting was done.

Yet Luke and Tindal were seemingly in a very
amiable mood. It had been decided to take advantage
of the fine weather to tow the disabled coble and the
small boat down to Burnharbour where eventually
they might be sold. Without waiting to be asked, the
two brothers assisted in launching them, and had even
volunteered to carry down some of their gear, which
was stored in Henry's warehouse. Sally hadn't
witnessed these proceedings. She had been too busy
keeping the bairns out of the way, and preparing a
hasty meal for the men, in which she hoped Tom would
join. Neither Tom nor Marney came up to the house,
and the meal had been ready half an hour when John
came in to report that the others were still busy,
although Henry would be coming up any minute.
John was gloomy. The noise of Jeff and Alice (they had
got a lump of wood and some rope and were playing at
hauling the coble up) irritated him, and Sally had to
quieten them by giving them some bread and jam. But
his spirits seemed to rise a little when he started to eat.

"By God, Sally," he said, "it's a treat seeing a meal
laid on a table again, and everything fresh cooked
instead of being warmed up. It's something even to
have fresh milk in your tea, and to be able to drink it
without having to balance yourself as though you
were walking a tight-rope in a circus."

Since the first trip, except for the week-end, all four
men had been sleeping on the mule at Burnharbour.
The success of that first night's fishing had not been

repeated, and they had been obliged to follow the plan of using the long lines chiefly for catching bait for the pots, and regarding lobsters as their marketable catch. There had been no opportunity yet for using the trawl. Lobsters had been scarce, which meant that they had to shift ground continually, and while the mule with all her faults made this an easier and quicker job than if they had been using the coble, it had meant almost continuous work from dawn till sunset, and a very small return.

John looked tired. He was unshaved and his hands and face were grimy with oil. Henry was in the same condition, and although he smiled at Sally when he came in, and had kissed both of the children, he seemed even more gloomy than John.

"Aren't the others coming up for something to eat," Sally inquired.

It was John who answered:

"I don't think so. I expect Tom will have to go up to his Aunt Rachel's to fetch his things, and Marney can think of nowt but getting everything stowed and getting away. He can't stand all those folks watching us. I tell you half Bramblewick's down in the dock or standing on the slipway. You know the way they can just stare, and tell you more by that what they're really thinking, than if they cursed you straight out."

John turned to his father.

"Did you notice Luke's and Tindal's expression when they helped us to put the coble down."

"No, I didn't. I was too busy."

"Pleased isn't the word for it. I've never seen them

look so delighted about anything all the time I've known them. I shouldn't be surprised if they ran up and down the scaurs waving flags in their hands when they see us tow the coble out of the Landing. There's only one fly left in their ointment, and that is, it's not all of us going instead of only Marney . . . And you can't see yet—or you *won't* see—that that's what Marney was scheming for when he persuaded you to go in for *Lucky Boy*."

"He didn't persuade me," Henry answered sharply, "and no one else did, not against what I thought right. Dammit, you can't let five minutes go by without yapping about that. Where should we be now if we hadn't got her?"

"We'd be here, of course. With some one to cook our meals, and a decent bed to sleep in at nights. You needn't pretend you wouldn't prefer this to living on board *Lucky Boy*. You've said youself that cabin's worse than a pig sty."

"What if I have. We're making a living and that is more than we could do here. If I've noticed one thing about Luke and Tindal to-day, it's that they're both about played out. They won't be fishing another winter. You talk so daft I've got no patience with you. Hurry up, and let's get down to the boat. The mistake we made was in coming here at all. Marney ought to have sent everything down by the carrier. It wouldn't have cost him more than a quid."

"Aye, and it would have been worth it too," John growled. "I can tell you I'm not looking forward to going down the slipway again, carrying a lot of pots

P

and pans, and having all those folks staring. But I'm
glad of one thing, and that is that mother's not here
to see. It wouldn't make her feel very happy thinking
maybe it will be her turn next."

Henry glared, but he said nothing, and Sally was
glad that the children created a diversion just then by
upsetting the coal scuttle, which apparently Jeff had
thought would make a good substitute for the piece of
wood in their game of hauling up cobles. She was
sorry for John, but she had a deeper sympathy for her
father. She could see that his nerves were on edge.
She knew that he was more perplexed than ever. He
had told mother about the mule, and that Marney was
going to Burharbour. But he hadn't told any member
of his family what she had said, and Sally's own opinion
was that she must have taken it badly. She had not
been able to see mother since, for the hospital rules
about visitors, relaxed in urgent cases, had been stiffened
and it wouldn't be until to-morrow, Saturday, that her
turn would come, and she was rather dreading it.

Marney and Tom did not come. When Sally had
washed up, she took the children on to the cliff and
she was just in time to see the mule and the coble and
the small boat in tow (and all three piled up with
furniture) steaming out of the Landing. She could
distinguish the figures of Luke and Tindal moving
slowly up the scaur, stopping occasionally and turning
to look seawards. Thirty years ago, the Fosdycks and
the other native born fishermen of Bramblewick must
have watched with deep resentment the cobles of
the Sledburgh foreigners sailing into the bay. Since

then all of the native fishermen except Luke and Tindal had either died or given up fishing. One by one the foreigners had returned, leaving only the Lunns. And Luke and Tindal might have felt a sense of triumph that now, after all the long years of the feud, the Lunns too, had to all practical purposes gone, even if their departure coincided with the brothers' impending retirement from fishing.

For Sally the event had no sentimental significance. She had neither a love nor a hate for Bramblewick and its people. She just wanted her own folks to be happy. But Bramblewick was dead; her own folks alive, and she suddenly felt she must do everything she could to get them out of it as quickly as possible and settled down in Burnharbour. As for herself, in her present mood she longed to be back in London. She wished she hadn't to go down to Burnharbour to-night to see Amy in her new home, to see her things filling that room in which she had experienced her most vividly intimate dream about Tom. She didn't want to see Tom again. She was not going to humble herself by running after a man who either hadn't the gumption, or was not sufficiently interested, to come and see her, when he was almost within speaking distance. She wanted to clear out, to get on with her new job, to make something big out of it, and she decided she would write the letter as soon as she was by herself, and get it posted. She would write that she was returning to London at the earliest possible opportunity.

Dusk had fallen when she reached Burnharbour. After Bramblewick, the town looked very cheerful, the shops were open and brilliantly lit, the streets were busy, and as the fleet hadn't put to sea there were plenty of fishermen about. Marney met the bus. The children had fallen asleep, and they carried them along the quay and over the bridge in their arms. Marney was in a good humour, and full of praise for Burnharbour.

"I'll tell you, Sally," he remarked as they turned left from the bridge, "it wouldn't break my heart if I never saw Bramblewick again, not after this afternoon. You were lucky to have been in the house all the time and missed everybody staring at us, and laughing to themselves, the way Bramblewick folk do. Burnharbour's different from Bramblewick as chalk from cheese. Everybody here was as pleased to see us come as Luke and Tindal was to see us go. Some one's been helping Amy in the house all the afternoon, and as soon as we got in there was Ted Stevens, and I don't know how many other chaps, ready to give us a help ashore with the things. We got everything into the house in an hour. Do you remember Ted? That chap that holds all the medals for saving life. Him who cheeked you and asked you to go to the pictures?"

"Yes, of course I do."

"He remembers you all right. Almost the first thing he said to me was, 'Where's that smart sister of yours.' Ted's at home now. We've been laying the floor canvas in the bedroom, and only just got it finished."

Amy, who had come to the door, took the sleeping child from Sally's arms. Looking past her shoulder into that room which had so excited her, Sally was aware first of Ted Stevens sitting on the edge of the table, swinging his legs (one of Marney's habits) and smiling at her. Except that he was not wearing sea-boots, he was in his rough fishing clothes, but he was hatless, and his very black curly hair made his teeth look whiter, and he seemed more attractive than when Sally had seen him first. In a peculiar way his smile, his unmistakable interest, gave Sally courage. It braced her against the shock of what she felt was going to be the spoliation of her dream. She returned his smile confidently as she entered the room, but instantly she knew that Amy had noticed Ted's interest, that with him as with Tom, she was asserting a prior claim. It seemed to Sally that she deliberately intercepted Ted's glance, as a racing yacht might steal the wind from a rival, and that there was a repressed hostility in her voice when she said to Ted :

"You know Sally, don't you," and half-turning to Sally, "Ted *has* been a help to us. I'm sure I don't know what I'd have done without him."

Ted had got down from the table and he reached out his hand to Sally.

"You bet I know her. Sally promised she'd come to the pictures with me if she liked me as much washed and changed as mucky. Damn it—I ought to have got a collar and tie on. Can you wait till I slip home and change."

Sally laughed.

"I'm afraid it would be a waste of time," she retorted readily. "Unless you can see me home to Bramblewick. The bus goes in twenty minutes, and there's not another to-night. That will be six miles there and six miles back."

Amy had crossed over to the far-side chair and was starting to take Alice's things off. She looked sharply at Ted.

"Don't take any notice of him, Sally. He's only joking. I've always heard Ted's a great one for that, particularly where girls are concerned. You ought to tell him you've got a young man in London. They'll be going fishing to-night anyway . . . Can you hand me Alice's nightgown from the line before you sit down again, Ted? Poor child. She's tired out and no mistake. It *has* been good of you, Sally, to look after them both. Did they give you a lot of trouble?"

Sally couldn't help chuckling to herself ironically, at the way Amy had so quickly diverted the conversation; at the way she was ordering Ted about. But she wasn't angry. She knew that Ted, at least, was more interested in herself than in Amy. She saw through his ragging and she knew that he wouldn't require much encouragement to have him more than interested. She answered Amy's questions easily.

"Oh, they weren't any trouble at all. They were as good as gold all the time."

"I expect there'll be a different carry on in the morning when they wake and find out where they are . . . You can take Alice up, Marney, as soon as she's ready. Give me Jeff."

Marney had sat down on the sofa with his son still asleep in his arms. Ted was on the table again, but Sally was aware that he was watching her out of the tail of his eye. She glanced round the room. It seemed half the size as when she had seen it empty. The floor canvas was laid, but as it was the one from the Bramble-wick living-room it wasn't big enough and there was a margin of bare board around the far-side wall. A large Victorian mahogany sideboard (Amy had bought it at a Bramblewick sale) took up half the space of the opposite wall. The sofa lay under the yard window, and most of the other floor space was occupied by chairs, boxes, bundles, sea-boots and fishing-gear, just as they had been brought in from the boats. An airing line, hung with napkins, reached across the whole room. The baby in its crib was under the table itself.

"Can't you find somewhere to sit down?" Amy remarked. "I hope you didn't expect to find us all straight?"

"Of course I didn't. I think you have done wonders. I only wish I had been here to help."

"It's having kids that makes flitting such a job," Marney said as he crossed over to Amy's side. "We seem to get six times as many things in the house for every kid we get. It's funny to think that when I was a sailor I could put everything I had into one bag, and fling it over my back."

"It's a pity you didn't stay a sailor then," Amy said quickly. "There wouldn't be one half the muddle if you kept your own things tidy. We're going to have a different carry-on in this house to what we had at Bramblewick, once we've got it straight. Bairns make less confusion than a man. Look at your sea-boots and all that fishing-gear. I'll say this much for Tom. He *does* seem to have got tidy habits. He's got all his things out of the way already, and I bet he's got his own room fettled."

Marney took hold of Alice with one arm, and lowered Jeff on to his wife's lap with the other. Sally, who had wondered where Tom was, heard his footsteps on the attic stairs. Marney grinned and looked at Ted.

"Listen to her. You want to look out you don't get landed with a wife and a houseful of bairns."

"You seem pleased enough with yours, anyway," Ted answered.

"I've got to pretend to be, or life wouldn't be worth living at all. The only good thing I've got to say about being married, is that you do know what's inside the trap as well as the bait. Even if you know the door's shut and you can't get out."

Sally laughed. She knew how fond Marney was of his wife and family; and if there was proof wanting it was there in the way he was holding the sleeping child, and smiling at Amy, who retorted swiftly:

"Aye, being married's a trap all right, but the door shuts harder on a woman than it does on a man, when she has bairns. All that a man has got to do with bairns is to kiss them good-night, or tell them to keep out of his way when he's busy. Still, if you hadn't got bairns, you'd only be doing your best to get them, and if you weren't married you'd be wishing you were."

Ted was laughing too, and Sally suddenly gave him a mocking glance.

"Perhaps Ted isn't one of the marrying sort anyway?"

He returned her glance boldly.

"Who says I'm not?"

"I've heard he's a great flirt," put in Amy.

"Is he? Does he ask every girl he meets to go to the pictures with him?"

"I do if they're bonny enough."

Sally could hear Tom's footsteps on the lower stairs, and she knew that he must now be within hearing. She knew that Amy was not pleased with the new turn the talk had taken, but for once she felt indifferent to her feelings and looking straight at Ted she said:

"Well, there's a late bus to-morrow. What's on at the pictures? I'd like to know what there is to see before I accept any invitations."

"It's a thing called *Destination Unknown*," Amy put in quickly. "I had a look at the photos as I went past the Regal this afternoon. It didn't look up to much. There was a champion thing on the first three days of this week though, that we missed."

"I've heard *Destination Unknown* is a good one," said Ted eagerly. "I've heard several folks praising it up."

"Who's in it," asked Sally.

"There's nobody big. But then it very often happens that a film with nobody anybody knows playing the chief parts is better than one with big names in it. There'll be a good comic anyway and a Mickey Mouse. What about it? What bus will you be catching from Bramblewick?"

Tom had opened the staircase door, but Sally gave him only a casual glance, and she answered Ted:

"I'm coming down early. I'm going to see mother

in the afternoon and take her for a little walk if it's fine."

"You'd better bring her in here for tea," said Amy. "I wonder what time she'll have to be back at the hospital. If they let her stay late she might look after the bairns, then we might all go to the pictures, to the first house, anyway."

"Don't talk so daft," said Marney. "They won't let her stay out all that time."

Amy was putting Jeff's nightgown on, and for a moment she was silent. Then suddenly she said, "I've got it. Tom could look after the bairns, couldn't you, Tom, if we all went to the pictures to-morrow night? We'd only be out a couple of hours."

Tom was standing near the staircase door. It might have been a trick of the light or the contrast between him and Marney and Ted, but he seemed taller than ever, and immensely strong. Sally watched him. He had given no sign that he was aware of her presence in the room. He was looking at Amy, but it seemed to Sally that his glance took in Ted too, and once more her belief that he was completely in love with Amy was confirmed. At the same time she had a more powerful conviction that his love was not returned, that Marney held an unmovable place in her heart. Tom (and now Ted, if she could land him) meant nothing more to her than some one on whom to exercise her feminine power. She felt a sudden pity for Tom. He had two men to be jealous of now. But it yielded quickly to anger. She felt, illogically, that he was to blame for the spoliation of her dream about this house. She felt that he had humiliated her, and was humiliating her now by his exclusive interest in Amy. She had a fierce wish to score off them both. If only Tom was in love with her and Amy with Ted, so that she could walk off with Ted and let them both feel something of what she was feeling herself. And yet still she could not say for certain she was in love with Tom, that she wanted him more than she wanted to go back to London. He was grinning now, stupidly she thought, and yet she detected an irony in his expression and in his voice, that saved his assent to Amy's proposal from meekness.

"Aye, I'll look after the bairns. I could always come for you if the house caught fire, or one of the bairns had a fit. Would you all be in the one-and-six-penny's?"

"No. We wouldn't, Tom. We'd be in the nine-pennies unless Sally objected. Seats may be hard, but you get quite a good view in the middle and not at the sides." She smiled at Ted. "Would you mind if we all went together, Ted? I reckon it's so much nicer if you've got a sort of party. Then we could all come back here for a bit of supper. We could buy some fish and chips on the way back."

Sally glanced at Ted. He was smiling, but it seemed to her that his voice lacked a complete enthusiasm when he answered.

"Why, of course. That would suit me all right."

"Well, that's settled then. It would certainly be a nice change for us, going to the pictures, and do you know, Sally, I'd sooner trust Tom to look after the

bairns than Marney. Last time I went out and left
Marney in charge of them he let Jeff and Alice have
my work-basket to play with and I found they had
unravelled a guernsey I was knitting and run the wool
half-way round the house. His lordship had gone to
sleep on the sofa . . . Come on, Marney, get them to
bed, and let me get tidied up. I'm sick of the sight
of all this muddle and mess. Will you take Jeff, Tom?
I'll come and tuck them in in a minute."

Tom reached over and took the boy in his arms.
Amy got up from her chair, and with what to Sally
seemed to be a triumphant smile watched the two men
go up the staircase. She was in her shabbiest clothes.
Her hair was tousled. There was a smudge of what
looked like blacklead on her chin. But there was
colour in her cheeks, her eyes were sparkling, her hair
had a glint and a colour as if it had just been washed
and dried in sunshine and blown by the wind; and
Sally had an almost overpowering sense of her own
inferiority until she glanced at Ted again and found
him staring at herself with the same unmistakable
interest. She smiled at him. At once Amy turned
and smiling at Ted, said sweetly:

"I *do* hope you don't mind about to-morrow night.
Say if you do. But it would be nice for us all to go
together."

Before Ted had a chance to answer the street door
opened and John put his head inside.

"Hey. Isn't Marney and Tom ready yet?" he growled.
"We're all ready for sea."

Marney and Tom were coming down the stairs

again. John stood waiting impatiently until they were in sight, then:

"Hey—come on, Marney. You know we want to get off early to-night so that we can get ashore early to-morrow, and father and me can get the twelve o'clock bus to Bramblewick. It's Saturday to-morrow, remember."

"Wouldn't you and father like a cup of tea before you go," said Amy. "I can mash a pot quick."

"Thanks," John snapped. "We've just had one. Whoever washed up last on board must have done it with paraffin. I've got the taste in my mouth yet."

"They say paraffin's damned good stuff for your health," said Marney as he sat down on a box and pulled on his sea-boots. "Better than Beecham's Pills. You ought both to have come in here for your tea when you were asked. We won't be a minute."

Ted had stood up.

"I'll have to be going too," he said, "it's early market to-morrow."

"*And* me," said Sally, glancing at the clock. "I don't think I've got two minutes left to catch the bus. I'll have to fly."

Marney and Tom had got their sea-boots on, and were collecting their gear. Ted was moving towards the door. Sally moved too, but Amy suddenly put her hands on her shoulders.

"Why, Sally, it's a daft idea your going back to Bramblewick to-night and nobody in the house. There's no sense in it. You can stay the night here."

Sally hesitated.

"Yes, but what about father and John? They'll want their dinner when they land home to-morrow. And there's mother's hens to be fed in the morning. I think I'd better not, Amy."

"But you could catch the first morning bus. There's one at nine o'clock. Come on, Sally, don't be daft. You know it will be miserable in that house all by yourself and I'll be all by myself here. I can lend you a nightgown. And you could sleep in Tom's bed. You wouldn't mind that, would you, Tom?"

Sally felt her cheeks tingling. She glanced at Tom, who showed no signs of embarrassment.

"Nay, of course not," he answered. "It wouldn't matter to me."

"It would be nice and warm for you when you turned in, if we weren't back too late," said Marney. "Where's my sou'wester got to, Amy? I saw it lying here only a few minutes ago."

"It's there on the sofa," said Amy, and to Sally. "You *will* stay, won't you? The two of us could get the whole place straight with the men out of the way. I think this room will look lovely when we get that extra bit of canvas down on the floor and all the pictures up, don't you. Do stay, Sally."

Ted with a general, "So long everybody," had gone. Sally suddenly felt intensely miserable. She felt that the moment she stepped outside the house she would start crying, and that she would never be able to face getting into the bus by herself, with the people in it staring at her, and the thought of going back to that empty house, of sitting there alone, thinking and dreaming about Tom who apparently was not even mildly interested in the fact that to-morrow he would be sleeping in a bed still warm from herself, filled her with dread. She hated him. She hated Amy for the calm way she had made such a proposal. She only wanted her to stay because she would be lonely herself with all the men at sea, when of course Tom and Ted would be safe from being attracted by any one else. Yet Sally found a curious comfort in Amy's touch on her shoulder. It was though something of Amy's real nature, something that belonged to her love for Marney and her children, was flowing into her through that touch. Her anger softened. She had a sudden desire to fling her arms round her sister's neck and cry, and be comforted. But she stiffened her lips and then smiled and said in just a vaguely trembling voice:

"All right, Amy. I'll stay."

11

FATHER and John got back to Bramblewick on the
midday bus. A stiff south-easterly breeze had sprung
up in the night, and, after hauling their lines for a
meagre catch they had been obliged to leave the
lobster pots unhauled, and make for port. As the
Saturday morning market was usually poor, this was
not exceptionally unfortunate. What lobsters were in
the pots would probably fetch twice the price on
Monday. But it had been a rough, uncomfortable
night; both men were tired. Sally could scarcely get a
word out of her father. John could do nothing but
complain about the mule and she was glad when
dinner was over and they both went to bed. She washed
up, laid the table for their tea and caught the two
o'clock bus back to Burnharbour.

She went straight to the hospital. Despite the wind,
it was a warmish day, the sun shining brightly. She
found mother sitting out in the grounds. For a
moment her fear that there was going to be trouble
was forgotten. She was so glad to see mother, still
thin and pale, but much more like herself again, and
mother seemed so genuinely pleased to see her. But
as soon as they had embraced and Sally had told her
how well she was looking, she saw a reproach growing
in her eyes, and she knew that the long-repressed storm
was not far from breaking. However, there was no

fear now that getting excited or even angry would cause a setback to her recovery. The matron had told Sally that the doctor was delighted with her progress and that provided she did not do any hard physical work, it would be all right for her to go home on Monday. A walk this afternoon would do her good, and unless it came on cold she could stay out till six o'clock.

"Do you feel strong enough to go for a little walk? I'm sure you must be sick of the sight of this place."

"Of course I'm strong enough," mother answered sharply. "If I'd had my way I'd have been back home a week ago, and I would have been too, I'd have got back by myself if the matron hadn't made me promise not to cross her . . . And I'm strong enough not to be told a lot of lies too, Sally," as waiving her daughter's helping arm, she stood up. "So you needn't think of starting. Has Marney flitted to Burnharbour?"

They moved towards the drive that led down to the town. Sally saw no reason why she should not be perfectly frank about everything.

"Yes. They flitted yesterday."

"How did they manage?"

"They put the furniture into the boats, and I looked after Jeff and Alice while Amy came down with Sam, and got things ready."

"And did they fetch the coble and the small boat too?"

"Yes."

"And so we haven't got a boat left in Bramblewick. There's no one left fishing there but the Fosdycks?"

Q

Sally was aware that she was being closely watched for any evasion, but she felt justified in answering:

"Well, there's only the Fosdyck boats left there: but our men seem to be fishing at Bramblewick more than they've ever done. Didn't father tell you about the big catch of ling they made the first time they went out in the mule. They caught them just off Bramblewick."

"Aye, he did," mother retorted drily. "It was about the only thing he *did* tell me that was true, without my having to worm it out of him. I suppose he thought I'd be so pleased about that I shouldn't mind owt else. Where are we going, Sally. Are we going to see Amy and the bairns now?"

"We will if you want to. But you mustn't walk so fast. You must remember you've been very ill, and take things easy."

Mother indeed was setting an alarming pace down the hospital drive, but she refused Sally's arm again, and it was only by deliberately lagging that Sally prevailed upon her to walk slower. She began to wish already that the walk was over, that mother was safe back in hospital again.

"Aye, I'd certainly like to see the bairns," mother went on, "but if I see Amy, I'll not trust myself not to give her a bit of my mind. I've always said she's made Marney a good wife, but it's my firm belief it's Amy who's at the bottom of all this carry-on. It's Amy who first put Marney up to leaving Bramblewick."

"Oh, I'm sure it isn't, mother," Sally protested, "I don't think that any of them would have wanted to leave if fishing hadn't been so bad, and looked like being worse this winter. And I'm sure they wouldn't have got the boat so suddenly if the coble's engine hadn't been smashed up. They've done better with the mule anyway."

Mother gave Sally a quick, reproachful look.

"So you're starting to argue for Burnharbour, are you, Sally?"

"I'm not specially, mother. It isn't my business. But I do want you all to be happy. And even *I* can see that fishing at Bramblewick's not much good now, and I don't see how any of you can be happy unless you're earning your living. And they *are* fishing at Bramblewick any way. From what I can see that was one of the main arguments for getting the mule. They'll be going ashore at Bramblewick regularly when the weather allows them to."

"Aye, and how often will that be. How often have they been ashore since they got her. I know all about Bramblewick Landing. It would be a wonder to me if they ever step ashore there once next winter. And just fancy, all of them being away from home the whole week. Eh—Sally, you needn't think I don't see what it's all leading to. If only you knew how I'm longing to be in my own home again and doing my work. What has father and John been doing for their meals. I should think they must have been half-starved living on that boat and fending for themselves. Have you been looking after the hens proper?"

"Of course I have, mother."

They reached the end of the drive and Sally again thought how lovely the old town looked with the sun shining on the harbour and the red roofs. They had passed several people going up to the hospital, for it was general visiting day, and they were in sight of one of the main roads into the town, busy with motor traffic and the carts and traps of country folk going in, or returning from their Saturday shopping.

"Don't you like Burnharbour, mother?" Sally remarked. "I do think it looks lovely from here. Do you remember how you used to bring me in when I was a little girl, particularly at Christmas time. How we liked all the shops lit up and decorated?"

"Aye, I *do* remember, Sally," mother answered, "But I can never remember ever wanting to live in Burnharbour, even when things in Bramblewick were harsh, and everybody was against us. There's too many folks about. You could live in a spot as big as this all your life, and not even know the names of half of them. Eh—I doubt Marney will rue what he has done. It was such a nice little house he had in Bramblewick. I can't bear to think of it being empty. Didn't Jeff and Alice cry when they were told they were going to flit? Eh— I reckon they will miss being able to run across to their grandma's for a jam tart or a cheese cake on a baking day. But I don't suppose Amy will mind that much. I don't know how many times she has gone for me for giving her bairns things in between meal times. That's another of her daft new-fangled ideas. As though a growing bairn oughtn't to have all the food it can stomach, provided it's good food and well-cooked. . . . Are we going straight to Marney's?"

They had crossed to the far side of the main road.

Sally had arranged with Amy that all being well she would take mother in for tea, but she didn't fancy the idea of spending the whole afternoon there, with mother in her present mood. She thought it would be a better idea to walk easily through the back part of the town to the public pleasure gardens, where they could sit down out of the wind, but in the sunshine and still have a pleasant view of the town and the harbour. After all, it wasn't doing mother any harm to talk and unburden all her pent-up feelings. Tactfully she steered along the main road.

"Amy's expecting us in for tea, but I think you ought to have a bit of a walk first, don't you, mother, and we can get to her place if we go through the town and out by the west cliff-gardens and down again. I wish you'd take my arm though. You must feel a bit shaky after being laid up for so long."

"Don't talk so daft, Sally. It isn't the first time I've been on my feet since I was taken bad. I must have walked at least a mile round my bedroom, backwards and forwards, worrying about what was going on at home. I'll let you know if I get tired. You've told me nowt yet about Marney's flitting. Was everybody out, staring?"

"It caused a bit of excitement, of course."

"What did Luke and Tindal Fodsyck do?"

"They helped our men with the boats."

"And what about Tom? Didn't they seemed vexed about him working for us?"

"I don't think they mind that much. You see they laid up their coble and started using their small boat when ours was smashed up, so that meant they could do without him and save paying him anything."

Mother was silent for a moment, then:

"Eh—Sally, fancy a Fosdyck working with a Lunn in the same boat, after all that's happened in the past. When we first came to Bramblewick I think they'd have almost murdered us if they could have done it without being found out. But it shows what time can do. If only we could have all been friends and worked together from the first. There'd have been no need then for all this carry-on and upset. I *do* want to be back home, but Bramblewick will never be the same place now that Marney's gone, and we've no boats there, and they'll only be coming ashore when the weather's fine enough. Has Tom been sleeping on board the mule?"

"Yes, until Marney flitted. But of course he's lodging with Marney now. Didn't father tell you he was going to?"

Mother looked at Sally in surprise.

"Tom lodging with Marney? No. Your father didn't tell me. It took me all my time to get what I did out of him. Next thing you'll be telling me will be that father's flitted too, and that our house is empty and that I'm not going back to Bramblewick next week. . . . Tom lodging with Marney and Amy. Well, I never did! And all this going on and me not knowing a thing about it."

Again mother was silent for a moment, then with a sharp look at her daughter:

"Sally, you don't think there's owt going on between Tom and Amy, do you? I've never said anything before but I did think once or twice it was queer Tom being so friendly and going into Marney's so regular."

Sally was blushing, but she answered steadily:

"No, I'm sure there isn't. I think Tom's fond of Amy, but he's just as fond of Marney and the bairns."

Mother looked relieved.

"Aye, that's what I really thought inside me. Amy, with all her faults isn't that sort, I'm sure. But Tom lodging with them! There'll be some talk about it. Eh—I don't know whether I'm standing on my head or my heels. I wish I was going home now. I feel I'd know better about everything if I was in my own home. I should think you'll be glad to get away out of it, Sally. Have you heard from your mistress? Have you written and told her I'm going to be home next week?"

They had reached the shops, and the beginning of one of the main streets of the town. Mother's question brought Sally sharply back to her own problems. She hadn't answered her mistress's letter yet, but she intended doing so to-night when she got home. It was true in one sense that she would be glad to be out of it all, back in London, getting on with her new job. The thought of going to the pictures to-night with Ted Stevens and Marney and Amy depressed her. She liked Ted. So far as appearances went he was more attractive than Tom. But he didn't affect her in the same way. There was a mystery about Tom. There was a mystery about her own feelings towards him. With Ted, she had felt that they had summed up and understood each other from the first. She could think clearly about him, and he was just the same in the flesh as he was in her thoughts. But the Tom she dreamt about and the Tom she saw, never seemed to fit, and she knew they never would, and she would never solve the mystery of him and of her own feelings until she got him by himself, away from the influence of Amy. Whether she had done so deliberately or not, it did seem clever the way Amy had made to-night's arrangements. Tom would be by himself all night, when the bairns were in bed, but safely so, with Sally at the pictures. It wouldn't be impossible for Sally to invent some excuse for not going, and instead for her to go to the cottage when the coast was clear. Yet however important it was that they should have that meeting, she wasn't going to lower herself either in Tom's eyes or in Amy's, that way. She would see Tom by himself, but she would do it fair and square and not resort to Amy's methods. She answered mother:

"Yes. I have had a very nice letter from London, and it's almost settled about that shop. But, of course, I'm not going back until you're quite strong again. I may go at the end of next week if you behave and do all the doctor says, but I won't if you go on like this. Can't you walk a bit slower?"

"Don't talk daft," mother retorted once more, "I'm only walking ordinary. You talk as though I ought to be in a perambulator with a dummy tit in my mouth. If we're going to Marney's place all that way round, we don't want to loiter. . . . Eh—but I'm glad you're still in favour. It's not many folks who would do for a lass what she's done for you. Isn't there a lot of traffic! You'd wonder where all the folks come from!"

They had reached the junction of the street with one that led down to the harbour. The old town hall was on their left, and on the opposite side of the adjoining street was the modest white-painted façade of the Regal Cinema, with a placard giving the name of the film DESTINATION UNKNOWN and a banner, MATINEE TO-DAY, 2.30.

It was a quarter to three by the town hall clock. They'd have shown the news, Sally thought, and perhaps started on the comic, but certainly wouldn't have started the big picture yet. She gave a quick glance at mother, but said nothing about what had come to her mind until they were across the street, and by that time she had repressed an instinctive reluctance at seeing (and paying for) something she was going to see again. She just knew that she couldn't face the whole afternoon talking to and listening to mother, and after that keeping the peace between her and Amy. She felt too miserable herself. Besides, it was clear that mother would tire herself out if she went on walking so fast and being so determined about it.

"Would you like to go to the pictures, mother?" she said.

They had halted under the canopy, and Sally was looking at the stills of to-day's and next week's pictures on each side of the vestibule and at the same time she was feeling for her purse. Mother clutched her arm.

"No, of course I wouldn't, Sally. It would be nowt but a waste of brass. Now, come on. We don't want to be standing here."

"But I've heard it's a lovely picture. I'd like to see

it. Come on, mother. I'm going to pay for our seats.
If you don't like it we can walk out."

"I don't want to go," mother said stubbornly, "I
want to go and see Marney and his bairns."

"But we can do that when we've been. It's a long
time from tea-time yet. Don't let's argue, or we may
miss the start."

Before mother had a chance for further protest,
Sally darted forward to the booking-office and bought
two one-and-sixpenny tickets. She turned, and this
time it was she who gripped mother's arm.

"Come on. It's settled now. We're going, and if you
don't like it, all you've got to do is say so, and we'll
come out again."

The seats were in the front row of the circle; and
Sally firmly held mother's arm up the stairs. As an
attendant opened the double doors for them, there
came from the well of the theatre a tumult of high-
pitched shouts and laughter, which continued as,
following the attendant's torch, they moved down again
to their seats. It was a children's matinee, Sally
realised, and on the screen was being shown one of the
adventures of Mickey Mouse.

Sally liked cartoons. It was her experience as a
regular picture-goer that the cartoon was the one thing
that never let you down. If the big film was good, then
the cartoon was a fillip to it; if it was bad, then after-
wards you could remember Mickey, or any of the other
cartoon stars and your sense of disappointment would
not be half so keen. Her first glance showed her that
she had seen this one before. It was Mickey's adventure

in search of sunken treasure. It had just reached its
climax when they sat down. Mickey, in a diving suit,
was trying in vain to hack an entrance into the hull of
the treasure ship with an axe. A giant swordfish
suddenly appeared behind him, charged. Mickey
turned in time, sidestepped. The monster charged on
into the galleons hull and (in the best tradition of the
cartoon film) crashed clean through, leaving a hole
the exact shape of itself. And from the hole gushed a
torrent of doubloons. The cheers, the shouts, the
screams from the tightly packed 'twopennies' was
ear-splitting, and did not die until the lights went up,
then quickly down again, and an announcement of
forthcoming attractions was shown on the screen. It
was not until then that Sally dared to look at mother.
It wouldn't have surprised her to have seen an expression of extreme anger on her face; if she had insisted
straight away upon walking out, and Sally felt that
she would not have the courage to protest. But she
did not look angry. She was sitting bolt upright in
her seat, staring steadfastly at the screen. The lights
went up again. Then she moved, and catching Sally's
eye leaned towards her and said in a chapel whisper:
"I wish we hadn't come in late, Sally. We missed
that one. Will they show it again? What's the next
thing do you think. . . . Eh—aren't these seats comfortable. But what a row those bairns make. There
ought to be some one to keep them quiet. I think——"
She stopped abruptly as the lights began to dim
again and the title of the big film was shown on the
screen to the accompaniment of orchestral music.

Sally breathed a sigh of relief, but as she read the names of the characters and the players (all quite unfamiliar to her) she had a sneaking fear that it was going to be just one of the many bad films that you are obliged to put up with as a penance for the occasional good ones. It was American, and there were gangsters in it. Gangster films usually were exciting, but it wasn't likely they'd appeal to mother. What would she make of it if all the characters spoke slang? It wasn't likely that she would know even what gangsters were. But the film had the merit of speed and intelligibility. In a very few minutes it was established that the villain was the chief of a San Francisco gang engaged principally in smuggling drugs. That the hero, an out-of-work ship's officer (victim of the slump), was the gang's innocent tool. Apparently down and out, he was shown wandering hopelessly along the waterfront, then being accosted by the villain, and offered the command of a luxury motor yacht just fitting out for a pleasure cruise. A quick scene on board the yacht established that its purpose was not mere pleasure cruising, and served to introduce various members of the gang, including a sinister Chinese steward, and a very beautiful lady, too dark and flashily-dressed to be the heroine. The heroine, indeed, was a reporter on one of the city's news-papers, worried by a threat of dismissal unless she can bring in a ' scoop.' A scene in her home, with an out-of-work father, a sick mother, and a baby sister showed how important it was that she should keep her job. Her assignment to expose the activities of the dope gang suggested that she was going to be involved in a perilous adventure.

The dialogue, as Sally feared, was rich in the slang of the American underworld and at first she whispered explanations; 'dope' meant opium, 'rod' meant a pistol, 'G-men' were police, 'bump off' meant murder; but suddenly mother gave her a nudge and whispered back.

"Ssh, Sally. Don't talk so much. I understand what it's about. It's a smuggling do. I know that without being told. Police are out to put a stop to it, and so is that young lass. Isn't she bonny? But I don't like that other one. I hope that young sailor isn't going to get mixed up in it and get blamed. He ought to have known better than have owt to do with that lot. . . ."

Sally did not attempt any more explanations. After all, the children downstairs were following the story, judging by the tense silence that had fallen on them, interrupted by an occasional united gasp as some dramatic point in the development went home. And the story was exciting. It moved so quickly there was no time to ponder on its possibilities. Besides, from what Sally had heard, things like this did happen in America. You read about them in the papers. She forgot her anxiety as to whether mother was enjoying it or not. She forgot all her own troubles in a complete sympathy with the heroine who, she felt, actually was a newspaper reporter and not some well-known actress playing the part. She liked the hero, too. In a vague way he reminded her of Tom, for he was very tall, and there was a reserve about him, a mystery.

She knew that he was the hero, and it was a pretty safe
guess that he was going to marry the newspaper girl
in the end and that therefore he must not be shown
as a willing participant in the smuggling business.

But as the story developed it began to look almost as
if he *was* willing, particularly when the dark woman
on the yacht showed that she was interested in him,
and he did not completely rebut her advances. This
clearly mystified the downstairs audience too, so that
when the heroine (who had adopted the bold expedient
of hiring a sailing dinghy and deliberately capsizing
it near the anchored yacht) was rescued by the hero,
the cheers seemed a little doubtful and were cut short
immediately when she was taken on board the yacht
and presented by the ' hero ' to his suave, villainous
employer. She was searched by the dark lady. She had
been foolish enough to keep on her person the identity
ticket of her newspaper; and it seemed that the hero
was almost as displeased with the discovery as the gang
chief, who promptly handed her over to the custody of
the Chinese steward. Was the hero so innocent? Why
did he glare in such an unfriendly way at the heroine?
Was it possible that the real hero was to be the officer
in charge of the G-boat which stopped the yacht for
examination soon after she got under way? He was
very handsome. He was coldly polite to the owner,
the captain and to the dark lady. The yacht's papers
were in perfect order however. A search yielded
nothing suspicious. The heroine had been locked up
by the steward in a closet hidden by a secret panel,
and it seemed that the supposed hero gave a smile of

relief when the officer returned to his own boat, and the yacht got under way again. But later, when the fate of the heroine was discussed and the suggestion made that she should be dropped overboard when darkness fell, sympathy towards the hero was restored when he advised against such action. This was a tense scene and Sally felt mother's hand gripping hers tightly.

"Eh—they're not going to murder that poor lass are they?" she whispered.

"No, of course not," Sally comforted her. "She's got to get married to some one in the end. Look, the captain's saved her for the time being anyway. . . . Don't talk mother," she added, "or neither of us will be able to follow the story."

There were loud cheers when the captain (a possible hero again) won his point, but again sympathy wavered when at nightfall he was shown on the bridge with the dark lady (dressed for dinner), apparently yielding to her fascination. But the scene at once shifted to a passenger liner, nearing the end of her voyage from Hong Kong to San Francisco, but still out of sight of land. Mysterious things were happening in one of her cabins. Two Chinamen, one a passenger, one a steward, were securing a number of packages at regular intervals to a long rope. Suddenly the passenger opened the port-hole, looked out, and saw a light shining across the sea. At once he heaved the first of the packages out of the port-hole and the steward helped him to pay out the rope until all the packages were gone. At the end of the rope was a mechanical buoy and, so that the audience would have no doubt as to what this was, the passenger explained to the steward how, an hour after it had been dropped overboard, the clockwork device would transform it into a flare.

"Why—it's like a fishing buoy really," mother could not resist whispering, "same as your father uses for night lining, only of course his has got just an ordinary lantern. That will be the opium they've put overboard. The chaps on the yacht——"

"Ssh, mother," whispered Sally. "Don't talk."

The yacht picked up the buoy, hauled the packages on board, but if there were still many doubts about the hero's innocence, there was none about the heroine. The Chinese steward had tried to make love to her. Momentarily, she had seemed to yield to his embrace, but what she had really done was to whip a knife from his belt, and breaking free she suddenly held it at his throat. To the shrieking delight of the audience, she had forced him into the closet, and while the opium was being hauled she had watched the operation from a hiding-place behind one of the yacht's dinghys. A minute later she was discovered, and it looked as if her fate was really sealed as two of the gangsters, pistol in hand, approached. She struggled, but she was overpowered. They heaved her towards the yacht's rails, and would surely have thrown her overboard had not the hero suddenly seen them.

But again the cheers that greeted his dramatic intervention were cut short as he explained to the chief that his reason for interfering was that the men were acting without either his or the chief's orders.

Did the chief really want to have her 'bumped off' like that? She was reprieved and locked up again, this time with an armed guard at the closet door. The yacht continued her cruise, but Sally had a growing conviction that in spite of everything, the 'hero' was the *hero*. There had been a swift interchange of glances between the chief and one of his lieutenants; a suggestion that the new captain might soon have outlived his usefulness and be a danger to the gang. . . .

And so it proved. The yacht's destination was a cove on a remote part of the coast, and above the cove was a palatial mansion with grounds fenced with unscalable walls. It was the gang's headquarters. The heroine was taken on shore and imprisoned. There was a council meeting of the gang attended by the dark lady, whose relationship towards the villain had been left rather obscure, but who evidently had fallen genuinely in love with the hero. It was decided that the 'bumping off' of the heroine should not be delayed and that it would be safer if the yacht's new captain was also silenced in the same practical way. The hero, all misgivings on the part of the audience allayed when he was discovered eavesdropping at the council door, was overpowered and locked up in a room close to the heroine. Both of them would be taken out in the yacht the next day and dropped overboard. But while the gang made 'whoopee' in celebration of its successful 'run' the dark lady slipped away to the hero's room. She would save him from death if he would promise to marry her. He agreed (but with a noticeable lack of enthusiasm) and when (to the delight of the

R

audience) he insisted that the condemned girl should
be saved too, and the dark lady pointed out that this
would imperil all three, and that anyway she deserved
what was coming to her, he did not hesitate to show
what he really thought about the proposal. He was not
rough, but he was firm. The dark lady was locked up
in his own room. It was a work of seconds for him to
overpower the heroine's guards. An unbarred window
in another room, overlooking the seaward side of the
estate, three sheets knotted together, gave them an
escape to the rocks below; and from there they quickly
made their way to the boat-landing place, where the
yacht's motor-launch was moored.

The children had become hysterical. Sally felt
mother's hand gripping her own tightly, and she was
just as excited herself. They reached the yacht. To the
gangster's sailors the hero was still their captain. They
went straight to the wireless-room. The scene shifted
to the wireless-rooms of G-boats, then to the mansion
with the orgy still in progress, back to the G-boats
travelling at terrific speed. The G-men, armed with
rifles and machine-guns, landed—the hero and heroine
with them. The mansion was surrounded on all sides.
The order for the advance was given by the hero himself, although his real identity was not yet known.
Inside the mansion the alarm had been given. There
was fighting, pistol, rifle and machine-gun fire, but
the sound of it was almost drowned by the shrieks of
the children. The chief made a deserate effort to escape
but was captured in a hand-to-hand struggle with the
hero. The triumph of the G-men was complete, and

Sally knew there was nothing left but the inevitable love scene. Who *was* the hero? She had half-guessed from the deferential way the other G-men had treated him. He was a special G-man sent from headquarters to break the opium gang. That was why he had resented the presence of the newspaper heroine on the yacht. But it did not matter now. The gang was broken. The heroine had got her 'scoop'; and although there was no kissing, the look the two of them gave each other in the final fade-out left no doubt as to what their future would be. The lights went up slowly. A notice had been thrown on the screen, NEXT PERFORMANCE AT 6.30.

Sally took hold of her mother's arm.

"Come on. It's all over. Did you like it?"

Mother did not answer. Her face was very white, and there were tears in her eyes. Sally, a little frightened, held her arm tightly all the way downstairs, and, as they reached the street, she wondered if she hadn't better take her straight back to the hospital. But, at the suggestion, mother woke up as though from a trance.

"Go back to the hospital, Sally? Don't talk so daft. We haven't been to Marney's yet. Come on, we don't want to be late. Which is the quickest way? I've got to buy some sweets for the bairns, too . . . I'm all right. I'm only a bit bewildered. Eh—I was glad those two escaped, and that all those bad people were caught and taken to prison. You know I thought all the time that that young man couldn't be a bad 'un. Now that other one, I just knew from the first what *he* was. Same with that flashy woman, although she did try to do the young man a good turn in the end by letting him out. But he was wise not to agree to marry her. She'd have only have led him into wrong-doing. Wasn't it all real! It was just as though you were there the whole time. If that's what you call the talkies, I'll say this, they're a great improvement on the old sort. That time I went before with your father, you couldn't make head or tail of what was going on. But what a pity we went in late. We must have missed such a lot. Why didn't you tell me we were going to the pictures. I could have been ready an hour sooner . . ."

Sally let her babble on without interruption. It was clear that the afternoon had been a success, that mother had thoroughly enjoyed herslf, and that for the time being at least her mind was free from thoughts of Bramblewick. Sally, too, had enjoyed the film. It had taken her completely out of herself. But now she was feeling a reaction. It might have been the shops and the traffic, the feeling that it was Saturday, but she had an intense nostalgia for London. She had a longing to have some new and very smart clothes on, to be going out to tea somewhere with a smartly-dressed young man, to have other people noticing them, to have the feeling that after tea they were going to walk through Piccadilly and Leicester Square and then spend the rest of the evening in one of the new super-picture palaces, finishing up with supper at the Corner House. And what she had to look forward to was going to the Regal again, to see a film she'd just seen, in company with Amy and Marney and a young fisherman she really didn't care twopence about, and who probably didn't care twopence about her; and for a finish up there would be a fish and chip supper, and then a lonely bus ride back to Bramblewick.

She felt miserable, and her state of mind was intensified when they got to the cottage. In spite of the fact that there were too many things in the room (and most of them the wrong things to Sally's idea) the place looked very bright and cosy. Everything was tidy. The bare patch of floor canvas had been covered with a new piece (evidently by Tom who had a hammer and a box of tin-tacks in his hands). The mantel-shelf had an array of vases and photographs on it—nothing else. All the pictures had been hung and there was no sign of sea-boots or fishing-gear. The table was laid for tea. The children were very neat and clean; and Amy herself had smartened up. She was wearing a clean blouse and had done her hair. She embraced mother with a genuine affection, and led her into a chair by the fire. At once Jeff and Alice were fighting as to who should sit on her lap and mother was evidently so overcome with the pleasure of seeing her grandchildren again she could not speak. But she had undone the packet of sweets she had brought and was handing them out and Sally knew by the quick disapproving glance Amy gave her that it wouldn't be long before she and mother were at cross purposes.

"Eh—you shouldn't have brought them sweets," she said, and to her children. "Now, don't you dare to eat more than one before your tea. You know you won't have any appetite. Besides, they're bad for your teeth

. . . Now, don't plague granny. Granny's been poorly, and you're to let her alone . . . Eh—I'm glad to see you looking so well, mother, but I should think you could do with a cup of tea. We'll not wait for Marney. He and Ted Stevens have gone to a football match. It's a Cup Final or summat. Lord knows when he'll be back. It's a good job I've had Tom to give me a hand. The place isn't ready yet."

Mother glanced at Tom and smiled.

"Hallo, Tom. So your one of us now I hear. I hope it hasn't made any ill-feeling between you and your uncle Luke and Tindal and your aunt Rachel, your fishing with us."

"Nay. That's all right, Mrs. Lunn," Tom answered a little nervously. "I'm very glad to see you getting about again."

Sally too had glanced at Tom. He had given her a vague sign of recognition, but he had said nothing, not even a ' now then,' and she suddenly felt relieved that she could look at him quite calmly, and really not care whether he spoke or not. Yet she was afraid that mother might soon get back to her Bramblewick state of mind if she pursued the topic of Tom's new partner-ship, and she put in quickly:

"You wouldn't have thought mother had been ill, the way she behaved all afternoon. She nearly walked me off my feet."

Amy had stepped over to the fireside and was making the tea.

"Did she? Where did you go, along the West Cliff?"

"No, we didn't go along the West Cliff," mother

said with an unusual sprightliness. "We *were* going, but we found ourselves in the market place, and suddenly Sally says, 'Let's go to the pictures,' and before I had time to say anything against it, she had bought two tickets. I don't know what she paid for them, but the next minute we were there inside, right in the front row."

Amy turned with the kettle in her hand.

"The pictures! Do you mean to say you've been to the pictures, mother?"

"Aye, of course I have. And why shouldn't I, there's no law against folks like me going is there? . . . Bye— you ought to have seen that thing we saw, Amy. We got in late and we missed a lot but we were in time for the main picture. Do you know it began by showing a young sailor walking about the docks looking for a berth, and it might have been any of our lads, except that none of our lads have been out of work very long. He did look fed up: but along comes a flashy looking chap and offers him the captain's job on a big motor yacht—such a fine vessel. Well, it looked as though all his troubles were over, but you soon saw that the yacht wasn't what she'd seemed to be. She was being used for smuggling opium and her owner and all her sailors were nowt but a lot of scoundrels. They had all got knives and pistols, and one of them was a Chinaman— such an evil-looking man. But the young sailor didn't seem to mind being mixed up with what they were doing. He seemed as willing as any of them when it came to getting the opium on board the yacht, but later on you found out that the reason was, he really wasn't a sailor but a police-detective in disguise, and he was sent out to find out all he could about the yacht and what her owners were, and get 'em landed in prison. . . . But I haven't told you about the girl that got all mixed up in it. It seems——"

Amy, still with the kettle in her hand, was listening with growing impatience, and suddenly she interrupted;

"—Oh, mother, don't tell us any more. We're all going to the pictures to-night, and you're telling us the whole story. You'll spoil everything!"

Mother looked abashed.

"Eh—I don't want to do that," she said apologetically. "I don't want to spoil things for anybody. I didn't know you were all going. Anyway, I haven't told you half of what really happened. I never said owt about the big house ashore, where they take the opium, and what that girl had to do with it. I hadn't come to the exciting part where—but I'd best hold my mouth if your going to see it for yourselves. Who's going. Are you going, Tom?"

Amy went on making the tea.

"No," she said, "Tom was going to stay and look after the house. It was to be me and Marney and Sally, and young Ted Stevens. We were going to have a sort of party and come back here for supper. But now Sally's seen it . . . Was it really a good picture?" she added, turning with a meaningful glance at Sally.

"It was very exciting," Sally answered smoothly.

"Well, I'm a bit surprised at your going when you knew we were all going to-night . . . But of course,"

Amy added, "it was nice of you to take mother. Will you mind seeing it again, now that you know what it's about?"

Instantly, Sally saw what was in Amy's mind. She glanced at Tom. If she didn't go, if Amy went with Marney and Ted, then she'd have the chance she'd waited for, she'd find out once and for all whether she was in love with Tom, whether Tom was unshakably in love with Amy. Her heart started to beat furiously. She knew what Amy was going to suggest. She knew that Tom wasn't so stupid he couldn't see that if he wanted to spend the evening with Sally, instead of with Amy and her husband (and Amy's latest fancy), here was a chance. Would he take it? She watched him when she answered.

"Oh, I don't mind one way or another, Amy. I'd rather see a good thing twice, than a bad thing once. Why?"

Amy moved to the table with the teapot.

"Oh, I was only thinking about Tom," she said quietly. "It does seem a pity, him missing it, if it's such a good film. Mother will have to go back to the hospital soon after tea, I suppose?"

"I don't want to, but I'll have to," mother put in with a grim smile. "I don't want to cross them, or they won't let me out next week. . . . Why, if Tom wants to go, Sally could look after the bairns for you, couldn't she? It would be a pity for Tom to miss it. I didn't tell you it's all about San Francisco. That's one of the places you and Marney went to on your first voyage, wasn't it, Tom? I remember Marney

sending a picture postcard of it, and I forgot to tell
you——"

"—of course, I'll stay if Tom wants to go," Sally
interrupted, and looking directly at Tom she said:

"Do you want to go, Tom, instead of me?"

This time she caught his direct glance, and suddenly
she felt an almost uncontrollable desire to rush at him,
to smack his face, to tell him that she hated him more
than she had ever hated any one in her life before. For
he grinned and said:

"Aye, I'll go if you don't want to, Sally."

"Well, that's settled then," said Amy. "So long as
you don't mind, Sally. Marney can take mother back
and meet us all at the Regal . . . I think I can hear him
coming now. Come on, let's have our tea. Are you
sure you don't mind, Sally?"

Sally had swallowed her rage. What did it matter
after all? She didn't love Tom. She felt suddenly she
didn't even hate him. She just didn't care. If he
wanted to go on being in love with a married woman,
and being her pet dog, well, let him. All she wanted to
do was to get back to London, to forget everything,
and she answered Amy in a cool voice:

"I don't mind a bit."

12

Sally's fears that things were not going to be too pleasant when mother got home were soon realised. Although she had cleaned the house from top to bottom and made everything look as cheerful as it possibly could be, mother hadn't been back an hour before she was finding fault, complaining that nothing was in it's proper place. Why had Sally put the tea-caddy in the pantry? She ought to know the pantry was damp, and that the tea-caddy always stood on the mantel-shelf. Why had father's chair been put on that side of the fireplace. He'd be sitting in his own light if he wanted to read the newspaper. Had Sally been using the best saucepan for making the mash for the hens? Whatever had she done with the baking powder? What had happened to all of father's and John's things? The airing line looked queer without a single pair of sea-boot stockings on it. Everything looked so different from what it had been when she had been taken away.

Sally knew that what her mother really found so different was not having father and John at home; that the only way for her to escape from her thoughts was to work hard, and that was the very thing she mustn't do. There had to be no washing, no standing on her feet for long, particularly no lifting. They had their first fight over making the beds, which Sally of course had made, but not exactly to mother's liking. She had wanted to turn and shake all the mattresses. Sally had won, but she hadn't been able to stop mother going out and fetching a pail of water as soon as her back was turned; and nothing short of physical force would have stopped her climbing the steep cliff path to look at her precious hens. She had come back with the complaint that they looked as though they hadn't been getting half-enough to eat, and Sally was very hurt, for she had punctiliously carried out her duties towards them the whole time she had been in charge.

Yet she was patient and tactful. Even in ordinary circumstances you could expect a woman of mother's age to be cantankerous after what she'd been through. She was really very miserable. Apart from going to the hens, Sally could not persuade her to go out. She knew what folks were saying! She didn't want to have any one asking her how Marney and his family liked living at Burnharbour, and if she wasn't going to find it lonely at Bramblewick with her men away all week. She didn't want to meet the Fosdycks, and see their grin now that they had the Bay to themselves, for let Sally say what she liked they *had* got it to themselves. It was rubbish to say that *Lucky Boy* was fishing at Bramblewick, when all they were doing was hauling their pots off Low Batts point and then steaming straight back to Burnharbour. It would be a surprise for her if ever they steamed into the Landing, and the men came ashore for a meal.

Yet, physically mother was almost well, and Sally saw no reason why she should delay her return to

London beyond the end of the week. She had written and posted her letter. She had finally made up her mind about Tom. Now, whenever she found herself thinking of him, falling into that waking-dream, she deliberately pictured him in Amy's room (which apparently he found as congenial as the old room at Bramblewick) calmly agreeing to take Sally's place in Amy's ' party ' and let Sally herself look after the house. And then she'd think about London, and the ' shop,' and having some new clothes, and going out with one of her young men; and she'd let her fancy wander further ahead, and see the shop a very great success, and herself coming back to Bramblewick and Burnharbour one day, quite a rich woman and perhaps with a husband too, and it would be such a joke to introduce him to Amy and see if Amy would try to fascinate him too. Only when she looked at the guernsey, did Sally find it hard to keep her thoughts of Tom at bay.

It was finished all but half of one sleeve. It did not make her think directly of Tom, but it made her think of the hours she had spent dreaming of him. She was tempted to destroy it. The housewife in her rebelled at the idea of wasting nearly ten shillings' worth of wool, and she thought of unravelling it and making something else. But it was wool that was made specially for fisherman's guernseys, and she decided at last that she would finish it, and perhaps after all give it or send it to Tom. She'd certainly have to make one more trip to Burnharbour to say good-bye to everybody. If she left for London on Saturday she might go down on Friday afternoon ; and it gave her a peculiar ironic pleasure that she could think of that farewell visit, even of seeing Tom, without getting worked up about it one way or the other.

The week passed slowly. On Thursday night John arrived home unexpectedly. He had cycled over and he was going to a band practice, and then cycling back to Burnharbour to sleep on board the mule. They were going to sea about four o'clock in the morning, so it wouldn't be worth while him going to bed at home. Mother was pathetically glad to see him. She fussed over him, insisting that he should change his socks and leave those he had got on to be washed. She got him a meal and indignantly refused to let Sally help her. Yet John was gloomy. So far it had been the worst week they'd had since they'd got the mule. Although the weather had calmed, and they had got to their pots on Monday they hadn't caught more than a score of lobsters and they'd only fetched sixpence apiece. They'd done no better with their lines. The keelers were now working about twenty miles out, and even they weren't doing so very well, seeing what it cost them in extra fuel steaming so far from port.

And John was even gloomier when he returned from the practice. It had been the worst attended ' do ' he'd been at since the band started. Only six out of the twelve members had turned up, and they'd spent most of the time arguing whether they'd learn a new march or just go on playing what they already knew; and one of them, Ted Sayers, who'd been so sniffy about the trawler ' do,' had told them all to go to hell and had walked out. It looked very much as though the

band was on its last legs and what could he do about
it now that he had to spend even his spare time at
Burnharbour? For two pins he'd chuck it himself.

"It's the biggest mistake we ever made, letting the
lifeboat go and setting every one against us," he
growled. "We're no better off fishing at Burnharbour.
In fact we're a damn sight worse. If we'd stayed
on at Bramblewick we'd have started salmon fishing
anyway. I heard to-night that Luke and Tindal had
got a start yesterday and got thirty their first shot.
That would be anything in the neighbourhood of five
quid and no petrol and bait to pay for. I'm going to
try and pursuade father to lay *Lucky Boy* up if we go
on doing so bad and bring the small boat back to
Bramblewick and fish for salmon all summer, but I
know I'll have them all against me."

"Aye, you will, John, you *will*," said mother, "and
it's Amy you'll have to reckon with more than father.
It's Amy who's been at the bottom of it from the start,
if you ask me. Bramblewick's too slow a spot for her.
She likes going to the pictures too much."

It was on the tip of Sally's tongue to point out that
mother hadn't been so averse to the pictures after her
Saturday afternoon's experience, but she had been
careful all week to avoid showing how she felt about
the Bramblewick versus Burnharbour controversy.
She would leave that until the time came for saying
good-bye, when there would be no chance for getting
embroiled in a heated argument; and she was glad
when mother switched off.

"Eh—I wish you hadn't to go back and sleep on that

old boat, John. It doesn't seem natural with your bed aired and waiting for you in your own home. Why can't you stay? You can as easy wake up here as there. I can wake you and give you a bit of breakfast. You'd get six hours' good sleep if you turned in early, and six hours in a real bed would be more good to you than a whole night in that boat. I can guess what it's like."

"I've no need to guess," John answered grimly. "But I'm not going to have the others laughing at me. Besides, we may be off before four. Marney's dead set on giving that trawl a trial to-morrow, if the sea's still calm . . . No, I'll be off."

"Then you'd best take some food with you. Wait. I'll see what there is in the pantry. I'll soon make you up a parcel. And you can take father a pair of clean stockings and tell him be sure and bring his soiled ones with him on Saturday. . . . Sally's going back to London on Saturday. Did she tell you, John?"

Mother had started getting her parcel ready.

"I should think you're glad you're going, aren't you, Sally?" John said. "I should think you'll have had about enough of this."

"It'll be a change," Sally answered. And later, as mother fussed with him to the door she said, very calmly:

"Oh, if you're seeing Amy, you might tell her I'll be down to-morrow afternoon to say good-bye. It'll be the last chance I'll get, of course."

13

THE mule did not put to sea early next morning. That day, which was to prove such a significant one in the fortunes of her crew, started badly. Henry, despite Marney's persuasions, had refused to alter his original plan of leaving harbour at four o'clock. They had shifted their lobster pots nearer to Burnharbour. Abandoning the idea of getting a marketable catch from the long lines, they had shot a couple of these with hard bait close in and left them overnight. There was the likelihood that some of the fish would be damaged by crabs, but that, so long as they weren't left too long, would not spoil them for pot bait; and as the hauling of both lines and pots could be carried out better by daylight, there was no point in a very early start. They would take the trawl, of course, and have a go with it if they got nothing to hurry back to market with. But that was no reason why they should start earlier than four; in fact, Henry would have said five but for the fact that the tide would be ebbing and there'd be a chance then of their not being able to get away from their berth.

Actually Henry was not to blame for what happened. At ten minutes to four, when Marney and Tom came aboard, he was on deck. John had got the engine running and the mule was clearly afloat, for although the sea was dead calm the river current, helped by the ebb tide, was sufficient to give her a gentle roll. She was berthed alongside the quay, seawards of the fish-market. Berthed close ahead of her were two cobles. Henry gave the order to cast off and because of the cobles told John to go astern, putting the helm hard over as he did so in order to swing her stern over towards the fairway. But the mule hadn't travelled her own length before she stopped. There was no unusual sound, no shock, but there was a significant cessation of her rolling.

"We've touched bottom," Henry growled. "Open her out, John. I reckon it's nowt but mud."

John opened the throttle, but apart from the increased noise from the exhaust and the churning of the propeller, nothing happened. It was still dark. The street lamps were out, and there was only a single light (kept burning for the use of the fishermen) on the quay. Henry seized a boathook and jabbed it overboard.

"There ought to be plenty of water here," he muttered. "But it seems we're on a bank of sand or summat."

"I know what it is," said Marney. "There was a keeler berthed here yesterday—*Guiding Star*, don't you remember? They had engine trouble and they let her ground. She must have scoured a hole in the mud with her keel and ridged it up each side. We've struck one of the ridges."

"Then why the hell didn't you say so when we cast off?" Henry snapped.

"I didn't think about it, of course," Marney retorted.

"And there'd be no need to think about it if we'd done as I wanted and got away at three o'clock. I reckon the crabs will have stripped our lines as it is. Can you touch the bottom?"

Henry ignored the question and shouted at John.

"Try her full speed ahead and see if she'll come off the way she went on."

John reversed the engine, but the mule did not move. The keelers had left port before midnight. There were no power craft in the harbour capable of giving her a tow. The tide was ebbing fast, and in less than five minutes it was manifest that the mule would not move until the tide flowed again; and, as it was now only half-ebb that would not be for six hours.

Marney rarely lost an opportunity for ragging his father, and usually Henry would take the ragging in good part and frequently would give as much as he took. But Marney also had a shrewd idea of how far it was safe to go, and there was something in Henry's manner on this occasion that warned him to keep a close guard on his tongue. It was ten o'clock when *Lucky Boy* cleared the pier ends, and it was eleven o'clock before they reached the lines and started hauling. The first fish they hauled was a conger that had been stripped almost bare of flesh by crabs ; and with the exception of a few small cod that had evidently taken the bait later, and were still alive, the remainder of what at best would have been a very meagre catch were in the same condition. But Marney, who as usual did the hauling (with Tom standing by with the unnecessary gaff) made no audible comment on this disastrous sequel to the morning's mishap, and it was John who, as the mule got under way again for the pots, voiced the repressed disgust that was evidently shared by them all.

"By God—this looks like a good finish up to a good week, doesn't it! I haven't kept count, but I reckon that when we put what it's cost us for line bait and oil against what we've sold our lobsters for, we'll be about two quid on the wrong side. Do you remember this time last year, father? We had just started salmoning in the little boat with you and Steve working the pots from the coble. I can't remember the exact figures, but I know we touched summat like twelve quid clear, either the first week or the second, salmon and lobsters combined."

"It was the second week," Henry answered dryly. "And the third week you chaps lost five nets, and that was a good seven quid out of our pockets."

"What you loose on the swings you make on the roundabouts," Marney put in. He and Tom were engaged in cutting up the few good fish for bait. "If I had my way we wouldn't bother to haul our pots at all. With a sea smooth as this we ought to be giving that trawl a try. We might easily make up for everything in one shot."

"Aye, we might," John answered sarcastically, and addressing Tom, but making his remark general, "Hey, did you know your Uncle Luke and Tindal had started salmoning?"

"No, but I guessed they would make a start first

fine spell," Tom answered, without looking up from his job.

"I heard they got thirty their first night," John went on. "They'll likely do even better to-night. I noticed salmon were fetching four-and-six a pound this morning. If we'd only got the coble engine fettled or a new one in, I reckon it would pay us to lay *Lucky Boy* up and get back to Bramblewick, for the time being anyway."

"We haven't got the coble engine fettled," Henry snapped. "And we're not likely to either, so don't talk such bloody daftness. If you and Marney want to, you can take the small boat and go back to Bramblewick and make your fortunes salmoning. But I don't want to."

"Nor me," said Marney loyally.

"Have you got that trawl warp fettled?" Henry suddenly asked.

"Aye. Everything's ready to put over."

"How much oil have we got, John?"

"Tanks are all full. The oil chap had his lorry down the quay filling up the keeler's tanks yesterday afternoon, so I thought I'd better take the chance. You get it cheaper buying it in bulk like that. There's forty gallons of paraffin and ten of petrol and five of oil."

"We could cross the bloody Atlantic with that," said Marney, and with something like his old enthusiasm. "What about it, father? Shall we start trawling and stay out till we do get enough to make up for this week's run of bad luck? There's plenty of food on board. We could fish all night if we liked. I bet we'll never get a more likely day for it."

It was a perfect day. There was no wind but for an occasional light puff of air from the land, and the sea was so smooth that the mule's roll was scarcely noticeable. They were still close in to the coast, about half-way between Burnharbour and Bramblewick. The sun shone brilliantly. The fields that came down to the cliff edge were flushed with new grass, and here and there patches of whins were showing their first blossom. It was so warm that Marney had discarded his guernsey for the hauling of the lines, and he was still working in his shirt sleeves.

"We may have a go," said Henry, after a long silence. "But I doubt we'll not do much good till the sun's gone down, and we're not going to leave our pots all that time without hauling. There's good trawling grounds straight off from where they're shot."

"Aye, but not so good as what there is off Bramble-wick," said Marney. "And *inside* Bramblewick Bay. I bet there's some soles and plaice on Church Steeples, seeing no one's fished that ground for donkey's years."

"And what would Luke and Tindal say if we start trawling there?" put in John. "I thought we'd argued all that out before. I reckon we ought to leave Bramble-wick Bay alone."

"Damn it," cried Marney, "it's only a minute since you were arguing for us to go back to Bramblewick."

"Aye, for salmoning, not trawling. It's all right salmoning and lining and potting there, because we always have done; but going there with a trawl, right in front of their noses—why—it would be asking for trouble. It's all right for you. You don't live there any more and have to see folks looking at you. You don't have to face the music. . . . What do you say about it, Tom? What would your Uncle Luke think if we trawled Church Steeples?"

Tom grinned.

"Why, it's not my affair. I don't suppose my Uncle Luke would be pleased, but then what would please him? I don't suppose he'll ever fish that ground again anyway."

"And if he did, what matter," Marney pursued. "It's not private. I say, let's go where the fish are and be damned to what any one thinks. They've got no cause to complain if they're doing so well out of salmoning. Shall we make for Church Steeples as soon as we've hauled and shot our pots again, father?"

Henry's jaws had set tight during this argument, a clear sign that it was not to his liking. He ignored Marney's question, but suddenly he said:

"Look out now, there's our first pot buoy close ahead. Slow down your engine, John."

The pots were hauled, and from three fleets, each consisting of forty pots, the haul was a box of crabs and five lobsters. They were re-baited and re-shot and then, without giving a word as to his intentions, Henry swung the mule round out to sea. They had steamed for about half an hour when he quietly told Marney to get the trawl ready. In a few minutes it was shot, and Henry still kept on a seaward course, the mule moving slower now that it had the weight of the trawl.

Although they were well inside the international three-mile limit there was nothing illegal in what they were doing. The right to use a trawl of limited size inside the three-mile limit was a privilege granted of late years to the inshore fishermen as a sop to their justified complaints about the general spoliation of their grounds by steam trawling. It was not a very valuable privilege. A small trawl could be used only on very smooth ground, and most of these close-in grounds had already been fouled by wartime wrecks, and among the majority of inshore fishermen trawling was regarded merely as a makeshift when there was a slump in long lining or potting. Even then it was looked upon with disfavour by the few coble men who were left. To them the very word trawl had an evil significance. It stood not only for spoilt fishing grounds, but for losses of fleets of pots, and lines, for the steam trawler, even when operating in legal waters, had little respect for anchored gear, no matter how clearly it was buoyed.

The weather continued to be perfect. Something like good humour prevailed upon the mule as the minutes passed and the trawl continued to drag clean and the time for the first haul approached. But luck apparently had deserted them. The trawl was empty but for a few crabs, and a bucket or so of whelks. Without a remark from any one the trawl went over again and the trawling continued. It was now getting on for two o'clock in the afternoon. Tom made some

tea. They had a meal on deck, Henry never leaving
the tiller. He changed his course southwards after
the second trawl, which again yielded nothing; and
after the third, which produced a dozen or so small
dabs, returned shorewards, and the trawl was not
hauled again until they were practically in the place
where they had first started, half an hour's steam from
pots. The sun by then was getting low. Again the
trawl was empty, and Henry, his mouth shut like
a trap, merely waved his hand for Marney to stow it
on board. He kept on shorewards towards the pots,
and it was not until they approached the first buoy
that he spoke.

"We'll try hauling lobster pots for a change," he
said ironically. "It's clear we're not going to make
our fortunes trawling."

Marney gave his father a sharp indignant look, but
he did not speak. He gaffed the buoy, coiled in its
warp until he got the weight of the first pot, and then
he and Tom started hauling. But now and again as
the hauling went on and pot after pot came aboard
empty, he glanced at Henry and observed that Henry
himself glanced repeatedly at the glow in the sky
made by the setting sun, and then to the south where
the jagged cliff of Low Batts point stood out in clear
relief against the curving sweep of Bramblewick Bay;
and he maintained his own tactful silence.

Marney himself subscribed unquestioningly to the
unwritten code of honour which was a tradition
among the inshore fishermen of the coast. The desire
to do well at his job, to find the best grounds, to use

the best methods of fishing, to land the biggest catch, was always fierce with him. In the rivalry that had existed between his family and the Fosdycks it had always given him immense satisfaction when they had beaten the brothers. But nothing could have ever persuaded him to do anything that was not in strict accordance with the code; such as setting gear so that it might foul or spoil another's fishing. In the old days, when the Fosdycks were more active, certainly it would have been an infringement of the code to have trawled Church Steeples. A beam trawl did not destroy immature fish (as a modern steam trawl did), but one or two shots on a ground such as this would spoil it for line fishing for a day or two. In the old days the Fosdycks would fish for salmon and soles too, working alternately at nets and lines throughout the night. Now they had concentrated all their energies on salmoning, and to Marney the ban on trawling was of their own choice lifted.

Of course Luke would hate it. Of course Bramblewick would talk, but they couldn't say anything worse than they'd said already. Yet, though his own inclinations were strong, he knew he would not gain anything by argument with his father. The pots continued to come in empty, and on that fact and on Henry's apparent continued interest in the view southward, Marney based his hopes. And those hopes rose almost to a certainty when they came to the end of the last fleet and Henry set a course to southward, straight for Low Batts point. For a time Marney said nothing, and again it was John who, poking his head through the engine-room hatch, was the first to comment on what was happening.

"Where are we off to now, father? You don't mean to say we're going to trawl in Bramblewick Bay after all?"

Marney laughed.

"Don't talk so daft, man. We're going ashore for our suppers, aren't we, father? Tide's just right for getting into Bramblewick Landing."

"Aye, I bet we are," John growled, and to Henry, "Well, if we are going to start trawling there, I hope you'll wait till dark, so no one can see us. . . . It wouldn't be a bad idea if we did go in to the Landing and slipped up home for our suppers. Are we going to?"

Henry did not answer, but Marney said:

"Hey—talking about supper, what about frying those dabs? There's not enough of them to take to market. They'd go champion with a few spuds and a drink of tea. I think we've got some butter somewhere. Shall we go down and put the stove on, Tom? Come on."

Marney and Tom went below and soon the acrid smoke of the stove, mingled with the smell of frying fat, was drifting down the deck towards Henry and John. But Marney had rejoined them before they had reached the point, and as they drew near it and the view of the bay widened, he was the first to observe a small boat lying close in to the cliff, just on the Bramblewick side of the point, and in the boat the familiar figures of Luke and Tindal Fosdyck. He said nothing, waiting for father and John to make the discovery for themselves. It was not a surprising discovery. In calm weather Low Batts point was a favourite berth for salmon fishing. The ironic significance of it was that Low Batts point, despite the rough scaurs that skirted its foot, was virtually the shoreward boundary of the Church Steeples ground, whose other extreme was known by the bearing of the steeple of Bramblewick old church in relation to a certain mark on the cliff. The ground stretched in a southerly direction across the bay. . . . Henry and John saw the boat at the same time. Marney watched them closely. He saw his father frown and a look of consternation on John's face as he turned to him and said:

"Well, that's put an end to it. Luke and Tindal right on the very spot. I reckon we can give the idea of trawling Church Steeples the go-by now anyway. Let's go straight ashore, seeing we've got as far as this, and have a real supper. We could sleep ashore if the weather keeps fine."

Still Marney said nothing, but he observed a new and grimmer look on his father's face as deliberately he steered the mule in towards the Fosdyck's boat. Then, as they drew near it, Henry said very quietly:

"I'm glad that they're there. There's no law to stop us trawling Church Steeples, or anywhere else we've got a mind to, so long as there's no one's gear in the way. But I know what Luke's feelings are."

"Damn it," said Marney, "you're not going to ask his leave, are you? We can come back at dark."

"Leave? Of course I'm not. It's not a case of leave.

But I want them to know what we're at. We're not going to act like a lot of thieves, waiting till dark. If we fish Church Steeples we'll do it open."

They drew near. Tindal was rowing. Luke was shooting a net outwards from the cliff, and they went on with the operation when Henry hailed them, although Luke had turned so that he had a clear sight of the mule.

"Now Luke," Henry shouted.

Luke answered in his customary gruff voice.

"Now Henry."

Henry swung the mule round so that she would pass broadside of the small boat and told John to throttle the engine down.

"It's a fine night," he shouted.

"Aye," Luke answered.

"Is that the last net you're shooting?"

"Aye! I'm coming to the end of it now. What for? Do you want to shoot your pots in here to-night?"

Henry answered smoothly.

"No. We've left our pots well to nor'ard of Low Batts, but I thought we'd have a go with the trawl along Church Steeples, so long as you've got no gear in the way."

Tindal had stopped towing and Luke stood with the buoy of the net in his hand.

"A trawl? You're not going to trawl that ground, are you?"

"Aye," said Henry very calmly. "You're not likely to be fishing it while you're salmoning, are you?"

There was no mistaking the truculence in Luke's voice when he answered.

"Nay. But no one's ever trawled it since I can remember. They'd have been stopped by the law."

"Aye, they would have been once," said Henry, still very calmly, "but not since that new law's been passed. How are you doing at salmoning?"

"Fair," Luke answered. "Fair."

He heaved the buoy overboard and glared with frank hatred at the mule, which was now swinging outwards again.

"Where are you going to start trawling?" he shouted.

"Close in here," said Henry. "But clear away from your nets, so we'll not do you any harm. But I just thought I'd come in and make sure where you'd got your nets. Good-night, Luke."

Luke did not answer.

"Get the trawl over now," Henry said quietly to Marney. "Shout to Tom to give you a hand."

"Keep Tom out of it while we're in sight of Luke and Tindal," John put in in a hoarse whisper. "I'll give him a hand with the bloody thing, if you've made up your mind to shoot it. . . . God! Luke's not half fed up. I knew he would be. He'd like to murder us."

John climbed out of the engine-room and he half closed the hatch behind him. The mule was heading out to sea and Luke and Tindal were becoming indistinct in the gathering dusk. The trawl splashed overboard. The warp tightened, and Henry, as Marney swung it over into the fairlead, put his hand on it to test by its vibrations if the trawl was dragging clear along the bottom. John was still on deck, standing close to Marney, both of them staring towards the now almost indistinguishable boat. They were all silent for a minute or two. Then suddenly Henry said:

"Hey—what the hell is Tom burning in that stove? It's stinking fit to make me sick."

"Garn. It's only melting butter," said Marney, "it smells all right to me."

Again there was a silence, then Henry shouted:

"That's not butter. It's burning paraffin. Can't you smell it?"

"It's the exhaust you smell," laughed Marney. "Keep your head over the other side. It's because of there being no wind. I can't smell paraffin."

"By God—*I* can," John shouted, suddenly leaping aft ; and at the same time Henry shouted. "It's the engine. Look sharp—*there's summat on fire.*"

He swung back the hatch himself, but John beat him and dived down into the engine-room and almost instantly there was a flash of light inside which lit up Henry's startled face as he followed his son below. There were three short steps into the engine-room, but with his feet on the lowest one Henry could go no farther, for John was in his way. He tried to brush past him. John, however, took a step forward and over his shoulder Henry saw a sheet of flame running along the floor from the starboard wall where the main paraffin tank stood, to the engine itself. The place was thick with fumes. The heat was intense. John, however, had seized a bucket of sand and had emptied half

of it on to the flames when he seemed to stagger
forward. Henry made a grab at him. With all his
strength he dragged him backwards to the steps.
But John suddenly broke free, and turning on his
father shouted in a choking voice:

"Get up on deck. There's that drum of petrol.
I've got to get it out somehow."

"Never mind that," shouted Henry, himself choking.
"Come on out."

But John had already turned and got hold of a
large petrol drum standing just inside the room. He
swung it up into Henry's hands and then, as Henry
swung it clear on to the deck, John staggered after him,
and he was pursued by a cloud of dark smoke which,
as he emerged through the hatchway, belched out and
suddenly flashed as though from a furnace chimney.
Henry and Marney helped him on to the deck. His
face was blackened. His eyebrows and lashes, the front
part of his hair were singed off. He was choking and
almost breathless, but as they let go, and Tom Fosdyck
with a bucket of water strode towards the hatchway,
he shouted:

"Water's no use. Paraffin tank has split a seam
and it's pouring out. The whole bloody show's on
fire. Throw that petrol tin overboard. We can do
nowt to put the fire out."

But Henry had anticipated Tom's actions. He had
already dropped the petrol drum over. He brushed
Tom aside, slammed the hatch to, and from that
moment took charge of what he knew was to be a
desperate effort to save not the boat but their lives.

The engine had stopped. The weight of the trawl had quickly arrested the way of the boat, but she was still pointing out to sea. Henry shouted:

"Get for'ard, all of you. Get hold of owt that will keep you afloat, and be ready to go over yourselves."

They went for'ard, but without panic, and dragging or carrying with them a number of buoys and fishboxes. Henry came last, and as he picked his way along the deck he looked earnestly shoreward. Even in that moment of intense anxiety it must have cost his pride something to do what he did. Many a time when he and his sons in the coble had been making Bramblewick Landing in heavy weather Luke Fosdyck, in his official capacity as cox, had summoned the lifeboat crew. It would have been a triumph for Luke if the boat had been able to carry out a rescue, and it had been Henry's special pride that never once had he needed its assistance let alone called for it. And now, having just shown his own independence by telling Luke he was going to trawl Church Steeples, it seemed that with Luke lay their only chance of escape. . . . But Henry did not hesitate. As he reached the others he cupped his hands and gave a hail shorewards. There was no audible answer. He hailed again, and then turning gruffly to the others, he shouted:

"Come on, shout as loud as you can. They must be within hailing distance."

They shouted, but they heard no reply. The mule still lay with her head to sea and between them and the shore the smoke, escaping now between the gaps in the

T

hatch, made an impenetrable screen. Again they shouted, and as they did so there was a loud noise aft; not an explosion, but a deep roar as the hatch was split asunder and a sheet of flame soared up the height of the mast.

A comparative silence followed. All four men now stood close together in the bows of the mule, their faces turned towards the fire and the still invisible shore. They knew their peril. They realised their absolute impotence to avert or even delay the progress of the fire. Like most fishermen and sailors of the coast, none of them could swim. They might, with the help of the buoys and the fish boxes, remain afloat until they were picked up, but there were no craft of any description in sight and the only available Bramble-wick boat was the one which now lay between them and the shore, and there was still no sign that their shouts for help had been heard or heeded. It might have occurred to each of them, even to Tom Fosdyck, that both men in that boat, in particular its master, had reason to rejoice in the disaster that had befallen them; that if ever there was a motive for not obeying the unwritten code of the sea, it was there in Luke's lifelong jealousy and hatred of the Lunns. Yet none of them would have dared to have given expression to that thought, and there was no trace of animosity in Marney's voice when he said:

"If they can't see that bloody flame and know we're on fire, they must be blind."

He turned to John and said calmly:

"Have you got a fag on you?"

John took a packet of fags from his pocket. His voice was hoarse but as calm as Marney's when he answered:

"Aye, here you are," and turning to Tom, "Will you have one?"

"Nay, I've got my pipe filled," Tom said just as smoothly. "I was just going to light up when Marney shouted down at me. But I haven't got a match."

John had already struck one.

"Did you take the frying-pan off the stove before you came up?" Marney asked.

Tom grinned.

"No. I'd just dropped the fish in."

"Damn it, they ought to be almost done by now. We ought to be down having our suppers while we're waiting." Marney looked at John. "By God—you won't need to go to the barber's this week. You're shaved as clean as a baby's backside. Never mind, you'll get what you wanted, supper ashore and a soft bed to sleep in to-night."

"Aye. I might if Luke gets to us in time. I can see no sign of them yet. I'm thinking about all that paraffin that must be in the tank yet. We'd have blown up before this if we hadn't got that petrol-drum overboard."

"Stop yapping, and let's give them another hail," Henry put in. "Come on now, all together."

They gave another hail, but it was drowned completely by a roar from the engine-room, the crash of rent ironwork and splitting wood. The whole deck shook beneath them. The heat suddenly became so intense that they were forced to shield their faces with their arms, and Henry shouted:

"Come on. It's no use waiting for them. Get your sea-boots off. Throw all that gear over near the bows, and see that there's summat handy when you drop. It'll be each man for himself. It wouldn't be safe for them to come alongside us in another minute anyway."

Henry seized a fish box and threw it over and started to kick off his boots, but as he did so, he (and the others too) saw the Fosdycks' boat with Luke and Tindal straining their utmost at the oars, bearing down on them, not from the direction of the shore but from the sea. They were not three lengths away. Suddenly Luke stopped pulling, and stood up with the light of the fire full on his face and shouted an inaudible command to Tindal. The boat slewed round, and began to back straight into the mule's bows. The roar of the fire grew louder. Luke was shouting, but it was impossible to hear what he said. The stern of the boat touched the mule. Luke moved aft, took hold of a rope that Marney had flung to him, and calmly John and Tom and Marney climbed into her, and last of all, Henry. They said nothing to each other. Tom took Luke's oars. Marney took Tindal's. They pulled with all their might and did not slacken until they had put a dozen lengths between them and the blazing mule. Then, after a few easy strokes they stopped completely and every man in the boat looked at the mule in silence.

The flames had spread almost amidships. The sail had caught fire and the tarred stays, burning fiercely with their deck ends severed, swung fantastically from the masthead. Aft, the fire had burned completely down to the water-line, leaving only the timbers that looked like the ribs of a burning corpse. Then gradually the pall of flame-lit smoke that hung above the mule grew whiter as an immense cloud of steam rose up from the stern. The bow of the mule began to lift until the keel was visible. The stern sank down; and suddenly there was a dull explosion; a cloud of steam rose up and seemed to envelop the smoke; there was a last burst of flame which silhouetted the mule's hull as her bow rose up until her keel was vertical with the water-line and showed her sinking, stern first. And then there was a sudden and complete darkness.

For a full minute no one moved; no one spoke. Then Marney said in a curiously subdued voice:

"Well, by God, who'd have thought that a boat even her size could have gone as quick as that. Damn it, it's not more than a quarter of an hour since we were lighting the galley stove. It's just like a bloody dream. How did it all happen."

"I don't know," said John. "I'll swear that paraffin tank wasn't leaking when I left it. But it must have been trickling under the bottom of the boards. It might have soaked into a bit of engine waste and the vaporiser or the exhaust pipe or a short-circuit from the magneto might have set it off . . . I don't know."

"Aye. Well, I've always said that engines in a boat are for those who like them," put in Luke. "Smoke was that thick we could scarcely see which way we were going so we pulled out to sea and came in that way."

"Aye, I reckoned you were having a job to find us," Henry said very quietly.

There was another silence, then Luke said:

"Well, it's a bit of bad luck for you, losing your boat. But I expect you'll have her insured."

"Aye, she's covered against loss, of course."

Their eyes were recovering from the temporary blindness caused by the fire. A thick pall of smoke still hung over the sea where the mule had sunk, but shorewards and towards the village of Bramblewick the darkness was not intense, for night had not yet completely fallen.

"Well," said Luke. "We'd better get you chaps ashore, hadn't we, Henry?"

"Why—I don't like taking you from your nets. You could put us ashore here. I reckon we would get along the cliff bottom before the tide flows. You'd only have to pull back."

"That doesn't matter," Luke answered quickly. "We weren't going to haul our nets till daybreak, and we're going home anyway for our suppers. We might put a hole in our boat trying to land under the cliff in the dark. We might as well take you into the Landing."

Henry would have preferred walking along the cliff bottom. Close to the north side of the village there was a rough way up the cliff which enabled any one to reach the village without walking up the slipway and through the Dock. It would have saved him and his crew the humiliation of passing the crowd which undoubtedly would have gathered there as soon as the news of a boat on fire had been flashed round. But this was Luke's hour of triumph, of his own defeat, and having tasted humble pie he was not going to jib at swallowing.

"All right, Luke," he said. "Thank you very much if you'll take us in, but we'll do the pulling." Then looking his old enemy straight in the face, "I reckon you got to us just about in time, Luke. It looks to me as though we've got to thank you and Tindal for saving our lives."

Luke did not answer Henry, but he said gruffly to the men at the oars:

"All right, then. Let's get home."

14

IT was dark when Sally got back to Bramblewick. She had spent a miserable afternoon and evening at Burnharbour. She had gone down for that farewell visit full of self-confidence. She had put on her best coat and skirt, taken particular pains with her hair and knew that she was looking her best; and she had taken the finished guernsey with her wrapped in a parcel so that no one would guess what it was. She had not gone with the idea of making a special last effort to interest Tom. Her real purpose was to say good-bye to everybody, but she had wanted at the same time to show up well against Amy, to give Tom a picture of her which might some day make him realise the opportunity he had missed through his stupidity. She had caught the two o'clock bus and had imagined arriving at Amy's just as the men were coming in; and she had experienced a curious shock when Amy had told her about the morning's mishap, how the mule hadn't put to sea until ten o'clock, and that the men might not be back until very late. She had tried to convince herself that she was not desperately disappointed. After all she was not leaving until tomorrow night, and she could come down again in the morning, and in any case father and John would be returning to Bramblewick in the afternoon. But she *was* disappointed. Her plan was muddled. She had

arranged in her own mind that she would stay to tea
and catch the six o'clock bus home; that throughout
tea she would show a complete indifference towards
Tom, just behave as though he wasn't there; and then,
when the time came for her to go she would politely
shake hands with him and perhaps, it would depend
on just how he looked at her, she would put the parcel
in his hands.

It had given her no comfort to feel that she was
looking her best and Amy her worst, seeing there was
no one else to mark the contrast. The mishap to the
mule had put Amy out too. When Marney and Tom
came back they had awakened the children and put
them in a grizzling mood for the rest of the day. There
had been an unexpected meal to cook for the men before
they made their final start, and she hadn't got half of
her housework done, let alone had time to think of
tidying herself up; and throughout the afternoon and
evening it seemed to Sally that Amy had never once
stopped talking to her, except to break off and scold the
children. Sally would have escaped after tea but for
the hope that the mule would return before she had
to catch the last bus.

Amy had not been worried by the non-appearance
of the mule. Marney had told her there was a good
chance of them staying out all night. Sally had no
fears as to their actual safety either; yet as she moved
up the familiar alley which led to her home (still
carrying her parcel) she felt a dread inside her. She
knew nothing of what had happened. She had noticed
that the people she had met on her way down from the

bus had stared at her, and that one or two of them had evidently said something about her after she had passed. But that was quite usual in Bramblewick. What she dreaded now was going back to her mother, having to spend the rest of the evening answering questions as to what was going on in Burnharbour, listening to mother's chatter about little things that didn't interest Sally a bit, to her complaints, doing her best to cheer her up, yet longing all the time to have some one in whom she could confide her own troubles and find sympathy. And worst of all, having to do her packing with mother helping and not bothering the least bit to hide the fact that she was delighted the time had nearly come for her to go. If only it was to-morrow night, and she had said good-bye, and was safe in the train for London! Once there she felt that she would never want to come back to Bramblewick or Burnharbour again, no matter how well she had done for herself. She hated both places. Burnharbour more than Bramblewick now that she had been so unhappy there.

As she opened the street door and wiped her feet on the mat inside there was no sound of talking from within to indicate that mother was not alone. She cried out, "It's only me, mother," carefully closed the street door, and her surprise was complete when she opened the inner door and saw Henry, John, Marney and Tom Fosdyck sitting at the table eating a meal, with mother at the fireside, a frying pan in her hand.

For a moment Sally just stared in astonishment, without fixing her particular attention on any one.

She was only vaguely aware that mother had smiled at her, but none of the men gave her a glance or spoke. Then suddenly she noticed John's hair and eyes and she said:

"Hello!—Whatever's happened? What's the matter with *you*, John—You *do* look queer."

John's mouth twisted into a wry smile.

"So you haven't heard," he said, "that's surprising. I'll tell you what's happened. We're the bloody heroes of Bramblewick again. You wait till you read next week's *Burnharbour Gazette*. It wouldn't surprise me if they bring out a special edition of this week's, to-morrow. Aye, with photographs too. I wouldn't be surprised if the *Daily Mail* gets hold of it."

Henry glared across the table at his eldest son.

"Hold your jaw," he snapped, "it's nowt to joke about."

He looked up and smiled at Sally and immediately looked down at his plate again, and the four men continued to eat in silence. But their gloom was not apparently shared by mother for she had turned from the fire and although her voice was hushed and dramatic, her eyes were sparkling with repressed excitement when she said:

"Haven't you heard what's happened, Sally? Hadn't Amy got a telegram before you left? Eh—I *do* hope it wasn't too late for it to be delivered. It would be awful for her if she heard about the mule in a round-about way and didn't know that every one was safe."

She had moved swiftly (the frying pan in her hand) to Henry's side.

"Will you have a bit more steak, Henry?" she said fussily. "There's plenty. What about you, Marney, and you, Tom? There'll be some more taties in a minute. Don't stint yourselves."

Sally threw down the parcel on to the chair, and cried impatiently:

"I do wish you'd tell me what's happened. Of course I've heard nothing. I've just come straight down from the bus."

Mother went on serving out the contents of the pan, moving round the table from plate to plate like a fussy hen with her chicks. She was back at the fire again and had filled the pan with potatoes before she looked at Sally and said dramatically:

"Eh—it was nearly a bad do, Sally. A very bad do. But I haven't got to the bottom of it all yet. I know no more than what Henry and the lads told me when they came in only half an hour ago. But the mule caught fire and she blew up, and now she's at the bottom of the sea. Praise God, none of our chaps are hurt, except John there having his hair singed off, but just think what it might have been."

Sally looked at John again, but this time he didn't look up. She had the sudden sensation that the whole thing was a dream and that in a minute she'd wake up and find herself in bed. Then she moved across to the fireplace and the illusion was broken.

"Is it true, mother?" she said. "Has the mule really been sunk."

"Aye," mother answered. "It's true. Isn't it a good thing I was here, and with my health back and plenty of food in the house. It was Mrs. Thompson, next-door-but-one, her who's scarcely spoken to me since they took the lifeboat away, who came and told me. I was just sitting by the fire wondering how long it would be before you came back, and she opened the door and shouted, 'Eh—there's a boat on fire just off Low Batts point. Do you think it can be your chaps, Mrs. Lunn?' Well, I didn't wait to put a shawl on even, but I dashed up on to the cliff and was just in time to see the end of it. I knew it was your father all right, for there's none of those Burnharbour boats ever come so close in; but I didn't know they'd been saved till they got ashore. Fancy, it was Luke and Tindal saved them, just in the nick of time . . . Now sit yourself at the table, Sally. I'm sure you could do with a bit of supper."

Sally's mind at last was working normally. She looked at the men, and then remembering John's ironic remark, she grasped the situation. She whipped off her hat and coat and turning to mother said:

"I don't want any supper, mother. You sit down and I'll get yours for you. I bet you've been on your feet the whole night long as well as climbing about that cliff. You know it's one of the very things the doctor said you hadn't to do. Now sit yourself down."

"Aye," Henry put in suddenly. "That's what I told her before you came in."

Mother turned round indignantly.

"Sit down? Don't talk so daft, both of you. I've never felt better in health in my life. Do as I tell you, Sally. And no more nonsense. Father will tell you better than I can what's happened. Can't you make room for Sally, John? I'll maybe join you when the taties are done."

Sally, realising the futility of arguing with mother in her present mood, sat down at the table and found herself opposite to Tom. Glancing at him she was surprised to see him half-smile at her and she felt herself go red. But he quickly averted his eyes, and like the others remained silent. The atmosphere of the room was tense, tenser than it had been the night the vicar had called about the lifeboat, and Sally felt a deeper excitement gripping her. Firmly she refused to have any food, but she let mother pour out a cup of tea for her, and then looking at Henry she said:

"I do wish you'd tell me about it all, father."

Henry smiled grimly, and answered:

"Why, there's nowt much to tell that mother hasn't told you. We'd just shot the trawl on Church Steeples, that's that bit of soft ground running southwards from Low Batts point, and the engine-room took fire. John did his best to put it out, and he saved us from blowing up by chucking out a big drum of petrol. We didn't blow up as it happened. There was a bit of a bang when the water poured into the engine-room but that's not blowing up. Anyway by that time Luke and Tindal Fosdyck had got alongside us and taken us off. That's all there is to it. We didn't even get our feet wet."

"Aye," put in John, "but you haven't said owt about what happened when we got ashore. I should think everybody at Bramblewick was down at the Landing, folks I'd never even seen for years. *And* the coastguards, *and* the policeman, *and* the doctor, *and* the district nurse, *and* that chap who came to live Up Bank a year or two ago, and writes up things for the *Burnharbour Gazette*. He wanted the full story from us. Wanted to know everything, what the mule was called, what time we left harbour, what was father's christian name, how had the fire started, had any other boats come to our assistance, and God knows what else. The bloody fool! I asked him if he wanted to know who was my favourite film star, and if I'd been to Oxford or Cambridge university. I'll say this for old Luke. He gave him it pretty straight. He just told him to go to hell and mind his own business."

"Aye, some folks *are* inquisitive, aren't they?" said mother. "Are you ready for another cup of tea, John. Say when you are. And don't be afraid of helping yourself to those cheese cakes, Tom! You're one of us now, remember, and it isn't often our men have to be asked to have this and that, whether it's on the table or not."

"The more reason why you should sit down yourself, mother," said Henry. "Sit down, I tell you," he added, raising his voice. "But don't any of you ask any more questions about the mule, for I'm about sick of it. She's gone, and there's no more to be said."

"No more to be said?" Marney broke in suddenly, "Damn it, we haven't said anything yet. I don't mean about the mule. I mean about what we're going to do. We've got to decide summat."

Mother had put the fried potatoes in the dish and placed this in the middle of the table. She poured

herself out a small cup of tea, drew her chair close up
to Henry's, and sat down, getting up again immediately
to reach for a plate of cheese cakes and push it in front
of Marney. But she sat down again, and Sally watched
her observing Henry's face closely and anxiously when
he answered:

"Aye, we've got to make up our minds what we're
going to do, but I don't see how we can decide quick
like this. It's come too sudden. I never expected owt
like this happening."

"*I* did," said John, "I've expected it happening every
minute since we got that bloody boat; not catching
fire, but rolling herself keel upwards and drowning us."

"Garn! There's been worse boats than her," protested
Marney. "She served us well enough, all things considered. I tell you when I saw her going down like
that, I had a lump in my throat I could hardly swallow;
and I'll tell you I wouldn't be sorry if we could get
another like her, although of course with a new engine,
and plenty of speed and a bit better accommodation
for sleeping."

"Aye. Maybe," said John sarcastically. "A new
boat in fact. It looks to me as though we're just back
where we started. We'll have to fettle up the coble
engine, or get a new one, and come back to Bramblewick. It'll be better for mother anyway, having some
of us at home . . . But you needn't think I'm so keen
on fishing here again; not after to-night's do, on top
of everything else . . . I'll say it again, we made our
mistake in father not taking on the lifeboat, and setting
every one against us. It's finished us here. It's finished

the band. Only six chaps turned up for the last practice. I tell you our name's mud in this spot."

"All the more reason why we should clear out of it for good," said Marney. "If I was so fond of making a bloody hullabaloo with a trumpet, I'd join the Burnharbour Salvation Band . . . Anyway, there is a proper band in Burnharbour."

"I know there is," said John. "The chap who taught us belongs to it and they'd have me in it any time I liked. But what's that got to do with it, now we haven't even got the mule . . . I know what you're thinking about. You'd like to persuade father to go in for a keeler. But you won't do that against mother."

"A keeler?" mother suddenly interrupted. "Do you mean those big new boats they've got at Burnharbour? Why, they must cost into thousands of pounds. How do you think father's going to get one of those?"

"How do you think Burnharbour fishermen get them, mother?" said Marney. "They don't buy them right out of their own pockets. Some one puts up the brass and they pay it back out of what they earn."

"Aye. But those who put up the brass will be rich friends or relations of those they lend it to. They wouldn't lend it to folks they don't know, like us."

Both father and Marney were looking at mother with a suddenly awakened interest, and John stared at her in frank astonishment.

"Eh—you don't mean to say that you'd favour a keeler, mother?"

"I can't favour owt I know nowt about," mother answered drily. "And it's not my fault if I know nowt

U

about all that's been going on while I've been shut up in hospital. It's the first time I've ever heard any of you mention a keeler, let alone go in for one."

"It isn't just friends and relations who put up the brass to buy them," Marney quickly explained. "It's any one who's got the brass and the mind to invest it. And I bet there's not any of them has regretted it either. Those keelers pay like gold mines. I reckon there's several chaps at Burnharbour would be ready to put up the brass for us so long as we put so much down, say fifty quid apiece. There'll be the insurance for the mule, remember."

"There's one chap at Burnharbour would lay down the full price to-morrow, if I gave him the word," said Henry with an unnatural quietness. "We wouldn't have to find a penny. But that wouldn't be my way of doing it. I'd want to lay down at least one-third, and arrange it so we could pay back the rest out of our earnings, so that we'd be owners in the end."

"Then why don't you ask him, Henry?" said mother.

It was Henry's turn to look at his wife in astonishment.

"Ask him?" he echoed. "You mean go in for a keeler? Why, it would mean us leaving Bramblewick, all of us. We couldn't work a keeler from here. We couldn't get ashore even in the calmest weather."

Mother smiled.

"So far as I can see you weren't so much better off for that in the mule. The only time you've landed here since you got her was once, when you took

Marney's furniture away, and now, when she's sunk.
. . . Eh—Henry, what I say is you've got to do what
you think best. I didn't want to leave Bramblewick,
but since the lifeboat do, and the feeling there's been
about us, the place has changed, and I've changed too.
There's Marney and his bairns gone to Burnharbour.
It's been nice having Sally for company this week, but
she's going back to London to-morrow. If you think
it's best to go in for a keeler, and us to flit to Burnharbour, well then I'm not going to go against it.
You wouldn't have to sleep on board of her always.
You'd be back home for most of your meals, anyway.
I'd get used to living in Burnharbour in time. You
and me might even like going to the pictures on a
Saturday night like the rest of them, but never twice a
week like Amy. I reckon that's extravagance. That
was a champion thing Sally took me to on Saturday,
although we missed nearly half the show by going
late . . . Eh—you do what you think's best, Henry.
I'll feel it I know, leaving this house, and I shan't like
giving up the hens, but I will do if I've got to."

Henry's face had turned very red. Sally saw what
effort he was making to keep his voice steady.

"There's no need for you to give up the hens, if we
went to Burnharbour," he said, "least I don't think so.
The chap I know who'd put up the brass for the boat
owns a house not far from where Marney's living, and
there's an allotment goes with it, somewhere up by the
old ropeworks. I think you could keep hens there as
well as on Bramblewick cliff. Me and John could soon
knock you up a hen-house. Of course I don't know for

certain it's still free. Why didn't you tell me before
you'd not mind leaving Bramblewick, mother?"

"Why didn't you tell me about going out to that
trawler and then buying the mule until so long after
you'd done it?" mother retorted. . . . "Eh—but let
bygones be bygones," she added quickly. "What about
this chap. Are you going to ask him, Henry?"

Henry glanced at the clock.

"It'll be too late to go down to Burnharbour to-night
—or——"

Marney had stood up.

"—it's not that late," he interrupted. "I can walk
there in just over an hour. I don't need two guesses to
say who it is. It's Captain Mowbray, isn't it? A very
decent chap from all accounts. I think I know where
he lives too. I say, the quicker we let him know the
better."

"Aye, but are we all agreed we want a keeler," said
Henry. "*You* are, I know. What about you, John?"

"Why—it would mean giving up the band. But I've
been expecting that anyway. And by God—those
keelers have got fine engines. I was looking at one the
other day. You could take an interest in driving one
of those . . . Aye, I suppose I'm for it."

"And what about you, Tom?"

Although she hadn't looked directly at him all the
time the others had been talking, Sally had been aware
of Tom, and in a subtle way she felt there was something different about him. She did look straight at
him now. He was looking at Henry. She felt suddenly
that she recognised the Tom who had helped her get the

water and coal the night she had arrived from London, the Tom she had dreamt about and loved, and a desperate excitement seized her. It was the first time since then she had seen him not in Amy's company, not watching Amy like a faithful dog. She saw, ironically, that here at last might be the chance she had waited for, a chance which for all her clever scheming Amy had not foreseen. She felt herself trembling when she saw him nod his head and say in his grave, self-deprecating, yet curiously dignified way:

"Aye. I'm willing, of course, if I'm wanted."

"Of course you're wanted," mother said briskly.

Marney had put his cap on, and was nervously glancing at the clock. Tom got up too.

"Eh—you're not going back to Burnharbour, are you, Tom?" said mother. "We can easily give you a bed here, you know."

Tom grinned.

"Why—thank you very much, but I think I'd best get back with Marney."

"What shall I tell Captain Mowbray, father?" Marney asked. "Just that we want to go in for a keeler, and that you'd like to talk it over with him, say to-morrow morning?"

"Aye. You'd best not say too much at first."

"But ask him about the house and the garden," said mother. "I think I'd better go down with father in the morning if you do fix up to see him. Perhaps Sally could too, seeing she's not going till late at night. But we'd best leave that until we hear from you what he says. How will you let us know? Will you send us a telegram? . . . Eh—I don't like you walking all that way in the dark, but I expect Amy will be pleased to see you. She's bound to be worrying a bit. Are you both going to say good-bye to Sally, in case she doesn't get down?"

Sally didn't wait for either of them to reply. She got up and reached for her coat and grasped the parcel with it.

"It's all right, mother," she said quickly. "I'll walk down to the Dock with them, and perhaps see them up to the top of the Bank."

As though afraid that something might yet be said to change his father's mind, Marney said a hurried general good-night, and Sally was close behind him as he and Tom stepped out; and it was she who shut the door; and as she did so she clutched at Tom's sleeve and said:

"Tom. I want to talk to you."

Her voice was high-pitched, nervous. As they both stopped and looked at her, she giggled, and then instantly she looked at Marney and almost shouted at him:

"Go on, Marney. We'll catch you up . . . Don't stand staring like a fool."

Marney grinned, and for a moment looked as though he was going to make some jocular remark; but something in his sister's face must have shown him how dead in earnest she was.

"All right," he said. "But don't be over-long. I'll wait on the Bank top. But I'll go on if you're not there in five minutes."

He swung round, and Sally watched him walk down the alley, under the street lamp which stood where it twisted down to the Dock, and finally disappear. Then she looked at Tom, who was regarding her with an expression of complete bewilderment, and she said:

"Did you know I was going back to London, to-morrow, Tom?"

He grinned, and answered:

"Aye. Of course. John told us last night. He said you were coming down to Burnharbour this afternoon to say good-bye. But of course there wouldn't be any one there, except Amy and the bairns."

"No. There wasn't. Wasn't it lucky you were all here when I landed home!"

Tom grinned again.

"Aye. I suppose it was, in a way. Otherwise we'd have missed you. But you'll be coming down to-morrow, won't you?"

"No, I won't," Sally answered quietly. "I'm saying good-bye now . . . Aren't you going to shake hands with me, Tom?"

He was standing so that the light from the street lamp was full on his face. He wasn't grinning now, but she saw him take a furtive glance down the alley as he held out his hand; and suddenly all her nervousness went. She ignored his hand. She laughed, and said in a deadly calm voice:

"Oh, don't bother, Tom. I hate shaking hands. And wouldn't it look daft if any one saw us. But I do want to talk to you. . . . Not here. Let's go up the alley on to the cliff. You once almost as much as said you'd take me for a walk along the cliff when we got a fine night . . . You're not afraid, are you?"

Again he looked at her in complete bewilderment.

"Afraid? Of course I'm not afraid. But it sounds a bit daft, doesn't it? What about Marney? We've got to get to Burnharbour to-night, to see that chap about the keeler."

"Yes. Marney has, but you haven't. And he's going to wait five minutes on the Bank top. And that's time enough for me to say what I've got to say . . . Will you come, Tom, or won't you?"

"Why—I'll come if you're bent on it, but it still sounds daft to me. How far do you want to go?"

"Just to the cliff edge . . . Come on."

She turned and walked swiftly up the alley, Tom walking at her side. Only two old cottages, used as warehouses, lay between them and where the alley ended in a pathway paved with old mussel shells, which, forking to the left, led to a narrow, level space on the edge of the clay cliff, close to Henry Lunn's own warehouse. It was a place from which Henry had invariably taken his first morning glance at the sea, for it commanded a full view of the shore and Bay; and to Sally every inch of it was familiar. There was a wide plank—part of a ship's hatch which Henry had found on the beach one day—let into the bank at one end of it. Here as a child Sally had often sat and played, and practised at her knitting on a summer's day; and from this very vantage point she could remember seeing her brothers quarrelling and fighting with the village boys down on the shore . . . There was no light except the soft sheen of the stars, but she walked up to the seat as surely as if it had been broad daylight and she flung down her parcel on to it and then stood perfectly still, looking not at Tom but across the sea, where far out the lights of two steamers moved steadily south. The night was still calm. The air was mild and very faintly Sally could detect the scent of whin flowers from a clump just below the cliff edge, mingling with the strong smell of the sea. Suddenly she turned and looked at Tom and said, still in a perfectly calm voice:

"Isn't it funny, Tom, us standing here, both grown up, and when we were kids I might have looked at you fighting Marney and John and praying to God to strike you dead with a thunderbolt. I did hate you then, and no mistake."

"Aye," Tom answered steadily. "We all hated each other then."

"And did you hate me?"

"I very likely did."

"And isn't it a queer thing that you're now living with Marney and that you're going with them on their new boat. Are you excited about it?"

"Excited? Why, I hadn't thought about it like that. I'm glad to get a job, and I'm glad to be with them, but it isn't a case of being excited."

"Have you ever been excited?"

"Why, it just depends what you mean by excited. If you mean losing your temper, I suppose I have, often enough."

"Were you excited that time you fought with those

men in Chile, and one of them came for you with a knife."

Tom laughed.

"Aye, I suppose I was. I must have lost my temper or I wouldn't have done owt so daft."

"And have you ever been excited by a woman?"

"You're asking me a lot of daft questions, Sally. Is that what we came up here for?"

"No, it isn't," Sally said quickly. "Will you sit down, Tom? Why don't you light your pipe? We've still got a minute or two to talk in."

"Why—I will, since you asked me."

She sat down, but Tom remained standing while very methodically he filled his pipe; and then he did sit down, leaving a wide space between them. He felt in his pocket, produced a match-box, shook it, took out a match, struck it, and put it to his pipe. And then as the match lit up his lean muscular face, Sally suddenly leaned over, snatched the pipe from his mouth, and threw it on the ground. Instantly she was on her feet facing him.

"No. You *won't* smoke that pipe." Her voice slashed at him like a whip. "You'll listen to what I've got to say without that to help you. That's what you do when you're watching Amy. Always that pipe. Always that look on your face. Why can't you be a man. Why do you let everybody boss you about as though you hadn't got any will of your own. Why don't you stop moping about your officer's tickets. You're as good a fisherman as any of our chaps, and fishing's as good a job as a sailor's. I persuaded you to come here to tell you what a fool you are, if you want to know. A fool—a fool! You're a fool to let Amy boss you about. You're a fool not to find some one you can really love, and you can marry and live with in a home of your own. You're a fool to think you're in love with Amy. Because she isn't in love with you. She's in love with her husband. And she'll have you or any other chap at her beck and call just to show him what a marvel he's got for a wife. Now put that in your pipe and smoke it, Tom!"

She stopped, still standing in front of him, but leaning her face towards his. She was panting, shaking. He remained where he was when she had snatched the pipe from his mouth, and he made no sound.

Her voice quietened, but there was a still more deadly sting in it.

"Isn't it true what I've said?" she went on. "Do you hate me because I've said it? Because I hate you. I hate you more than I ever did when we were kids. Why don't you say something? Haven't I excited you? Haven't I made you lose your temper yet? Don't you want to hit me? Or are you just wanting to run back to Burnharbour and Amy? Are you so much in love with her you can't speak?"

She could not see his face, but when she stopped she could hear him breathing heavily. And then she was startled by a loud, ironic laugh. He still did not move, but he said in a voice that seemed charged with a profound bitterness.

"Love? Love's no use unless there's two of you for it. I'm not in love with Amy. She's Marney's wife. I like her. She never made me do owt I didn't want to

do. I don't believe in love. I don't believe in owt . . ."
his voice suddenly grew stronger. "Hold your jaw,
Sally. I've had enough of it. You've told me nowt I
didn't know for myself. It's none of your business
anyway. I'm off."

He stood up, towering above Sally. She looked up at
him. She said quickly:

"Would you believe in anything if you knew that
some one loved *you*? That I loved you, Tom?"

He laughed again.

"You? A swank like you, loving a failure like me?
You've got to get back to London to-morrow. I suppose
the next time you come up here it'll be in a Rolls-
Royce. Hold your jaw, Sally. I don't want any more
of your mocking. Stand out of my way. I tell you
I've had enough of this daftness. I'm off."

He put out one hand, as though to push her out of
his way, and suddenly Sally reached out her own hands,
clutched at him, drew her head tight against his chest.

"Tom, I love you," she cried passionately. "*I love
you*. For God's sake don't go. I only talked to you like
that because I love you, because I'm jealous of Amy.
I'm not a swank, I don't want to go back to London
and be a lady. I want you. I think you're wonderful.
I'll do anything for you. I want to marry you, Tom.
I want us to have a home of our own in Burnharbour
and have kids, kids of our own. I fell in love with you
when I saw you first that night at Amy's, and I tried
to forget you when I went away, but I couldn't. I'd
have shown you that I loved you only Amy never gave
me a chance. And I knitted you a guernsey and I was

going to give it to you to-night. It's there on the seat
if you don't believe me. Oh, Tom. Can't you speak
to me?"

She suddenly raised her hands until she felt his face.
She moved them until they were round his neck, and
she clasped them, and pulled with all her might until
his face lowered nearly to her own, and she panted:

"Tom, kiss me—kiss me."

And suddenly she felt a contraction of his body as
though every muscle of it had become taut under an
immense strain. She heard him gasp; felt his breath
hot in her face, saw the whiteness of his teeth in
the starshine; and then his arms tightened across her
shoulders as he drew her whole body to his in a fierce
embrace, and she heard him gasp with an incredible
passion,

"By God, Sally. You—you loving me. By God—
I'll kiss you. . . ."

THE END

Devotees of the writings of Leo Walmsley are
commended to join the Walmsley Society.
Details of membership may be had from:

Secretary
The Walmsley Society
'Sherbrook'
16 Newlands Drive
LEOMINSTER
Herefordshire HR6 8PR